Darling

INDIA KNIGHT

PENGUIN BOOKS

PENGUIN BOOKS

UK | USA | Canada | Ireland | Australia
India | New Zealand | South Africa

Penguin Books is part of the Penguin Random House group of companies
whose addresses can be found at global.penguinrandomhouse.com.

First published by Fig Tree 2022
Published in Penguin Books 2023

001

Copyright © India Knight, 2022

The moral right of the author has been asserted

Typeset by Jouve (UK), Milton Keynes
Printed and bound in Great Britain by Clays Ltd, Elcograf S.p.A.

The authorized representative in the EEA is Penguin Random House Ireland,
Morrison Chambers, 32 Nassau Street, Dublin D02 YH68

A CIP catalogue record for this book is available from the British Library

ISBN: 978-0-241-95505-5

www.greenpenguin.co.uk

Penguin Random House is committed to a
sustainable future for our business, our readers
and our planet. This book is made from Forest
Stewardship Council® certified paper.

Darling

HUN

'A triumph! Brilliantly done, faithful but ι
tremendously romantic and very funn
Nina Stibbe, author of *One Day I Shall Astonish the* ?r

'It takes a brave author to attempt a contemporary reimagining of such a
beloved novel. Luckily, India Knight has courage and talent in
spades . . . Beautifully and meticulously done' *Sunday Times*

'Sheer brilliance. *Darling* is hilarious and heartbreaking and
vivid and clever and utterly compulsive – I absolutely loved it'
Francesca Segal, author of *Mother Ship*

'The delight is in the details. Knight's are bang on, and there's joy in
spotting them . . . There's heart as well as humour: it was, and remains,
a sincere romance . . . *Pursuit of Love* diehards can rest easy: your blood
vessels are safe with this faithful, fiercely funny homage' *Spectator*

'Total escapist bliss. A joyous updating of the Mitford classic.
I loved every page' Sabine Durrant, author of *Finders, Keepers*

'In less talented hands, Knight's retelling of this classic novel
might have gone horribly wrong. But *Darling* is a treat,
with whip-smart dialogue, larger-than-life characters, witty
observations and a heartbreaking twist' *Daily Express*

'An absolute triumph. Romantic, clever and oh-so funny' *i*

'Fans of Nancy Mitford's *The Pursuit of Love* will adore this
brilliant contemporary take . . . The writing is as sharp,
the details as perfect, the jokes as funny as the original' *Daily Mail*

'[A] lively modern update of a passionately loved classic . . . A sizzling
modern-day comedy of manners. Plenty of Mitfordian wit but with UKIP
peers and mobile phones' *The Times*, Best Fiction to Read This Autumn

'Knight nails the wit and satire' *Grazia*

'I found myself tearing through, beguiled by Knight's faithful
channelling of Radlett ways, wiles and speech patterns . . .
Reinventing anything so beloved is a formidable challenge,
and Knight has risen to it admirably' *Bookseller*

About the Author

India Knight is the author of four previous novels: *Mutton, Comfort and Joy, Don't You Want Me?* and *My Life on a Plate*, as well as several non-fiction books. She is a columnist for the *Sunday Times* and lives in Suffolk.

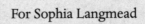
For Sophia Langmead

I

I found an old photograph of us all at Alconleigh, a 6x4 print, tattered with age but as vivid to me as flashing neon. It was taken at breakfast twenty-odd years ago, and as I gaze at it with that rush of yearning that you get when you look at old pictures – it's loss, really, an ache, the feeling that you can never go back, that time has fled and that you are bereft – I can smell the coffee pot sputtering on the Aga, feel the worn, waxed oak of the kitchen table, hear the soft pad-pad of the dogs fossicking for crumbs on the rug beneath it. I can hear my cousin Linda too, as clearly as if she were standing next to me, her laughter laced with indignation: 'I remember that picture! I wanted really short shorts that made your bottom hang out, but Ma got me those giant, old-man dungarees from a charity shop instead, and cut them off at the knee, and I was supposed to be *pleased*.'

There were always two teapots at breakfast, one, yellow and chipped, containing PG Tips for Uncle Matthew and one, printed with small spongeware donkeys, containing Aunt Sadie's loose-leaf Assam. In the picture, Uncle Matthew is triumphant because he has 'finished' the crossword, which usually involved getting fed up halfway through and writing in words like BATTO or CORPID to complete the clues that eluded him. Then he would push the paper aside with a satisfied grunt and carry on with his medium-boiled eggs with toast (six minutes exactly, this occasioning a fudgy yolk, the only acceptable kind – all other eggs were denounced furiously, compared to phlegm or worse, and liable to be hurled). Occasionally one of Uncle

Matthew's children would glance over at the nonsensical cross-word and say, 'But Pa, what's MIRONS?' and he'd reply that mirons was mirons, in a very categorical way that, like Uncle Matthew himself, brooked no dissent. We sort of believed him about mirons, because we all, adults and children alike, constantly made up words ourselves. Sometimes, in adulthood, we'd use the words in the outside world and be surprised to find they weren't real to other people, or at least that their meaning wasn't as immediately, glaringly obvious to them as it was to us. 'Grooble', for instance, meant to touch or paw in an annoying or overly intimate way, as in, 'Ma, she won't stop groobling my pencil case,' or, when we were older, 'Did you meet the husband? Bit groobly.' As well as the words, there were endless phrases. If people were short – all the Radletts were long-limbed and rangy and viewed short people with fascination and envy ('It must be so *cosy* to be short,' Linda said) – we'd say they were 'still growing', even if they were adults: 'What's she like?' 'Dark hair, hazel eyes, still growing, very nice.' If people were clingy, we'd say they 'wouldn't flush'.

Anyway, here we all are. My beautiful cousin Linda – also known as Linny, Linoleum, Lino, Linguine, McCartney, Macca or sometimes Paul – is looking crossly at a dish of sausages, the presence of which suggests that the photograph was taken when the Radletts still kept a few pigs, a short-lived enterprise that perished when Linda's vegetarianism became militant. Or perhaps she is cross at the thought of her dungarees. Aunt Sadie had told her that she looked very sweet. Jassy had said that she looked like someone American who lives in the woods and whose brother is also her husband. 'I can't believe my own mother dresses me like an incest,' Linda had cried. Aunt Sadie had snorted with laughter at this and told them both not to be so silly, but said, 'Howdy, y'all,' every time she looked at Linda that morning. Uncle Matthew shouted that he was against incest in all its forms and that shooting was too good for them, enraging Linda further by directing the remark at her with a disgusted look on his face. Jassy, chewing languidly on a toothpick, kept telling Linda that they were 'kin' and that Miss Linda was mighty pretty. By lunchtime the dungarees had been discarded, which Linda said was actually a shame because the bib pocket had made a perfect home for her mouse, Lucky Fernandez.

Here is twelve-year-old Jassy, clear-eyed and wild-haired, looking straight at the camera with an amused and detached expression, as if to say, 'I don't know who these people are or why I am among them, but I don't mind for now.' Louisa, the eldest, is sketching something on the back of an envelope, most probably a girl wearing normal teenage clothes, these being denied us in favour of not only dungarees but also corduroy trousers and hand-me-down jerseys, an injustice most acutely felt by seventeen-year-old Louisa, who longed with all her being for something tight and short and made from synthetic fabric. She had also longed, from the age of eleven, for marriage to a lord, preferably Scottish and in possession of a castle, so perhaps she is sketching a wedding dress. Robin, more usually called the Baby despite saying, 'I am not a baby,' at least once an hour, is three and wearing one of his older siblings' T-shirts as a dress or sack; he is carefully drawing a triceratops on the wall. Aunt Sadie has improvised a matching neck frill for him out of a crumpled tea towel.

Aunt Sadie, stately and serene, is planning supper and holding down the pages of a food-splattered recipe book with one hand while feeding herself home-made spelt toast with the other. My mother must have been staying because here she is, smooth-skinned, glossy-nailed, perfectly made-up, a narrow silk scarf tied jauntily around her pretty neck. She is peeling a peach and laughing at something Uncle Matthew has said. My mother is Aunt Sadie's sister. She is called Georgina but everyone calls her the Bolter, including herself: 'Darling, it's me, Bolts,' she'll say on the phone in her husky voice. She always sounds like she's spent the night screaming. The Bolter is much married and rarely single – she wears all her wedding rings at once, in a stack that reaches her finger joint – which is how I came to be living at Alconleigh. There is a third sister, my beloved Aunt Emily, who more or less adopted me when I was seven and my mother bolted to follow a man called Rémy to Uruguay (it lasted six months but the Bolter's Spanish remained excellent). Aunt Emily and I had lived together happily in a cottage near the main house ever since. She was a part-time academic, kind, serious, less alarmingly glamorous than my mother and with none of her brittleness, and I adored her.

I am in the photograph too, sitting next to Linda. We are both fourteen, though we look much younger. I am gazing at her with a half-smile on my face and a shine of perfect delight in my eyes. That the rest of the morning will involve lessons – we were home-schooled by Aunt Sadie – does not dampen my enthusiasm. Linda scattered her glitter wherever she was.

'But *why* did you make us live here, Pa? It's so cruel. I do love Norfolk, but we are vital young women, and – well, look.' Linda gestured at the window. Fields surrounded the house as far as the eye could see.

'It's not much to work with,' said Jassy. 'Admit, Pa.'

'It's such a waste of us,' said Linda.

'We considered New Zealand,' said Aunt Sadie, 'so bear that in mind.'

'But I'd love to live in New Zealand!' said Linda.

'Bloody nonsense,' said Uncle Matthew. 'It's much emptier than Norfolk. You'd just waft about all day with koalas clinging to your legs, wailing like Kate Bush.'

'Who's Kate Bush?' asked Jassy.

' "WUTHERING HEIGHTS",' shouted Uncle Matthew. 'Give me strength.'

' "Running Up That Hill",' said Aunt Sadie. ' "The Man with the Child in His Eyes". "Babooshka". You know, darling.' She hummed a few bars.

'Nope,' said Jassy. 'Do you know, Lino?'

'No,' said Linda.

'We are *young* people,' said Louisa.

'Anyway, the koalas wouldn't be climbing my legs,' said Linda. 'I'd carry them in my arms, like babies. Like twins.'

'Would you breastfeed them?' asked Jassy with interest.

'I don't think so,' said Linda uncertainly. 'I suppose I might if they were orphans.'

'Koalas is Australia,' Louisa tutted. 'New Zealand is possums.'

Everyone ignored her. Aunt Sadie pushed back her chair and got up.

'Help me out, Matty,' she said. 'The children can't not know who Kate Bush is.'

'Bloody fools,' said Uncle Matthew, glaring at each of us in turn, even Robin. 'Bloo. Dy. Fools. Right, which one?'

' "Wuthering", I think,' said Aunt Sadie, smoothing down her dress and ruffling up her hair. She held her arms out in front of her and shook them, shifting from foot to foot.

Uncle Matthew said, 'Give me a sec,' leaned back in his chair and then made a sound uncannily like notes being picked out by one finger on a jangly piano. 'Ready,' he said. 'From the top.'

Aunt Sadie suddenly crouched on to the kitchen floor. We were still seated and it took me a moment to work out where she'd gone. We were all looking at her, wondering what she was doing, when she sprang up again with great vigour and started to sing.

'I don't like that eee-eee noise,' said Robin after a while.

'SILENCE,' Uncle Matthew bellowed. 'This song is a masterpiece.'

'Why is Ma doing wavy arms?' Robin asked, undeterred.

'Because I am a ghost,' said Aunt Sadie breathlessly. 'I am the ghost of Cathy and I miss Heathcliff and I am expressing both these things through dance.'

'I don't know them,' said Robin. 'Ma! I don't like your angry eyes.'

'More mad than angry,' said Jassy. 'Pa's the one with angry eyes.'

Uncle Matthew, gazing enraptured at Aunt Sadie, ignored this.

'Have you nearly finished?' enquired Linda.

'No,' said Aunt Sadie. 'Give me space, I'm about to do a cartwheel.'

'That's my girl,' said Uncle Matthew fondly, reaching out to grab Aunt Sadie as she landed awkwardly – the cartwheel had been more of a bunny-hop – but with an expression of triumph. 'Here, Sades, am I your Heathcliff?'

'Yes,' puffed Aunt Sadie. 'It's powerfully moving, "Wuthering Heights", isn't it?'

'If we told someone that this was our life, they wouldn't believe us,' said Linda, helping herself to coffee. 'They would literally say we were making it up.'

'We'd probably be taken into care,' said Jassy.

'Don't be silly, darling,' said Aunt Sadie.

'Would the animals come into care too?' asked Linda. 'I'm not going without them.'

'No,' said Jassy.

'Then I'm stuck here,' said Linda.

2

People often say that they live in the middle of nowhere, but we really did. North Norfolk is not overpopulated at the best of times, but the hamlet of Alconleigh – population: us – really was the very definition of emptiness, with no near, or even vaguely near, neighbours. If it hadn't been so pretty, it would have felt desolate. 'Ah, here we are, the absolute arse end,' Uncle Matthew would say with deep satisfaction whenever we drove home from somewhere. (Driving with Uncle Matthew could be an ordeal: he barked, 'WHY IS IT FUN?' out of the car window at every single group of Lycra-clad cyclists we ever passed. It wasn't really a question, and there were more pelotons in Norfolk than one would imagine. Uncle Matthew also cried every time we drove past a particular very old, very decrepit, very sweet-faced corgi who lived in the nearest village – a village we unavoidably had to drive through to get home – with its equally ancient and doddery owner. She would carry the dog carefully from front door to front garden every afternoon at five, there to let it take the two or three hesitant, tottering steps that were all the walk it could manage. In the end, Aunt Sadie timed all outings so that we would never travel through the village between the hours of five and six p.m., but it didn't really work because even knowing they were inside, old and weak but devoted to each other, caused Uncle Matthew's eyes to glisten with unshed tears.)

The Radletts lived in the farmhouse; Aunt Emily and I lived a few hundred yards away in the cottage; there were a couple of barns and agricultural outbuildings, a handful of tenant farmers an hour or more's walk across the fields, but that was it. You could – and we did – walk for miles and miles without leaving Alconleigh land, and assuming you'd managed it, there was, in any case, nowhere to go, apart from the marshes and inlets and estuaries, and then the grey sea and its beautiful, vast shore. The Radletts all swam year-round, in all weathers and without wetsuits, as joyfully and frolicsomely as otters, and travelled the creeks in a lovely old wooden sailing dinghy, a Twinkle 12 that was ironically referred to as HMS *Freedom*.

We were in the absolute arse end because Uncle Matthew used to be a rock star. He'd been the singer in a band called Sin, and a proper rock star, as in global fame, album sales – back in the days when you could measure these things in album sales – in the tens of millions, chart toppings on both sides of the Atlantic, wives, girlfriends, groupies, lurid gossip, more gold discs than he knew what to do with (they were stacked up neatly in their frames in the loft) and a vast entourage. There were six unauthorized band biographies called things like *Sinner: Deep into Hell*, one of them a top-ten *New York Times* bestseller for forty-nine weeks, and, for quite a while, a life of well-documented excess on two continents. This was never discussed on pain of banishment, though we had a souvenir in the form of a Brit Award which Uncle Matthew, high on pharmaceutical-grade cocaine, had once used to whack the head of Styx, the drummer of his band. Styx had never been overly concerned with the life of the mind and reportedly didn't care about the additional loss of grey cells once the headache wore off. The Brit Award, which lived in the downstairs loo, still had a brown splodge of blood and a few matted Styx hairs adhering to it. We weren't allowed to touch the Brit, which lived high on a shelf, even though we desperately wanted to. 'Fucking Styx, man,' Uncle Matthew would say affectionately about twice a month, shaking his head fondly as he came out of the lav.

Unusually for a rock star, Uncle Matthew conquered the charts and the critics, made a considerable fortune, counted his blessings, eventually got clean – he subsequently abhorred all drugs with the incandescent fervour of the absolute convert – auctioned off his guitars at Christie's for charity and called it a day in early middle age. It must have helped that he'd fallen in love with Aunt Sadie, though they only got together officially after he'd cleaned up because Aunt Sadie said that people who used narcotics had bad karma and that the drugs were an issue, even though she found Uncle Matthew powerfully attractive and fun to sleep with every now and then. 'What your pa doesn't know about sex isn't worth knowing,' she once remarked. 'It's because he has farm-cat traits.' This had caused Jassy to collapse to the floor and pretend to die.

The Radletts lived at Alconleigh because Uncle Matthew and Aunt Sadie felt that their children should have as wholesome and unpolluted an upbringing as possible, far away from London, he because of his own rackety past and because he knew that his children would forever be objects of deep curiosity, Aunt Sadie because, as she once said, 'Clean air is worth more than gold, and anyway I didn't want weird men masturbating at you on the Tube. I didn't want you travelling everywhere by taxi like spoilt babies either.' (When quizzed about this, she said that as a young woman in London, such occurrences were 'constant', painting a picture in our heads that was both alarming and powerfully intriguing.) As well as New Zealand, they'd considered moving to the west coast of Ireland, to the wilds of west Wales and to one of the remoter Scottish islands before settling on Norfolk. Uncle Matthew sold the house in North Kensington and the small cottage in Somerset he'd bought with his first pay cheque and bought Alconleigh Farm, which sat in 10,000 acres a few miles from the Norfolk coast. Linny and I always thought that the thing that swung it must have been the total absence of mobile signal, not only at Alconleigh but throughout much of our part of the county. High-speed broadband had bypassed us completely, though this was academic as we were not allowed electronic devices of any kind. We were analogue children in a digital world, or, as Linda frequently wailed, 'utter freaks'. Fortunately for our development, the almost comical wholesomeness of our geographical circumstances was countered by the fact that Uncle Matthew and Aunt Sadie treated us like grown adults in all other respects. We may have been shielded from the perceived dangers of urban life, but no subject was off limits, no topic deemed unsuitable for children, no question evaded, though our more explicit queries about sex were sometimes answered by Aunt Sadie by means of allusions to animal husbandry that always managed to be both annoyingly vague and troublingly evocative. 'Ugh, I can't believe that it's how we were *made*,' Jassy once said, idly watching one of the horses cover a mare. 'It's ruining my childhood.' Linda concurred. For far longer than might seem feasible, she had assumed that women laid babies, in the contented, strawy way that hens laid eggs.

3

Uncle Matthew had been married twice before meeting Aunt Sadie and having four children with her, first briefly at eighteen to his childhood sweetheart, Pat, now deceased, and then, marginally less briefly, to a former groupie called Cloud Nine, whose real name was Sophie Bridport but who was known to us as Auntie Cloud. Uncle Matthew and Auntie Cloud had two grown-up sons, twins called Cumulus and Cirrus, who now went by Marco and Adam and were, respectively, a middlingly successful character actor and a tattoo artist. They were kind to us when we saw them at family gatherings, but they seemed ancient, too old to hold any glamour. They lived in London, which might as well have been Ulan Bator. London was unimaginably strange to us, both longed for and frightening. We had been only a handful of times; once, in Soho – a friend of Uncle Matthew's was playing a secret gig at Ronnie Scott's – we'd seen an unaccompanied poodle lick up some human sick, the pity of which had made Linda cry inconsolably for the rest of the evening (eventually Uncle Matthew, swearing like a trooper, had gone out to look for the poodle so that we could rescue it and bring it to live with us. He looked for an hour, but it had disappeared. This made Linda cry more, and spoilt London for years).

Our nearest equivalent was the seaside town of Cromer, more manageable in size, which to us held as much dazzle and louche glamour as Las Vegas. We didn't go to Cromer very often either, only to get our hair cut by an old lady called Marie who smelled exhilaratingly of cigarettes and Listerine, or for birthday fish and chips by the beach. The town seemed to us the acme of sophistication, with its year-round pier show, once-grand Edwardian hotels and uncomplicated sense of fun. Its dogs seemed well cared for. Once, coming out of Marie's at dusk and heading for the chip shop, we'd seen some Traveller boys hanging out near the taxi rank, shouting and laughing and wearing gold necklaces, and had fallen in love on sight despite being too shy to speak to them. 'When we first saw them – I want that feeling all the time,' Linda said on the way home, her eyes shining in the darkness of the back of the car. 'I *love* that feeling. Like being a firework or an electric eel.' From then on we dressed up, inasmuch as we owned anything to dress up in, every time we went into Cromer, but we never saw them again ('They're probably travelling,' Jassy pointed out, rolling her eyes). Linda and I had decided to live together in Cromer when we grew up, in a candy-coloured house with neighbours and mobile phones and boys everywhere. We longed for boys and we didn't know any, apart from Creepy Jared, the son of a tenant farmer who sometimes helped out with the animals and who was the only boy roughly our age for miles. We didn't like him because he always wanted to show us dead, mangled things, and seemed to enjoy my disgust and Linny's distress. He had thumbs that looked like toes and talked about sex all the time, using the phrase 'gagging for it' even about wood pigeons. We'd had endless discussions about whether, despite this, he was worth losing one's cumbersome virginity to when the time came. (Within a year or two, we would shift our attention to the adult farmers, whom we called the Reds because that was usually the colour of their trousers when they were off duty. The blameless Reds would occasionally appear in Aunt Sadie's kitchen, where she would give them tea and cake, or sometimes chai and samosas. They briefly became, faute de mieux, the sole focus of our nascent sexual obsession, even though they were ancient and looked like gnarled beetroots. Linny and I would force ourselves to find something attractive about them. 'Mikey Payne has the nicest little brown eyes,' one of us would say, falling on to the sofa in a desperate approximation of swooning. 'Really close together, like a kind monkey. I love that about him.')

As we never tired of complaining, my cousins and I were ridiculously old-fashioned. We were the kind of children who shouted excitedly about the swallows and swifts returning. We ran about outside because there was nothing else to do. We were twentieth century in the twenty-first, like our Fair Isle jumpers, our board games, our flat, navy, rubber-soled sandals, our love of frogs, whom we named from tadpolehood and were bored enough to pretend to recognize thereafter. As teenagers, we once found a pile of Aunt Sadie's old Ladybird books in one of the attics, and Linny observed that we looked exactly like the illustrations, which was mostly true.

Twice a year we went inland to Holt, a charming, well-to-do market town that we considered boringly wholesome and unseedy, there to see the dental hygienist, a South African called Mr Van Der Pant – 'Panties', inevitably. There would be old magazines, ancient copies of *Grazia* on the little table in the waiting room, and we'd fall on them and boggle and hoot with incredulous laughter, like primeval fish-creatures being given an insane, unimaginable glimpse of the biped, mammalian future. We lived on the idea of a *Grazia* double-page spread about buttock implants for about six months. Whenever there was an overlong, dull silence, one of us would say, 'Bum implants, though,' and we would reanimate instantly, sometimes stuffing cushions down our woolly tights or trousers to bring the words more vividly to life. Lip implants had almost the same galvanizing effect until the Bolter appeared sporting some, at which point the others kindly fell silent on the subject, at least in front of me.

4

I'd been staying in the main house rather than the cottage that autumn because Aunt Emily had, unusually, been away for three long weeks. Alconleigh, surrounded by fields and framed by that East Anglian overabundance of sky, was a large Dutch-gabled farmhouse, built in the seventeenth century but much extended subsequently, and made of knapped flint cobbles. It sat at the bottom of a twisty half-mile drive. The house was huge, full of little rooms, nooks, crannies and secret stairs – Uncle Matthew and Aunt Sadie had a pathological aversion to anything open-plan: 'Not a speck of cosiness, no privacy, no wonder most people are neurotic,' Aunt Sadie said, this being one of her many Rules to Live By, which covered everything from the importance of regularly ingesting turmeric to the grave dangers, never quite specified, of radiation from micro-wave ovens.

Despite its size, Alconleigh was sprawling rather than grand, friendly rather than forbidding, comfortable rather than smart. The Bolter was never without the name of a new, hot interior designer – 'I must get Philippe Parrochino to redo my tiny housey' – and was forever redecorating her Chelsea mews house to resemble something she'd seen in a magazine, or at a party, or in a dream. By contrast, Aunt Sadie disapproved of ostentation, valued cosiness above all else and was of the opin-ion that as long as you had squishy sofas, old rugs, cookery books and dogs, you couldn't go far wrong. The dogs, a terrier called Beppe Colombo and a lurcher called Ribston Pippin, both of whom had theme tunes to which they came when called, were welcome on all furniture and beds; any visitor saying, 'Are the dogs *allowed* on the furniture?' in a polite spirit of enquiry earned themselves Uncle Matthew's undying enmity: '*They* are. You're not.'

I loved staying at Alconleigh. I was often nervous around Uncle Matthew, but I adored Aunt Sadie, and the house felt like a hug. Uncle Matthew was a man of extreme and simple emotions, and he loved Aunt Sadie extremely and simply, to the exception – or so he always claimed – of all others, 'from the moment I clapped eyes on her'. For her part, Aunt Sadie used to say, 'It was all over once I met Matthew,' and we had no reason to disbelieve her, for they were demonstratively, cringe-makingly in love, even now. This is why the Radletts were, despite everything, so profoundly grounded and secure, I think. That, and the love that permeated the house like the smell of a pie baking and that made it such a comforting place to stay in, regardless of the fact that Uncle Matthew was quite frightening even to his own children.

He was, to all of us, the very incarnation of masculinity: magnificent, handsome, noble in profile, intensely intimidating, more than human. He was also unpredictable, a man of violent passions and explosive, random-seeming dislikes and prejudices. He objected furiously to many things, the objections forming a vast and elastic mass that expanded and contracted wholly without warning, governed only by Uncle Matthew's erratic internal temperatures. It was impossible to keep track. If you'd asked him directly, he would have told you that it was straightforward, that he simply hated upper-class people ('poshos') because he was working class and had got where he was by grafting, and people who had not got on his nerves. The posho-phobia made only partial sense: he had, after all, married one – Aunt Sadie was the daughter of an Indian diplomat and an English debutante – and our part of the county was tormentingly stuffed full of them. Besides, he might have been *born* working class but few people would have described him as such now (Aunt Sadie once astutely observed that not being working class any more made Uncle Matthew very happy and utterly livid at the same time).

But none of this made a speck of difference to Uncle Matthew. As well as hating the posh, he also considered many 'posh' things intolerable, although again his interpretation of posh was in places individual to the point of eccentricity. Some of his pet hates were obvious enough: cravats, yellow corduroy, Little Englanders, loud braying voices, people who said 'shampoo' or 'fizz' for champagne ('Rather snobbish of you,' Aunt Sadie had once pointed out, to his fury). Some were less so: soap with a pump dispenser, cufflinks, thin socks, overcoats, which he considered both posh and effete, umbrellas, pugs, 'virtue signalling', Dijon mustard, scented candles, English nursery food, including, to our sorrow, mashed potato. Curry, on the other hand, could do no wrong, though he also hated the generic word 'curry' and always used the dish's specific name. He hated aftershave, claret, all tweed excepting that from the Isle of Harris, Englishmen who wore tartan, or sashes, or cummerbunds ('Just admit you're fat, fatso'), anyone with any kind of special food regimen or intolerance whatsoever, people who said 'huzzah', electric gates, 'feelings', water features, blazers, 'smooth drives' (ours was pitted and potholed to the point of no return), hardback novels, people who thought of themselves as literary and said things like 'I'm a great reader.' Uncle Matthew would later claim to have read one book in his entire life, under extreme duress, while forced to convalesce after an early hip replacement. The book, *A Street Cat Named Bob*, moved him so profoundly that he did not, he explained, face wet with tears, need to read anything else ever again, since nothing could ever be as good. When Aunt Sadie had pointed out that Uncle Matthew hated cats too, he'd looked at her strickenly and said, 'Not Bob, Sadie. Never Bob.' In no particular order, Uncle Matthew also hated wallpaper, polyglots ('It's just showing off'), euphemisms in general and euphemisms for swearing in particular, hence our own salty vocabulary, people who abbreviated names and added an S on the end – Matts, Robs, Linds, this last absolutely guaranteeing full-blown apoplexy, even though he often called Aunt Sadie 'Sades'. He hated pot pourri, handkerchiefs, tissues and, by extension, any kind of public nose-blowing, gratuitous thrift, as when people didn't heat their house properly when they could afford to, or bought the cheapest product to save a few unnecessary pence ('penny-pinching poshos, nothing worse'). Also frayed collars and ancient holey jumpers worn in public places ('disrespectful'), being called 'mate' by said poshos, who, he claimed, when male often spoke one octave below their natural speaking voice in an artificially deepened voice to add patrician gravitas, fooling most people but not him. He hated people from southern England who said 'aye', overconfident public school girls with loud voices, imported mushrooms, salted caramel ('not a flavour'), spindly sofas ('not sitting on that'), unfaithful men with 'liars' eyes', high-pitched yawning, all breakfast cereals, privileged women with rich husbands who pretended their hobby was 'work' and always talked about how busy and exhausted they were, skiing, racists, 'poncy' sunglasses (meaning any that weren't from the Shell service station on the road to Cromer), prolonged coughing ('Go and do that elsewhere'), boxer shorts ('no support, what's the point?'), double-breasted suits, people who considered themselves 'characters', non-native wild flowers, feet, any kind of utility wear worn by people who weren't manual workers, with especial loathing reserved for baker-boy caps, tooth veneers, hunting socks and breeks ('Have a look in the mirror, *mate*'), kiwi fruit, ostentatious swimming pools, people who said chin-chin or santé instead of cheers, people whose arms he considered too long, dietary supplements, bath oil ('bath grease'), members' clubs, cars with bull bars, these causing him to aggressively enquire about their owners' moose problem, artichokes ('don't trust them'), facial hair, chicory, Surrey, the colour teal ('not a real colour'), fountain pens, people who dropped Latin phrases into conversation, including 'QED'. Also overly fussy egg dishes, yoga mats (Aunt Sadie once told us that during their courtship she had arranged to meet Uncle Matthew at a yoga class and he had brought along a medium-sized Persian rug), minimalist flower arrangements, especially of the lone-sculptural-bloom kind, minimalist interiors generally, adults who talked obsessively about their school or university days, people who called their parents 'parentals', women who said 'hubby' and men who said 'my other half'. He hated starters, which he found pretentious: we only ever had a main course and a pudding, though there was always cheese, which for some reason he considered wonderfully proletarian. Recent additions to this ever-expanding list included 'wellness' ('Why would I take advice from posh girls with eating disorders?'), enoki mushrooms ('creepy') and the use of the word 'cis' to describe anyone who wasn't one's sister. When Uncle Matthew wasn't furious, he was excessively sentimental. You could see where Linda got it from. All of the Radlett children were creatures of extremes: they loved or they loathed, with nothing in between. They existed in a world of superlatives, and anything dull or ordinary cast them into despair. I don't use the word lightly: Linda in particular had a kind of furious intensity about her, the flip side of which was a disconcerting blank emptiness. They were all incredibly bad at being bored, which was perhaps why they could make almost anything interesting.

5

Although an agonizingly slow modem eventually appeared in the kitchen, we had no computers other than a mostly decorative antique iMac, bulgingly triangular and boiled-sweet pink, which Aunt Sadie would occasionally try and use to send emails, to no avail: the admin got outsourced to Uncle Matthew's assistant Olivia, who would come in once a month and blitz her way through piles of paperwork. We begged for laptops, tablets, smartphones, any kind of device at all; we pleaded, we cried, often, out of sheer frustration, indignation, rage, but no dice. Uncle Matthew was convinced that the internet was a cesspit of vice and that even one look would radicalize us into crazy fundamentalism of some kind or another; Aunt Sadie developed strong and implacable views about the undesirability of social media early on: that it eventually drove even the sanest people stark staring mad was one of her articles of faith. The newspapers got delivered every day, although Aunt Sadie had stopped reading them. 'They're so fattening,' she explained. 'Everything is terrible and then I have to comfort eat, which is heaven once in a while, but not every day or I'd turn into a ball.' And we had books, and nature, and a landline, and terrestrial television – what more, they thought, could we possibly need or want? Never mind that no normal child had watched television in years, or played music on a CD player.

And that was that, except that, unbeknown to the adults, you could get two bars of signal on the other side of the donkeys' paddock, in a fallow field which housed a large, abandoned former pig ark that we had mucked out, scrubbed clean and filled with fresh straw. Uncle Matthew and Aunt Sadie had kept pigs for a while despite Linda's increasingly indignant protests, but stopped when they found her hiding in the trailer that was taking Lolly and Poots, two especially nice Large Blacks, to the local abattoir, sobbing that it was horrible beyond words to murder two of her closest friends. The empty pig ark made a lovely and surprisingly spacious den, cosy and sweet-smelling, and in the warmer months Linny and I often carried across our bedding and camped out in it, waking up with straw in our hair, like medieval peasants. Being made of metal, it got too hot in high summer, but it was wonderfully dry and comfortable on an autumn day, with rain pattering down on the tin roof and hot chocolate lugged across the field in our Thermos flasks. On warmer days, the donkeys, Bingo, Tina and Noble George, would potter over and stick their head above the fence and we'd share our snacks with them. We called our den Da Sty, a name that struck us as the very height of gritty urban sophistication, the sort of establishment you might read about in *Grazia* the next time you were at Panties'. Two bars wasn't much – it took a couple of minutes to access, let alone open, a web page on my ancient Pay As You Go phone, the lone handset available to us, a gift to me from the Bolter – but it was all we had, and so Da Sty became a sort of clubhouse for the children. It was where we would gather to discuss urgent questions that might have arisen during the day, and sometimes attempt, with varying degrees of success, to look up the answer.

This particular meeting at Da Sty had been called for two purposes. The first was that we'd overheard the phrase 'vaginal laxity' on *Woman's Hour* before Aunt Sadie turned it off and got back to teaching us maths, and our curiosity was high ('But Sadie, what is it? Why is she saying it in such a sad voice?' 'Nothing that is relevant to trigonometry,' Aunt Sadie replied, though her eyes flicked to the radio and she murmured, 'poor things'. Uncle Matthew was out inspecting some fencing. *Woman's Hour* was on his list of hatreds due to, he claimed, its preoccupation with mooncups and body hair.

The second topic for discussion that day in Da Sty, more convulsively intriguing still, was that Aunt Emily was expected back that evening, with, according to Uncle Matthew, 'her fella'. But Aunt Emily didn't have fellas: that was her whole point. When I said as much to Uncle Matthew – which took some effort: I was intimidated by him and the thought of a fella had made my stomach plummet – he waved his hand about and said, 'You're a bit slow on the uptake, Fran, for someone who's been to proper school.' That I had spent a few unhappy years in the formal education system before being rescued by my aunts, was mildly nerdy and lived in Aunt Emily's book-stuffed cottage was a source of great amusement to him: he was always testing me and finding me deplorably ignorant compared to his erratically home-schooled children. 'Here, Fran, how come crows attack buzzards even though they're so much smaller? Show me. Act it out. Do the wings', 'Say you're keeping sheep. Roughly how many fence posts in a two-acre field?' and so on. I never knew the answers, unlike his own children, though I learned some by osmosis, eventually. On one particularly excruciating occasion, he asked me what I knew about Louis XIV. I mumbled vaguely that he was the Sun King and lived at Versailles 'in great splendour'. Uncle Matthew repeated 'in great splendour' in a mimsy, nasal voice, then sniffed. 'Lino,' he said. 'Stop drawing that vole for a sec. What about Louis XIV, then?'

'Let me think,' said Linda. And then, more or less in one breath: 'Oh yes. He lived at Versailles and everyone there had to grow one really long fingernail to scratch at doors because knocking was considered rude. Also there were no loos, so ladies in amazing dresses just crapped where they were, like horses. Louis had *loads* of mistresses and *loads* of children, mostly illegitimate, and then when his old wife died he married the nanny, who was quite grand, not like an au pair, I wish we had an au pair, maybe she'd let us wear normal clothes, and then can you believe when he got bored of her he married the *new* nanny – I know! What an old goat, as Ma would say. He had to get up in the morning twice, once with just his friends watching and once with everybody else watching, literally the whole court, plus anyone at all could also turn up and gawp, and it was the same at night when he went to bed. The valet would come and say, "Sire, voilà l'heure," and poor Louis would have to organize himself in bed, in his big nightie. Then when he got up he would have to go to the loo in front of his courtiers, with everyone just standing there staring. I'd have hated it so much and so would you, Pa, you'd die. His brother was called Monsieur, like my mouse who died in childbirth' – here Linda blinked rapidly a couple of times but gamely carried on – 'and he wore red high heels and lovely long curly wigs. He was gay but he got married twice and had seven children, so personally I would say he was an adaptable person. He was an extremely brave soldier. Also Louis loved dancing all by himself in public. He had chubby little fat legs and he wore stockings with ribbons, I don't know how they didn't fall down because I don't think elastic had been invented. Hmmm . . . Oh yes – men at Versailles were always sending their old wives off to convents so they could get new ones, even though the old wives were young and sexy and not at all religious. Do you want to know about the Princesse de Conti? Or Madame Bouillon? Only I can't get the nose right on my vole, look, it's more like a shrew's, so if I could carry on that would help my life.'

Long look at me from Uncle Matthew.

Now Uncle Matthew said, 'She's got a bloke,' and idly spread his toast with Aunt Sadie's thick-cut marmalade. 'She's in love,

Franny. You know.' I absolutely didn't. 'At least I assume it's a bloke. Actually, *is* it a bloke, Sadie, d'you know? You never know, these days, and she's at that age where she could go lezzer.'

'As far as I know,' said Aunt Sadie vaguely. 'Technically, I think she just said, "I've met someone." Let me think. Yes – "I've met someone and I'm bringing them."'

'Ah,' said Uncle Matthew. 'Could be a lady friend. Stocky and capable. Or tremendously feminine and fey, of course.'

'I don't *think* Emily's a lesbian,' said Aunt Sadie. 'I'd have noticed by now, and besides she'd have said. And anyway, don't tease Frances. Apart from anything else, there's nothing wrong with a lesbian, stocky or otherwise. Look how happy Margot Shrimpling is now she's taken up with Rose from the shop. An awful lot of older women become lesbians, I think. So much less alarming than dealing with cantankerous old men, somehow.'

'Do you have a specific cantankerous old man in mind?' asked Jassy.

'I'd totally take up with Rose from the shop,' said Linda.

'We all would,' said Aunt Sadie. 'She's divine.' The shop was a shed two villages away that sold milk, newspapers, bread when Rose could be bothered to make it and boiled crabs in season.

'Classic profile for middle-aged lezhood, I was saying,' continued Uncle Matthew. 'Too clever, bit cross, single for ages, bookish –' here his eyes settled on me – 'set in her ways. Although Em's jolly with it, I'll grant you. The ones who go lezzer . . .'

'Don't say "go lezzer", darling,' said Aunt Sadie mildly. 'It makes you sound so old.'

'Yeah, but they're of a type, aren't they? The ones who go gay later in life. You know. Hard work. Bit intense. Low on laughs. Then they end up together and they cheer up because they can talk to each other about the Liberal Democrats and cats, and suddenly they're really into it.'

'Yes,' said Aunt Sadie. 'And then one night there's some tentative touching, and wham, their lives start anew. I think it's lovely. So romantic. But anyway, I don't think any of this applies to Emily.'

'Would you like an auntie, Fran?' This was to me. 'Another one, I mean.'

'Not really,' I said.

'So is Aunt Emily gay now?' asked Jassy with interest. She looked up from *Ducks and Duck Breeding*, the book she'd been nose down in. 'She kept that quiet. Oh, lucky Franny, having an auntie for a stepdad.'

'I suppose I wouldn't *mind* an auntie,' I said hesitantly. 'I'd rather a nice auntie than a horrible uncle.'

'Do you know, ducks have actual penises,' said Jassy. 'A male duck's penis lives inside a sac in its body.'

'That's so sweet,' said Linda, meaning it. 'All cosy in a little sac. I *love* ducks.'

'Some ducks have helical penises,' Jassy continued, 'but I don't know what helical means. If only I had an instant way of looking it up, like a normal child.'

'Fran will know, she went to school,' Uncle Matthew said. 'Is there more bacon, Sadie?'

'Ugh, bacon,' said Linda with feeling.

'Don't worry, darling,' Aunt Sadie said to me, patting my arm. 'I'm sure whoever Emily brings home will be lovely. She doesn't enter into these things lightly.'

'True. She's not the Bolter,' observed Uncle Matthew.

'Exactly,' said Aunt Sadie.

'Not that it matters who she comes back with,' said Linda sternly. 'Anyone can love whoever they like. Like me and Beppe Colombo, who is my Platonic ideal, except a dog.' Beppe was under the table, his tail sticking out, being fed bits of leftover scrambled egg and toast.

'Beppe Colomboooo, kiiiing of doooogs,' sang Robin, who had left the table and was dancing around the room in Jassy's old hoody, which reached down to his knees. 'I wish I had a tail.'

'I wished that for years too, Bobbin,' said Linda. 'I could never decide between a useful one, like a possum's, or a cheerful one, like a dog's.'

'Or a dinosaur tail,' said Robin.

'Too long. Where are you on beaver tails?'

'Dunno,' said Robin. 'I don't know them really well.'

'Too cumbersome,' said Aunt Sadie. 'You'd want something thinner, Robin. More wieldy. Anyway, where were we? Oh yes, Emily and her friend. Have you quite finished, Matthew? Because it really doesn't matter.'

'Course it doesn't matter,' said Uncle Matthew. 'I was just speculating. Anyway, soon find out. Eh, Fran?' He winked at me unreassuringly.

'They'll be here at six. That reminds me,' said Aunt Sadie. 'There's quite a list of dietary requirements. I need to go and get things for supper.'

Uncle Matthew stopped chewing. Dietary anomalies were one of his many bêtes noires ('load of fucking nonsense'). 'Why is there a list? Fella's not a vegan, surely to God?'

'No, not exactly,' Aunt Sadie said. 'It's just all quite . . . specific. Girls, get on with revision, it's all laid out upstairs. I'll be a couple of hours.' And she exited, wondering aloud about coconut aminos.

'Well,' said Uncle Matthew, turning back to me. 'Helical. What does it mean, Miss Jean Brodie?' But, as usual, I didn't know.

6

Aunt Sadie had, in a previous life, been a private chef, and then ran her own place at the bottom of the King's Road in London – she'd met Uncle Matthew when he stumbled into her cafe, Peas and Paneer, in search of a hangover-busting breakfast. Later that morning, revision perfunctorily dispatched – Aunt Sadie took the sourcing of food very seriously and was still out scouring Holt for exotic ingredients – the emergency meeting took place in Da Sty. Vaginal laxity would have to wait. The bombshell concerning Aunt Emily and her 'lover', as Linda insisted on calling him, needed urgent addressing.

'I mean, he might be nice,' said Linda, not looking especially convinced.

'They rarely are,' said Jassy, shaking her head dolefully.

'How would you know?' I asked.

'From your mum's husbands,' Jassy said. 'At least three have been very weird indeed. At *least* three. Do you remember the one who always went on to Pa about knowing loads of famous people, and Pa pretending he'd never heard of a single one, even the ones who were old friends, just to annoy him because he was so awful?'

I sighed. 'He was called Stafford,' I said. 'I do remember.'

'And thingy, what was his name – the one who always went about in T-shirts with rolled-up sleeves to show off his buff arms? Pa *hated* him.'

'That was Richard,' I said. 'He was still growing and I think he minded.'

'Still,' said Linda. 'At least they don't get the hots for you.

You know, because you're all peachy and pubescent, or post-pubescent, or whatever it is, with your snowy orbs.' We had found a really old Mills & Boon novel of Aunt Sadie's years before and 'snowy orbs' were what we called bosoms, on the basis that 'breasts' was too anatomical, 'tits' reminded us of the teats of livestock and 'boobs' seemed too comical to be digni-fied. We were tragically romantic in our expectations of life.

'Yes, at least you've been spared that,' Jassy said sombrely. 'So far. Inappropriate behaviour. "Tickling games".'

'Jassy, how do you even know about things like that?' I asked.

But I did know how: it was from the time we'd accessed a porn site using my ancient phone – it took about twenty minutes – and glanced down the list of categories (the images wouldn't load) before the signal went again. 'Incest!' Linda had cried. 'That is so awful. Like on puppy farms.' Linda felt things far more deeply when they happened to animals than when they happened to humans. When she was younger, we could make her cry by reciting a poem that went:

A tiny little robin
Frozen in the snow
Nothing on the bird table
Nowhere left to go.

Sometimes all it took for a build-up of tears was for Louisa to silently mime pecking at nothingness at her younger sister, and then mime keeling over, beak-mouth downturned. Some years before, Linda had been so traumatized by reading an old copy of *Black Beauty* that Aunt Sadie had had to throw it into the fire.

'I think if it's a woman, you know, if Aunt Emily has become a lesbian, then it's less likely, tickling-wise,' said Jassy. 'So that's a cheery thought, Franny. It could all be fine.'

'But who is this person?' I cried. 'I've never heard a single thing about them. Not one mention! Why wouldn't she say anything to me?'

Linda, who had fallen silent and who – I could tell from her damp eyes – had been privately musing again on the horror of puppy farms, now said, 'You never know. He might be Bonting.'

'He won't be Bonting,' I said gloomily. 'Bontings are rare. That's why they're Bontings.'

'Not that rare,' said Jassy. 'We know loads of Bontings. Us, for starters. Robin. Louisa. All the animals, obviously. Ma and Pa. Aunt Emily. Auntie Bolts . . .'

'Not sure about Auntie Bolts,' said Linda. 'Sorry, Fran.'

'Yes, Auntie Bolts,' said Jassy firmly. 'Don't be so rude. She is . . . well, she is at least part Bonting. She is genetically Bonting, because Fran is Bonting. And there's loads more. Hopkirk.' Hopkirk was the gardener and looked after the estate. 'Mrs Hopkirk. Olivia. Jared's dad. Josh in the stables. Rose from the shop.'

'I love Rose from the shop,' said Linda. 'She is 100 per cent purest Bonting.'

Being Bonting was the highest accolade we could bestow. The name came from a picture book that Aunt Sadie read to my cousins when they were little. It was by Shirley Hughes and called *Bonting*, and in it a little boy called Alfie finds an exceptionally nice stone, which he calls Bonting and cherishes dearly. Bontings, to us, were the absolute apogee of greatness and lovability, the sorts of people you wished you could carry about in your pocket and place on your bedside table at night.

'The thing is,' Linda said, 'that Aunt Emily is nice. And so it would be weird if she didn't have a nice lover. It would be counter-whatsit.'

'Intuitive,' said Jassy, who was quite advanced. Her self-improvement project – she had embarked upon it aged ten, citing dissatisfaction with the narrow scope of Aunt Sadie's curriculum – included learning as many new words as possible, 'so that despite my criminally dull early life, I will be fascinating when I talk'. We all read a lot, through boredom. Many of the words we read in books didn't come up in everyday conversation, and so we were never quite sure of our pronunciations – 'megalomaniac', for instance, was said by us for years with a Spanish flourish, as 'mejalo-manny-ac'. We often put the emphasis in the wrong place too, the realization that we couldn't say 'hyperbole', 'archipelago' or 'anathema' emerging only in adulthood.

'Yes,' Linda continued. 'I just don't think it's very likely that she's going to appear tonight holding hands with some sort of horrible monster.'

'Kissing him,' said Jassy. 'All over his monstrous warty countenance.'

'He's not a toad,' I protested.

'You never know,' said Jassy.

'Imagine Aunt Emily having sex,' said Linda. 'Being really into it.'

'Don't.'

'Gagging for it,' Linda said, quoting Creepy Jared. 'COME ON, SON. THASSIT. COME ON. GET IT IN THERE, LAD.'

'We're only teasing you,' said Jassy. 'It'll be fine. He'll be Bonting, just wait and see. I feel it in my insides, like Mrs Hopkirk and perimenopause.'

But I was only partly reassured. Before I went to live with Aunt Emily, I had been painfully aware that my mother could marry anyone – any kind of person at all, at any time, and that we could end up living anywhere, in a castle or a caravan, in Hampshire or Eswatini, and that they might like me or not like me, or be kind to me or mean, and that I would have to fit, to make it work. Like all children who have learned to bend themselves to the whims of a careless parent, I was good at becoming whatever was required: you could pour me into any vessel and I'd take on its shape. Which is why I had a wariness that was absent in my open-hearted cousins, a watchfulness that made me a good observer. I was less nice than them. But I never thought the thing I'd always feared about my mother could happen with Aunt Emily. Aunt Emily and I were a pair, bonded for life, like swans. I felt anxious for the rest of the afternoon.

7

We children went riding along the vast, empty beach that afternoon. I was increasingly distracted by the imminent arrival
of Aunt Emily and her depressing-in-advance partner, and
couldn't concentrate on anything. Riding, like playing a musical
instrument, was considered an essential part of our education,
and factored into the elastic timetable that also included lessons called things like 'A Proper Lasagne', or 'My Composting
Method', or 'Drawing the Smaller Birds'. Needless to say, my
cousins loved their horses more than life, a passion I did not
fully share. This wasn't helped by the fact that my mother had,
by all accounts, been a remarkable horsewoman in her youth –
nerves of steel – whereas it was all I could do to hold on and
not fall off when we galloped along the shore, the Radletts at
their wildest, all of them in a sort of glittering-eyed frenzy –
faster, faster, whooping and hollering like cowboys. Sometimes
Linda rode side-saddle just because she could; sometimes she
rode with no saddle at all. My cousins were tremendously
physical, completely at ease in their own bodies, athletic without being particularly aware of it. One of their greatest treats
in life was the Child Hunt, an invention of Uncle Matthew's,
whereby the children, on foot, would be hunted by Uncle Matthew, on horseback, and by four bloodhounds borrowed for
the purpose from Mikey Payne, he of the little monkey eyes, a
neighbouring farmer and keen huntsman. Uncle Matthew
loved horses and dogs but didn't like killing things, hence this
ingenious compromise. Two children – the designated
hares – would be given a head start, and run about laying the

trail, already breathless with the excitement of it. After a while, Uncle Matthew would follow at full pelt, the baying, slavering hounds leading the way. In the winter, in low light, with Uncle Matthew in top-to-toe black astride his huge grey, the scene sometimes called to mind something from the Book of Revelation – 'and behold, a pale horse' – which sounds awful but only added to our hysterical excitement. We would run as fast as we could, screaming with fear and adrenalin, pause briefly to catch our breath and then take off again. The whole thing took upwards of two hours. When the hounds found us, they would be rewarded with pats and kisses and pieces of raw liver. We realized only years later that some people took a dim view of the idea of hunting children, but we loved it.

The weather really turned, suddenly and dramatically, after half an hour or so. The heavens opened, the rain whipping round, which thrilled the cousins. Their laughter and shouts of delight only got louder as the enormous sky darkened and a black storm started rolling in. They were magnificently impervious to weather, but I felt increasingly sodden and miserable, so I left them to it and despondently ambled my way back home, shivering from the icy rain but too wary to go fast in case my horse slipped in the mud on the lanes. I was soaked by the time I got back to the stables, my hair stuck to my head, my T-shirt glued to my snowy orbs. I handed Alan, my horse, to kind Josh, the groom, and ran across to the house in sheeting rain. To my shock, Aunt Emily's car was already parked outside.

She got up to embrace me as soon as I came into the kitchen, dripping on to the stone floor – 'Franny!' she cried. 'There you are! I've missed you so much, my darling.' She looked and felt comfortingly the same, still smelled familiarly of Shalimar, like an especially delicious vanilla custard, and yet she seemed brighter somehow, more luminous, like a switch had been flicked. All that sex, I thought to myself gloomily ('GET IN THERE, LAD'). She was beaming at me. 'Now, do you want to go upstairs and change before I introduce you to my friend? Or shall we . . .'

'Aha!' said a tall, slight, fair man, walking in from the sitting room. 'Frances. We meet at last. What joy. I'm David Warbeck. Davey.' He had a kind, open face and he was smiling broadly as he approached with his hand held out, which I liked – my mother's husbands usually hugged or kissed me hello even if I'd never met them before. His handshake was slightly limp and his hand lovely and smooth; his entire manner was friendly and boyish; he even had a floppy haircut, like a schoolboy's, with a long fringe pushed sideways. The first thing I thought was that he looked likeable; the second was that Uncle Matthew was going to hate him. He'd probably taken one look from the window and gone away to his bear cave to roar. Davey was wearing a soft, worn tweed jacket on top of a frayed shirt; this alone would constitute grounds for hostility. And this Davey was, undeniably, posh.

'You're absolutely soaking, you poor thing,' he now observed. 'We mustn't let you get a chill, and Lord knows I mustn't catch one off you – I am an absolute *magnet* for germs, it's a desperate situation, a constant frontal assault against the poor body. You mustn't linger in the dampness like a poor, sad mushroom for a moment more. Why don't you go and get changed, and we'll make you a nice tisane?' Tisane! But Davey didn't stop there. 'I have some eucalyptus oil in my kit,' he said. 'I'll dig it out. Very good rubbed briskly on to the soles of the feet. The foot is linked to the sinus, as you know, and a quick massage along Ayurvedic principles, pressure points and so on, the very *firmest* touch, works wonders.'

I stared at him in astonishment, then at Aunt Emily, who was beaming happily at both of us, as though the situation was perfectly normal, as though she wasn't a person who came from a family that didn't really believe in illness, let alone in herbal remedies and things to do with feet. 'Do quickly change out of your wet clothes, darling,' she said. 'Have a nice hot shower, and then come back down and we'll all have tea together.'

'I'll make the tisane now,' said Davey cheerfully. 'Brought some with me, I always do. I harvest the blooms myself along biodynamic principles, Frances, dead of night, by moonlight, with my lovely scythe. Makes a powerful difference to the medicinal outcome. Let me think, now, what did I bring with me? Lemon verbena, obviously, mint, camomile, all the basics. But what we really need here is some of my mallow root and rosehip, so deeply, deeply warming. I think you might be in luck. And of course I've my kombuchas. Very potent against the germ in their own right.'

'Thank you,' I said. 'Um, are you a . . . herbalist?'

'Ha ha, no, no, nothing of the sort. As a matter of fact, I used to be a major in the British Army,' he said. 'But I'm an absolute martyr to my ailments and I've always had a keen interest in healing the body. *Mens sana* and all that.'

'Right,' I said. Latin too: Uncle Matthew was going to eat him alive. I wasn't sure I could bear to watch.

But when I came back downstairs after my hot shower, braced for the worst, I was amazed to find the adults sitting around the fire, roaring with laughter, none louder than Uncle Matthew, whose face was pink with pleasure. It quickly became clear that he had taken a passionate and immediate fancy to Davey Warbeck, and since he never changed his mind about anybody or anything, that was that. 'Come and join us, Franno,' he said expansively, his good mood radiating in warm waves. 'Have you met Davey? Marvellous man. Nothing he doesn't know. So clever. He writes books! He takes pictures! Knows all about everything. Have you read *A Street Cat Named Bob*, Davey? It's a masterpiece.'

'I suffer, with cats – allergic, you know how it is, people always think it's the fur but really it's the protein in their urine and dander – but I did very much admire Bob,' said Davey. 'Quite a cat.'

'I knew it!' Uncle Matthew roared ecstatically, slapping the arm of the sofa. 'I knew you'd love Bob the moment I saw you. There's a fella, I thought to myself, who knows what's what.'

Quite how he had thought this to himself remained a mystery: on paper, Davey was the incarnation of all Uncle Matthew's worst prejudices, with more sprinkled on just for fun. And yet here he was, besotted. Davey seemed equally keen. 'Now,' he said, stretching contentedly. 'Would anyone like to try my sauerkraut? Medicinal rather than feasting purposes, in this instance. I brought a couple of jars, house gift, you know. It *is* rather pungent but of course that's where all the goodness lies, in the ferment, which combats the pathogenic bacteria one is so riddled with. Just what the doctor ordered after this wonderful but rather rich tea you've so kindly laid on. All those probiotics – a dream for the gut. Matthew, can I tempt you?'

At supper that night, Davey, who it turned out wrote and photographed well-regarded, lavishly produced books about (mostly Georgian) interiors, chatted companionably to Aunt Sadie about gardening and cookery, two of her favourite topics, about which he seemed extremely knowledgeable. 'Thank you so much for making me this delicious food,' he said. 'I hope I haven't put you to too much trouble.'

'Not at all,' lied Aunt Sadie. 'I couldn't get my hands on nutritional yeast, which I must say does sound revolting, but I managed to get hold of everything else on your list. When I had my cafe, Peas and Paneer . . .'

'I remember Peas and Paneer very well,' said Davey. 'We called it Peas. It was quite the scene, back in the day.'

'Thank you,' said Aunt Sadie. 'Yes, I suppose it was. Anyway, we used a lot of tofu before it was fashionable, and I became very fond of it. But tell me, what exactly is tempeh?'

'Excellent source of protein,' Davey said. 'Same sort of idea, compressed soya beans, but coarser in texture. Madly meaty. Would you like to try some? Only, would you mind using your own fork? I work desperately hard at my inner ecology and your saliva would transfer on to my fork, you see, along with bits of your oral microbiome.'

'Are you a vegan, Davey?' Uncle Matthew asked amiably, with no hint of the roiling, tooth-gnashing fury the question would ordinarily evoke.

'Oh no,' said Davey. 'I'm a wretched invalid, too delicate, I'm afraid, to align myself with any existing alimentary movement, though I have a lot of time for the late Dr Mayr's method. Have you taken the cure? Austria? No? Oh, you should, you'd love it. Stale buckwheat rolls, deeply thoughtful chewing, tiny sips of vegetable bouillon. It's heaven. And of course the Germanic races really *understand* about faeces.'

'Ce sont, comme d'habitude, les voies urinaires,' said Jassy.

'Quite right, Jassy,' said Davey, looking nonplussed but also rather impressed. 'Clever of you. Can you say it in German too?'

'No,' said Jassy.

'Right. Where was I? Ah yes. The answer, Matthew, is that I follow a regime of my own devising. Decades' worth of research. A life's work, really. And anyway, today's veganism is far too processed for me.'

'Jackfruit,' said Uncle Matthew with feeling. 'They give it to you instead of pulled pork.'

'I abhor the jackfruit unless I am in Myanmar,' said Davey. 'The Burmese do the most delicious things with it. In fact, I abhor all of these ersatz approximations. Provided I knew the pigs personally and had been able to reassure myself regarding their welfare and upbringing, I would rather eat pulled pork than pulled jackfruit.'

'See, Linny?' said Uncle Matthew approvingly. 'Davey's right. These things aren't as clear cut as you think.'

'Yes, but I still don't eat my fellow creatures,' said Linda. 'Especially if I know them personally.'

'I quite understand,' said Davey disarmingly, earning himself a dazzling smile. 'Neither would I, if I weren't so desperately frail.'

'Davey seems Bonting,' Linda said that night in the attic bedroom we children always retreated to after supper. 'Super Bonting, actually.'

'He does, doesn't he?' I replied. 'Thank God.'

'Did you notice how he yawns? He opens his mouth really, really wide before the yawn actually begins, in readiness. I could have watched him for hours.'

'Bit weird, I thought. You could see all his teeth.'

'No, I liked it. I might start doing it like that too.' Later we would discover that Davey also ate his home-made Scotch eggs as though they were apples, taking hearty sideways bites, and held carrier bags by the very extremities of his fingertips, with a faintly repulsed expression, as though disgusted by his own consumption.

'Do you think he's a bit, well . . . ?' I asked. 'What's the word, Jassy?'

'Effeminate,' said Jassy. 'He is effeminate. Do you know, he's killed people. In the army, not in normal walking-about life. I asked him earlier and he said that alas he had, but only when it was absolutely unavoidable, and not for a very long time.'

'It's hard to imagine,' I said.

'He says he had wonderful therapy for twenty years afterwards,' said Jassy.

'I don't think he's gay,' said Linda. 'I thought he might be at first, but no. It's just how he is. He is himself. I think that's why Pa likes him so much. Also he wouldn't look at Aunt Emily like that if he was gay. They clearly have enormous amounts of the hottest sex. I really like him, Fran. You're so lucky you're going to have him as a stepdad.'

Supper – raucous, laughter-filled and lasting late into the night – had concluded with a toast to Aunt Emily and Davey, who'd announced their engagement just after pudding. Uncle Matthew was so delighted that he went off to find a bottle of his finest champagne, and we all toasted the happy couple with genuine pleasure, and in my case the most enormous sense of relief. Davey took only the tiniest 'symbolic' sip of champagne because he said that anything fizzy distended him horrendously in the tender organs and turned the night into a Calvary.

'Oh, Davey,' Uncle Matthew had chortled happily. He looked at Davey with shining eyes, as though he were a child and Davey a new puppy.

Dear Davey. When I went up to bed that night, he followed me out and quietly said, 'I want to reassure you, Franny, about the future. Nothing will change. I'll move into the cottage, but I know how important your relationship with Emily is and I respect it. I will try my hardest never to get in the way of it. I will try to nourish it, as the soil nourishes the grain, though I myself have difficulty with the more modern grains – selectively bred, you know, hybrids, all the wholesome strength-giving goodness removed. Anyhow, I think you're terrific. This must be strange for you, but you're not to worry about a single thing. I come to add, not to remove. To nurture. And I'm perfectly aware that I'm not your father.'

It had taken one night for all of us to love Davey Warbeck. I love him to this day.

8

Things did change, though, over the course of the next couple of years. For a start, our rather ramshackle, untidy cottage got a mini-makeover courtesy of Davey, who seemed to know an infinite number of 'sweet' people – these in turn all seemed to adore him – who appeared in a series of vans and spruced and prinked and repainted, who made loose covers and new curtains in beautiful fabrics – 'but still rustic, I think, don't you? À la fermière. Important to preserve the Norfolk vernacular.' The result, which I had worried might make our home into something alien or odd, improved it dramatically: the cottage, if anything, became even cosier; the new lampshades that popped up everywhere seemed to make it glow (because they were lined with golden paper, Davey explained, Norfolk vernacular temporarily forgotten, 'which makes absolutely everyone look about a hundred times more attractive').

'The charm of it!' Davey would say, walking into a room and eyeing it appreciatively. He took great delight in his creations. To my joy, as well as a newly decorated bedroom, I was given a four-poster bed and a new mattress which proved so comfortable that Linda used to come for sleepovers especially, groaning with pleasure every time she lay down – 'The firmness, Franny! It's so *civilized*.' The outside of the cottage got a makeover too: the window frames and front door were painted a cheery poppy red, and a plethora of pots and containers, planted with daisies, cornflowers, nicotiana and tumbling nasturtiums in the summer, flanked the front door. Davey sprinkled a kind of magic dust into our lives, while appearing to float around doing not much at all except wave his hands about and pop vast quantities of vitamins and supplements, which he kept under the kitchen sink in a huge, compartmentalized storage crate that took up the whole space.

The other thing that changed was that there was a minor – but definitely noticeable – improvement in Uncle Matthew's variable temper. He was still prone to explosive rages, but a little less frequently than before, and these days he and Davey seemed to spend much of the week laughing. 'Men don't really have friends, you see,' Aunt Sadie explained. 'Not in the way that women do, poor things. And now Matthew's found one, and he's beside himself with the goodness of it.' Uncle Matthew became marginally less frightening to be around. Davey, who was very clever in his apparently guileless way, had even convinced him that formal education had a couple of benefits, this in the context of me harbouring dreams of university – a situation monitored closely by Jassy, who had similar ambitions. As for Linny, she thought she might become a circus rider.

The Radletts hated going anywhere: Uncle Matthew's irascibility made the outside world challenging, plus, as he pointed out whenever they were asked to dinner somewhere, 'WHY? Why should I sit in a stranger's house eating lasagne when there's such good food at home?' Aunt Sadie occasionally dragged everyone out when it became too rude to refuse an invitation for the umpteenth time; on one occasion, Linda, who sometimes narrated whatever situation she found herself in to herself out loud, had quietly murmured, 'He was the greediest man she had ever seen,' about the host, who heard her and looked very put out. But Davey was intensely, proactively sociable. He knew people all over the place and was forever popping off to visit them, or having them over ('Strangers!' we would say, as mysterious cars pulled up in the drive, but there were so many of them, and they came so frequently, that our initial excitement soon abated). Most of Davey's friends were called things like Bobo or Honks, and yet were largely able to be present without incurring Uncle Matthew's wrath, though he did take exception to a very loud man called Oinker, who did another one of Uncle Matthew's most hated things, which was to make noises when someone else was speaking – 'Mmm, yep, yep, uh-huh' – to indicate that none of what he was hearing was news to him and that he fully understood all the references. It drove Uncle Matthew almost mad over the course of a weekend. We all wanted to know why Oinker was called Oinker, but Davey only murmured vaguely about 'the army, you know. Things can get quite ribald.' 'I never want to set eyes on that Oinker again, Davey,' Uncle Matthew told him. 'Man's a moron, with his stupid sounds.' 'Right ho,' said Davey, amiably.

9

More incredibly still to us children, it turned out that Davey knew our neighbour Merlin Berners, through being old friends with Merlin's artist father, Tintagel. Uncle Matthew had taken violently against Merlin Berners from the moment he became aware of his existence, and was implacable in his loathing. According to Uncle Matthew, Merlin was a terrible creature – 'I won't hear his name in this house' had been the refrain for the previous two years – which only added to our fascination. Though he was a relatively recent neighbour, they had never met; Uncle Matthew had simply woken up one morning and decided that Berners was intolerably dissolute. Jassy said that Uncle Matthew was triggered by Merlin because he reminded Uncle Matthew of his wayward past. Uncle Matthew replied that he was triggered whenever Jassy opened her mouth.

Merlin was a famous fashion designer, an enfant terrible whose catwalk shows were known for their faintly sinister beauty and fantastically elaborate staging – engineered thunderstorms, artificial forests, wan girls dripping weeds as they emerged from real-looking lakes. As I have said, we got the newspapers every day and were usually bored enough to read them. Merlin and his crowd were stalwarts of the gossip columns: beautiful girls staggering out of nightclubs and parties, beautiful, muscular young men looking moody, and always a thrilling suggestion of loucheness. Merlin was only in his mid-twenties and his cool, detached gaze looked straight into the camera, impassive, amused, a ringmaster, seemingly in perfect control even as his friends were falling over. There was something borderline menacing about him, even in photographs. 'Gosh, that boy is unwholesome,' Aunt Sadie would say, peering intently at paparazzi shots. 'Quite attractive, though.' Linda said that he looked like he drank his own blood, 'in a good way', which set Uncle Matthew off again. Merlin Berners was, to us, a figure of utmost glamour.

Merlinford, his country retreat, was only five miles away from Alconleigh; at certain points, his estate abutted Alconleigh land. Here Merlin had his own staff, imported from London. They were androgynous types in improbable clothing – hessian trousers, leather harnesses, wimples – that you'd occasionally catch sight of locally, wandering about looking strikingly out of context. Mrs Hopkirk sometimes helped with the cleaning at Merlinford if weekend parties had got too out of hand, which, judging by the frequency of her visits, they usually did. She tried her best to be discreet, but nevertheless managed to relay a sense of great debauchery and decadence, bustling into the kitchen almost thrumming with the urge to impart gossip. Merlin's parties would go on all weekend, she said, and sometimes well into the early part of the week; nobody seemed to go to bed before dawn, and the debris and paraphernalia they left behind often shocked Mrs H to her core, or sometimes reduced her to a giggling heap. We children were sustained for weeks by an overheard mention of 'a gigantic dildo, Mrs Radlett, you'd never think they made them that big, and *made of metal*'.

Merlinford was hidden from the world by an especially dense, high, aggressive-looking geometric hedge, and Merlin kept black-shouldered peacocks and doves that were dyed pink (Mrs Hopkirk reassured Linda that they were dried in the airing cupboard after their dunking, so that the dye took, before being released – 'they don't seem to mind it, bless them'). He had two whippets; these wore diamond necklaces instead of collars, though no one was quite sure whether the diamonds were real or imitation. The whole set-up was so alien, so provocative and forbidden, that it jarred thrillingly with the wholesome aesthetic of our own surroundings. Merlin had long fascinated us children, and never more than now, when Davey casually mentioned that he knew Merlin himself, which was, to us, a bit like knowing the Devil. When Davey eventually went to tea at Merlinford a couple of months later, in the early summer, we lined up in the hall like the Von Trapp children, waiting for his return and fizzing with anticipation.

'Tell us everything,' said Jassy. 'Please start at the very beginning. A very good place to start.'

'We need *every last scrap of detail*,' said Linda.

'Don't think some bits aren't important, Davey,' said Jassy. 'Because they will be, to us. Please could you start with "I turned into the drive."'

'I turned into the drive,' said Davey obediently, 'and about two seconds later there was the house, because the drive isn't very long. Lovely place, I must say, and so improbable somehow to have a Palladian villa surrounded by farmland, though it's hardly the only one. One thinks principally of Holkham, of course, and Houghton Hall . . .'

'Stay on task, Davey,' said Jassy.

'What? Oh, yes. So, Merlinford was built around 1750, I should think. Perfect classical proportions, square and solid. Acres of meadows. Dull garden immediately around the house, though, and of course that brutalist hedge. Merlin thinks borders are bourgeois.'

'Are they, Davey?' asked Linda. Davey had quickly became our arbiter on all matters of taste.

'No,' said Davey. 'Although I suppose it depends on what you put in them. Your ma's are mostly full of wild flowers, which is divine. But Merlin's too young to care much about plants.'

'Anyway, then you went inside,' said Jassy, 'and what did you see?'

'Wait,' said Linda. 'Who opened the door?'

'A young woman called Thalia,' said Davey. 'Very polite and efficient, tailored clothes, like an assistant in an office.'

'Oh. I wanted her to be naked or something. *Then* what did you see?'

'A great big hallway, a double staircase conjoining down the middle, a chequerboard marble floor – black and white squares – grand, formal, you know. Giant urns on either side. Very correct and assured.'

'I want to know about him now,' said Linda.

'Hang on,' said Jassy. 'I want to know more about the rooms because I want to imagine him walking about in them, being all weird.'

'Big square rooms, pillars, ornate plaster ceilings, great big chimney breasts,' said Davey. 'Superficially conservative, but with this layer of, what shall we call it, dark glamour.'

'Ooh,' we said, savouring the phrase. 'Dark glamour!'

'Yes. Almost oppressive, you know. You couldn't get away with it in a low-ceilinged house, you'd suffocate. Quite a lot of taxidermy, including – Linda, cover your ears – a giant brown bear, about ten feet tall.'

'No!' said Linda. 'Ugh. I'm going right off him.'

'Gay men often love taxidermy,' Davey shrugged. 'I expect it's to do with a veneration of things in their prime. Peak perfection, preserved for all eternity, sort of thing, except it never is, though I must say this particular bear is in marvellous condition. Lovely fur, still quite soft, no moulting, I had a feel. Anyway. Lots of pretty things too, some very good glass, trinkets, little sculptures, *objets*. Wonderful paintings, though all rather brooding and dramatic. Flowers everywhere, but not garden flowers – lilies in dark colours with those phallic stamens, really erect, you know.'

'I really don't,' sighed Linda.

'Lilies everywhere. And orchids too, unusual ones, fleshy-looking things in blush colours. Carnivorous, almost. Thank God I didn't have a sneezing fit because lily pollen plays absolute havoc with my breathing, I literally choke, the throat seizes up from all those aldehydes. Where was I? Oh yes. Outsized, very deep velvet sofas, cabinets of curiosities – I think I spotted something horrid pickled in a jar, you know the sort of thing, rather Gothic, unexpected in a classical house.' One of the things we liked about Davey was that he always included us in his observations, as though he were describing things we'd personally encountered a hundred times, or witnessed or heard of, as though we were sophisticated and urbane adults instead of teenage yokels. 'And interesting colour combinations everywhere, everything very slightly off, but in an intriguing way. As far as I'm aware it's all his concept, no interior designers. He's quite the aesthete. Excellent eye.'

'And Merlin?' asked Linda. 'Please get to Merlin now.'

'Ah, Merlin,' said Davey. 'Merlin is always . . . very much Merlin.'

'What's that supposed to mean? We don't know Merlin,' said Linda. 'What is he *like*? What was he wearing?'

'Just jeans and a T-shirt,' said Davey. 'Or what passes for them. The jeans were rubberized.'

'Oh,' said Jassy, very put out. 'I wanted him to be wearing at least a cape.'

'Yes, disappointing,' said Linda. 'Me and Fran thought maybe a dress, like a blood-red crinoline, really low cut, showing all his tattoos, and maybe a crown. Dripping with jewels and raven feathers. Quite sexy.'

'The suggestion of raven feathers is never far away,' said Davey with a faint smile. 'Anyway, you'll meet him soon enough, because I have invited him to Louisa's twenty-first. He said he'd come and bring a few people with him.'

This was such outlandish news that for a moment we all just gawped at Davey in silence.

'Pa will never go for it,' Linda eventually said. 'Not in a gazillion years.'

'Absolutely no way,' said Jassy. 'Over his dead body, he will say. He'll cancel the party rather than have him here.'

But in the event, Uncle Matthew did not cancel the party. He roared for weeks about Merlin attending – 'That depraved shithead! It's a bit bloody much, Davey' – but, following patient, immaculately judged daily intercessions by Davey, eventually reluctantly conceded, on the grounds that Merlin would indeed add a much-needed injection of glamour to the proceedings, depraved shit or not. Aunt Sadie said that it would be impolite not to ask an immediate neighbour, since everyone else locally had already been invited. Uncle Matthew had strangely old-fashioned manners for someone so rude and perhaps this struck home too. He was also aware, at some level, that without a dramatic intervention like this one, his eldest daughter was likely to have an extremely dull party. And so the invitation stood, and overnight Louisa's ploddy birthday bash was sprinkled with gold dust. Before Davey's bombshell, the guests had been mostly made up of old family friends and their children, as well as the local farmers and landowners and various employees and acquaintances, none of them exciting to us because we'd known every single one of them for ever. Aunt Sadie had been fretting for weeks about the lack of younger people and was delighted that Merlin and his gang were coming, though she'd taken Davey aside and asked him about the possibility of drugs, trying to swerve an Uncle Matthew explosion.

'I did mention it to Merlin,' said Davey. 'Gave no impression of having heard me. He's quite vague when he wants to be. I'm sure it'll be fine, though, and anyway, we'll keep his lot and Matthew well apart. I gather the young people favour pills these days, rather than anything one might snort. Or possibly in addition, so hard to be sure, but potentially more discreet, at least. Now, I'm assuming the party will be in the barn, Sadie?'

'Yes.' There was an old black agricultural barn that was sometimes used for events – charity cake sales, the odd plant sale, an annual quiz – to the left of the paddock. 'I thought long tables down the middle and big bales of straw,' Aunt Sadie said. 'Garden flowers everywhere.' She waved her hands vaguely about. 'Champagne on ice in old bathtubs and a bar to the side. Dance floor at the back, stage somewhere for the band – Matthew's organizing that part – front and back doors open on to the fields. Braziers for later, and for the mozzies. Little lanterns in the trees so they're all lit up. It'll be lovely. I could get the children to help me make garlands.'

'Yes, it sounds sweet,' Davey said. There was a tiny pause. 'But it could be so much lovelier, Sadie. You could go the full fête champêtre, you know, very eighteenth century, think of that marvellous painting by Giorgione in the Louvre – well, no, the women are naked, that wouldn't work. But imagine Louisa as a shepherdess, with a divine crook, beribboned, and pavilions all over the garden . . .'

'One, Louisa would never dress as a shepherdess,' said Aunt Sadie, 'and two, it's sounding a bit Marie Antoinette, Davey.'

'Oh, Sadie – how clever. Yes! That could be the theme. Le hameau de la reine.'

'No,' said Aunt Sadie firmly. 'That story doesn't end well and besides I don't want to encourage her. She's already obsessed with aristocrats for reasons none of us can fathom. We can't have people dressing up as doomed French royals pretending to be peasants. Plus, think of the neighbours. They'd be appalled. I'd be appalled, to say nothing of Matt.'

Deep sigh from Davey. 'Darling, very unlike you to worry

about that sort of thing. Anyway, there's good-appalled and bad-appalled,' he said. 'This is *stratospherically* good-appalled. Could I at least just make a few quick sketches of what it might look like? Please?'

No party had ever been more keenly anticipated by us than Louisa's twenty-first. We thought of nothing else. We looked forward to it far more than Louisa did herself; she had requested a party in London, the hiring of a bar or nightclub and a celebrity DJ, but this had been flatly turned down, and she was cross about it – 'I only know about five smart people and they're going to think I'm a grockle. Who has a party in a barn? I'm not six years old.' By this point, Louisa's unwavering desire for the life of a lady was reaching its peak: despite her youth, all she wanted was to meet someone titled, kind and not freakishly unattractive as soon as possible. She was painfully aware that this person was unlikely to present themselves at her twenty-first-birthday party, and this was making her additionally bad-tempered. But Linny and I, and Jassy too, to a lesser extent, were electrified by the prospect of the party, not only because we didn't have big parties in the barn very often – the last one had been a fundraiser for the RNLI – but because as far as we knew Merlin hadn't yet cancelled, and there was every possibility that he would actually turn up. And with an entourage! We were beside ourselves. Louisa, who was tremendously square, was further put out by the prospect of Merlin and his crew.

'I hope they don't come,' she said. 'I don't even know them, and it's my party. I can't bear people like that, with piercings and God knows what.'

'That's because you're massively uncool,' observed Jassy.

'No, I'm not. I'm just a grown-up.' That Louisa was, in fact, massively uncool was evident even to us. She continued:

'They're just going to stand around sticking out and looking mad, and everyone's going to gawp at them.'

'People who dress like that want to be gawped at,' Linda said. 'That's the whole point. They don't mind. They like it.'

'Yes, but I mind,' said Louisa.

'Because you're so uncool,' said Jassy. 'Squares feel threatened by cool people. You hate them because they don't wear tartan trousers and cummerbunds.'

'There's nothing wrong with tartan trousers,' said Louisa crossly.

'There bloody well is if you're twenty-one years old in the twenty-first century,' said Linda. 'Even I know that. You just fancy old fat men. You want to marry Toad of Toad Hall.'

'What's wrong with you, anyway, wanting to get married all the time?' said Jassy. 'It's such a weird thing to want to do with your life.'

'There is no nobler calling than wanting to be a wife and mother,' Louisa replied, 'so you can pipe down, Jassy, and anyway I'd hardly call a lifelong obsession with running away very sensible.' Jassy had started her Running Away Fund when she was ten and stored every penny she was ever given under her bed in a series of Kilner jars; these days there was also a bank account.

'I want to get married, have babies, live somewhere really nice and become a lifestyle influencer,' Louisa continued. 'If only you'd listen. I've explained a hundred times.'

We had a rough idea about lifestyle influencers – by this point Louisa had explained certain things to us, like porn, though we weren't sure at all about whether she was telling the truth or making up the most amazing lies purely to freak us out; we suspected the latter ('I mean, I don't think that's physically possible, do you, Franny? Despite the elasticity.'

'No, of course not. She's just teasing us'). But we still didn't fully understand what being an influencer entailed and now told Louisa so. 'For God's sake,' she said. 'Why do you three never know anything? So I marry my lord, then we have children, then I take pictures of the house and the children and of me, looking all golden with the light streaming in, and then I get tons of followers who love me, and then people give me things.'

'Why?' said Jassy. 'Why do they give you things?'

'What sort of things?' said Linda. 'And would you call him My Lord, or were you just saying that as a figure of speech?'

'I would call him by his name,' said Louisa.

'Lord Buttock of Bot,' Jassy said. 'Most likely. Lord Fatarse of Bum.'

'Shut up, Jassy. When you're an influencer you get sent all sorts of things,' said Louisa. 'Holidays, clothes, jewels . . .'

'Are you sure?' said Linda, frowning slightly. 'I can't see why anyone would send you anything. Really, jewels?'

'Because I would be an influencer, stupid. People would look up to me and want my life.'

'What, with your lord in his comedy trousers?' said Jassy.

'Yes,' said Louisa.

'And,' said Jassy, 'please don't be rude about my Running Away Fund. At least I'm self-reliant, not standing around waiting for some fat old lord to fall on top of me with Herr Pippo, banging away and making babies until I become a stupid influencer.' At some point that year we had adopted Herr Pippo as an alternative to 'penis', though I can't remember why. 'And anyway, why are you so greedy for free things?'

Being greedy for material things was the worst sin, according to Aunt Sadie, if you were lucky enough to have a nice life in the first place. (She was in favour of people who did not have a nice life being as greedy for nice things as possible, driving gold cars and having diamonds in their teeth, and was always disappointed when she met such a person and found them to have tastes more akin to her own.)

'I hate your future life, Lou. I'm marrying for love,' said Linda. 'God, I can't wait, can you, Fran? I wish the love would hurry up and come. I am so ready for love.'

We had, all that spring and summer, become fixated by the passage of time, or rather by the agonizing slowness of it. We sensed that we were on the verge of freedom and newness, of life really beginning, just round the corner, within reach, but when we stretched out our hands like supplicants, hoping to grab it, there was nothing but thin air. I was going to university in the autumn. Jassy, working in conjunction with Aunt Emily and Davey, had formulated a plan to go to the local – fifteen miles away – sixth-form college after home-taught GCSEs. Davey had taken the matter in hand, aided by Aunt Sadie claiming, falsely, that she no longer understood the A-level syllabus and was too busy to go off and learn it. We'd all expected yet another detonation from Uncle Matthew, and it came, but it was less loud than it might have been, and Davey was confident of eventual success, since even Uncle Matthew understood that it was neither kind nor practical to keep his children at home for ever. Encouraged, Linda had developed vague notions about art history courses in Florence, based on the perceived beauty of Italian boys rather than on any particular appreciation of the quattrocento.

Wheels were turning. The future beckoned. You'd think that our lives might suddenly take on a bit of acceleration. In fact, the opposite thing seemed to happen. Time now treacled by; the bud seemed to wither on the branch. It ticked by so slowly that, mooching about lethargically all that unseasonably warm spring, sweaty and languid, we would play a game of guessing what the time was. 'Guess the time, Fran.' 'Four p.m.' 'Not quite that good.' We lay about for hours, hot and listless, in slow motion, watching dust motes dance in the light and listening to music. We couldn't wait for the future to start and for life to begin.

Linda's future, unbeknown to her, would start on the night of Louisa's party. Davey had failed to get his way with the fête champêtre, but Aunt Sadie's casual talent for scene-setting had not let her down. She'd been beavering away for a week, ably aided by the Hopkirks, their grown-up son Callum and us children, excepting Louisa because Aunt Sadie wanted the finished barn to be a surprise. She'd clambered up ladders and placed stubby church candles all across the horizontal ceiling beams, around which she'd also twined long strands of ivy and jasmine, their ends tangling down prettily, their scent already heady. Davey had arranged for one of his elves to drape the ceiling in fabric, hiding and softening the more agricultural aspect of the space. Four old clawed bathtubs – Aunt Sadie could never resist a clawed bathtub at auction – were brimful of ice, ready for the champagne. The floor space had been split up into separate parts. We'd made a chatting area, with rugs on the ground, four huge squishy sofas placed into a square and an inviting pile of Moroccan floor cushions. Two bars had been set up at either end of the barn, and two tables, each about twenty feet long, were dressed with crisp white table-cloths, glittering glasses and cutlery and the entire cutting garden's worth of flowers arranged in an assortment of mis-matched jugs. In the golden light of a warm June evening, the old barn looked enchanting.

So did Linda, in a faintly glimmering leaf-green floor-length slip dress, her dark hair loose, her skin tanned, feet bare but toes painted the colour of geraniums. She wore no jewellery except for a pair of gold hoop earrings. Linda had extraordinary eyes, somewhere between navy and the colour of dark violets, and in her green dress I thought she looked like an iris, a comparison she did not care for. 'I don't want to look like a stupid iris. I want to look like a woman of the world. I know it's Louisa's party, but I want everyone to look at me and not think I look like a flower. Fran! What a thing to say. I'm going to get changed.' But she didn't, in the end. She just added lipstick.

'You look really beautiful,' I said. I knew Linny was beautiful – I had eyes in my head – but I took it for granted and stopped noticing after a while, and we never wore the sort of clothes we were wearing now. We were absolutely delighted with ourselves: getting dressed, Linny had sighed happily and said, 'You know, I'd be quite happy staying here with you, staring at ourselves in our dresses. This is already the most fun we've had in years.' My mother had arrived from London for the party with a new nose job ('Darling, how cute is my snoot?') and a big box from Selfridges for me, containing the prettiest dress I had ever seen or owned, a pale pink silk and organza gown with a fitted bodice and a sweetheart neckline. Like Linda, I was barefoot – we only wore shoes if we really had to, and although heels had been purchased for the party at Louisa's insistence ('Can you try for once not to look like savages?'), they were so uncomfortable that we decided against them – though not before Linda, in front of the mirror in her underwear, admired her legs in them. 'I have very good legs, I think, Fran. Look how long these shoes make them look! Wow. I have *amazing* legs. Who knew? No wonder people totter about, if it makes their legs look like this. Do you know what I'd do if I had a party? I'd tell everyone it was fancy dress, but very specific fancy dress, like "come as a troll" or "come as a penguin", and then I'd ignore it completely and just appear in the most beautiful dress with all my legs sticking out.'

Jassy wore a black, sharp-waisted, close-fitting two-piece suit that she'd found in a charity shop in Cromer. She had tried to wear it with nothing underneath, but Aunt Sadie put her foot down and insisted on finding her a thin, strappy silk vest. The outfit was accessorized with a great deal of glittery eyeshadow and an old top hat from the dressing-up box, embellished with pheasant feathers collected on a walk; her hair tumbled down to her waist in an unbrushed mass of curls. Jassy looked entirely like the essence of herself: original, eccentric, not conforming to anyone's expectations of an adolescent girl, with something of her father's panache about her. Louisa – we had to keep reminding ourselves that it was her party more than it was ours – had been taken to London by Aunt Sadie to shop for her outfit, and looked statuesque ('and ancient,' Linda said cattily) in an elegant strapless navy-blue column dress and very high heels. Her hair, unlike ours, was up in an artfully messy chignon. Davey came in full white tie and Aunt Emily in a ball gown she'd had for years and that smelled faintly of the cedarwood balls she used to guard against clothes moths. Uncle Matthew loomed, rangy, in his softest pair of leather trousers and a Sex Pistols T-shirt underneath an impeccably cut tuxedo jacket. Aunt Sadie wore a sari and armfuls of bangles, her standard solution to anything that involved having to look smart. Robin was in his favourite astronaut outfit, the helmet already slightly fogged.

At first nothing much happened – though nothing much was exciting enough. People had started arriving earlier that day: first the caterers and then the house guests, including my mother (in diamonds and a black, liquid-looking gown that was slashed to the navel), Uncle Matthew's second wife, Auntie Cloud (in a gold-sequinned kaftan), along with their children, Marco and Adam, one in black tie and one in smart streetwear, although we didn't know what smart streetwear was and he had to explain. The members of Sin were already here with their wives and children: Uncle Styx, cheerful as ever, with a very pretty, seemingly mute Danish girl called Freja in tow; Uncle Paddy, the bass player whom Uncle Matthew had once snogged on stage, here with his wife, Carol, and their three round-faced, ordinary children, whom Uncle Matthew had called the Lumps ever since they were born – 'Lumps! Do you want pudding?'; and Uncle Jimmy, the lead guitarist, who was slim and elegant as a museum curator: you'd never have guessed at his former career. He'd married a woman called Perdita, who loved telling unbelievably dirty jokes, called her bosoms 'my boys' and could drink most people under the table. Perdy and Jimmy had brought along their friend Charlotte – 'So posh I can't understand a fucking word she's saying,' huffed Uncle Matthew – and her son Jonty, who was in his mid-twenties and, we couldn't help but notice, seemed to have taken an instant shine to Louisa ('Well, Jonty's not ever going to run out of forehead,' Linda said. 'No worries about that at all. And have you noticed how he stands? His hands just hang there, like paws').

This would have made a party in itself, though a very cosy one where, in the main, everyone knew everyone else too well. Aunt Sadie had declared that good parties were just like good recipes, and that no one wanted a party that felt like comfort food. She'd invited elderly relatives and anyone who lived even remotely locally, while conceding that these were perhaps not the exotic and glittering additional ingredients one might have hoped for – 'more like old carrots from the bottom of the veg drawer, really'. But Davey had come to the rescue and imported a dozen or so glamorous-seeming friends up from London – as usual, they were called things like Grebe and Tooter – and of course Louisa had her own guest list. It consisted, predictably, of tremendously conventional-looking variants on the 'slightly fat boys in tartan trousers' theme so beloved of Jassy. But the barn was packed with people, which was what mattered. The impression was of great, somewhat aged jollity.

Linda and I realized that neither of us actually knew how to dance within half an hour of Davey's London friends hitting the dance floor. There was always music in the house and we danced a lot to stave off the boredom, but – it was now clear – in a wafty way, a Bush-like way, with much trailing of arms and cod-balletic legwork; we also liked interpreting lyrics entirely literally, so that our dancing often closely resembled mime. We did have a more urban version of dancing, which more or less consisted of jogging on the spot, occasionally pumping our arms horizontally, like pistons. It became crushingly obvious that neither of these approaches would do – that what we considered dancing would, in fact, look deranged were we to attempt either of our styles. Linda elbowed me and said, 'How is she doing that with her bottom? I don't think my bottom could do that, do you?' and, seconds later, 'Oh my God, look at that man, what's he doing with his torso? We must copy them. Fran, why are we such freaks – look, even Louisa can dance pretty much normally. Why didn't she teach us? She is so cruel. She said the joggy dance was cool. She said sometimes people did the haka on dance floors. She's so mean.'

We stood by the edge staring at the dancers for ages. They were much older than us, but instead of feeling the ordinary contempt of youth for old people, we were fascinated. It wasn't just that they could dance without jogging or sticking their tongues out angrily – Linda and I had painstakingly learned the haka the moment Louisa casually told us that it was 'very, very cool in London clubs' – but also the way they looked, the way they held themselves, the way they chatted and laughed – everything about them was just right, or so it seemed to us. They were glossy, polished, confident, completely at ease at what was, after all, the party of someone they didn't know. They were the sharpest contrast to us imaginable, with their easy gaiety, their lack of awkwardness, their smooth moves. On paper, our background should have made us blend in seamlessly with people like this, but our upbringing was so peculiar that they seemed completely alien.

Linda had taken a shine to one of the waiters and was making her way towards him when a loud burst of laughter came from just beyond the entrance to the barn. At the same time, a sort of hush gradually fell on the guests. The music kept playing, the waiting staff kept circulating, but there was a palpable shift in the room's energy. For a start, there was now an enormous and magnificent black horse standing just inside the barn door. The horse wore a garland of dark red flowers around its neck and its rider apparently had every intention of riding it right into the room. Around the horse and the rider were a dozen or so people on foot, dressed so spectacularly oddly that within moments the entire population of the barn had turned towards them in gradual increments to stare. The rider was Merlin, wearing a kind of customized, sexed-up black tie, a crown apparently made of greenish-black feathers, and about twelve gold necklaces. He looked handsome, odd and otherworldly, and being on a horse, towered like a prince above the throng. We had never seen anyone that looked like him before in our entire lives, not even, as Linda said, 'in a book or a film'.

Merlin's friends were also wearing extraordinary clothes, mostly black, all stiff fabric and outlandish shapes – exaggerated shoulders, wasp waists and the like, many cut to look as if they were torn or slashed. One woman wore what appeared to be a floor-length mantilla with nothing underneath. The effect of all this was electric – 90 per cent of the older guests were in smart clothes they'd owned since the 1980s, because no one local really ever dressed up – and no one was more electrified than Uncle

Matthew, who, leaping out of nowhere, was suddenly standing by the horse and tightly holding its reins.

'What the fuck is this? Who the fuck are you?' barked Uncle Matthew, though he knew perfectly well.

'Merlin Berners, sir,' said Merlin, very politely. 'It's an honour. Great fan. And these are my friends. We were invited by Davey Warbeck.'

'You're not bringing that horse in here like Bianca Jagger at Studio 54,' Matthew said.

'Clever you,' said Merlin. 'That was exactly my reference.'

'Don't patronize me, you arse,' snarled Uncle Matthew. 'Can someone find Josh, please?' He turned back to Merlin. 'Josh will stable your horse. Well, come on then, dismount. Do you know how, or do you just sit about on horses like a prat who wants to make a grand entrance?'

'Like a prat,' said Merlin, nevertheless dismounting elegantly. He put out his hand. Uncle Matthew did not take it, but gave a heartfelt snort.

'And who are these people?' asked Uncle Matthew. 'Your *entourage*, I suppose?' Another snort. 'Why are they dressed like escapees from some Victorian loony bin? What's with Widow Twankey in the full-length veil? And why is that boy,' he spluttered, 'wearing a *codpiece*?'

'Hello,' Widow Twankey said, coming forward. She had enormous breasts shaped like butternut squashes. 'We're all friends of Merlin's. We're staying at Merlinford for the weekend. I love your music. I grew up listening to Sin, my parents loved you too. *Wrath: Sin VI* is the soundtrack to my youth.'

'You're banned from listening to it,' said Uncle Matthew. 'Effective immediately.'

'Davey said to bring a few people,' interjected Merlin, entirely calm despite Uncle Matthew's rudeness and agitation. 'Yes, that is a codpiece, from a couple of collections ago. Do you like it? I'm sure we could make you one.' His tone was courteous.

Josh had been located and now led the horse away to the stables, eyes on stalks.

'Merlin, dear boy, welcome,' said Davey, who had suddenly appeared by Uncle Matthew's side and was now beaming rather fixedly. Uncle Matthew, by contrast, was as red as a freshly boiled crab. 'Matthew, I brought you a nourishing cocktail,' Davey said, handing him a frosted glass. 'Vodka, but full of berries. Terrific source of manganese. Berries generally are absolutely bursting with antioxidants. Now, Merlin and, er, Merlin's friends, come in, come in. Welcome. No, please don't kiss me, germs, you know, ghastly. The bar's over here. Have a drink and I'll introduce you to people.'

'Fun crowd,' said Merlin, as Davey led him and his cohort away.

The other guests parted to let them through, trying not to gawp. There were a few giggles, but within ten minutes the strange new visitors had been absorbed and the party had settled into its rhythm again. To their credit, Merlin and his coterie did not self-isolate but mingled with the others and seemed, despite initial appearances, to be quite jolly and in high spirits. They politely wished Louisa a happy birthday, even though she flinched and physically shrank from them with a nauseated look on her face. They chatted to whoever they found themselves next to, ate the food, drank the drink. Merlin danced with Mrs Hopkirk, whom he already knew, and later with Aunt Sadie, who said she'd enjoyed it enormously; the woman in the veil, who couldn't eat because doing so would have involved full nudity, was a particular hit with the farmers. 'Not surprised,' said Linda, 'what with her enormous knockers, like livestock.' It turned out she'd grown up not twenty miles away and that although she called herself Electra, her name was in fact Daisy.

The party went on all night; breakfast was served at six a.m. Two significant things came out of it: one, Jonty Fort William, in fact Lord Fort William, he of the excess of forehead and dangly paw-like hands, would be engaged to Louisa within the year; and two, Linda had been asked to tea at Merlinford. She'd kindly mentioned me, and I was to go with her.

'What was he like? What did he say?' I asked as we lay, galvanized with excitement, on the double bed in Linda's attic bedroom. 'God, Lino, what a night.'

'Yes,' agreed Linda. 'The night of our lives. So he said, "And who are you?" and I told him, and he stood very close to me and really stared at me, and then he took my chin in his hands and turned my head from side to side, a bit like I was a horse except without looking in my mouth or at my hooves, and then he said, "Hmmm." I don't fancy him at all, not even a bit, but it was almost sexy, like he could really *see* me. And then he asked me to tea at Merlinford, any time I liked, and then I said could I bring you, and he said yes, he supposed so. He is the most fascinating person I've ever met. And now I won't be able to sleep, is the problem.'

'That's not the problem,' I said. 'The problem is that there is no way Uncle Matthew will let you go.'

'She would find a way,' Linda said to herself. 'Because she knew her life depended on it.'

'I hope so,' I said. 'Now come on, let's talk about the whole party from the beginning.'

II

The solution to the apparently intractable problem of tea with Merlin was in fact perfectly simple, in the end: we said we were going for a long ride and trotted over to Merlinford instead. Linda wanted to go the day after Louisa's party, but she also wanted not to seem desperate ('even though I am so desperate that I can hardly breathe'), so we left it for forty-eight interminable hours. Merlinford was exactly as described by Davey, and the set-up unexpectedly formal: we were given afternoon tea, with two kinds of cake, tiny crustless sandwiches and lapsang souchong. 'She wanted to spit the disgusting tea out,' Linda murmured to herself when Merlin briefly excused himself to go and get a book he wanted to show us. I say 'us', but it was clear from the start that Merlin and Linny were extremely taken with each other, and that my role was more that of a lady's companion, smiling politely in the background. This was fine by me. All of the things that appealed violently to Lino – Merlin was exciting, glamorous, self-obsessed, extravagant and had the whiff of sulphur about him – were less attractive to me. In some ways he reminded me of my mother, though at least there was nothing sulphurous about the Bolter. But he seemed to live for pleasure and self-gratification; like a child – and like Bolts – he sought only amusement, and tired of things, and people, the minute they stopped being entertaining. He demanded constant attention, and became sullen and absent if it was not given to him. I was too dull for Merlinford, which made me uncomfortable. Linda, by contrast, was made for it. She had been waiting to be enchanted all her life.

Our visits to Merlinford grew increasingly frequent. We had a new excuse: we said we were going to visit Lavender Davies, known to us children, not without cause, as Norfolk's Dullest Girl. Lavender was the only child we properly knew – her mother was an old boarding-school friend of Aunt Sadie's – but since she was almost outlandishly boring, we rarely had anything to do with her. Still, she now came into her own, and she had the virtue of living much further away, which bought us extra time at Merlinford. Aunt Sadie never saw Mrs Davies and they certainly weren't in regular touch, so she was unlikely to check up on our new-found passion for Lavender, who, we informed Aunt Sadie, had recently become much more interesting. In between these pretend visits and the always acceptable 'we're just going for a ride', we were left pretty much to our own devices.

Linda could not get enough of Merlin – what he said, how he lived, what he thought, what he wore, how he spoke, the words he used, the facial expressions he made, how he held his long-fingered and unusually expressive hands, how he walked, what he ate, what he liked and disliked. If she could have knelt at his feet wearing a rapt expression, she would have, for days, but she was too much herself to take up any supplicant role. Instead, she sat next to him on an enormous velvet sofa, nestled among fur throws – Merlin's interiors always felt odd in summer, seemingly being designed for Siberian winters – wearing clothes he found for her. He would disappear upstairs, or send one of his assistants, who were called things like Achilles and Ganesha, and return with one of his own creations, which he would then dress Linda in, rather in the manner of someone dressing a doll. Not all his clothes were mad – 'I'd never make any money if they were,' he said. 'The catwalks are just to show what I'm capable of' – and, as Merlin had surely worked out on the night of Louisa's

64

party, they looked incredible on Linda, who was tall, skinny, long-limbed and strikingly beautiful. 'What I love about your face,' Merlin told her, 'is that you're so much more than pretty. Pretty is so boring.'

'I am pretty, though,' said Linda, slightly put out. 'Everyone says so. Well, no, that's a lie, nobody ever tells me I'm pretty at home, which I call rude, because I am.'

'Yeah, you're pretty,' said Merlin. 'But you're much more interesting than that. More weird.'

'She was not weird,' said Linda to herself.

Merlin laughed. 'I mean, that thing you do, talking about yourself in the third person – that's pretty weird. I love it. I love your face, darling. It can be very pretty, boringly pretty, like a nice drawing of a nice girl, but then it can be this whole other much more fascinating thing. Much *darker*. There's a duality. I guess what I'm trying to say is that you're not only pretty. And that I'm not sure you're a nice girl.'

Linda looked startled at this, but didn't reply. I could see her thinking about what Merlin had just said.

'Anyway, I'm going to teach you how to walk now. What's your shoe size?'

'Merly, don't be so silly. I know perfectly well how to walk,' said Linda, snapping back to the matter in hand. 'What's wrong with you?' She stood up and started loping around the drawing room. 'Look, I'm walking. Walk walk walk. Step step step. With my feet and legs, like this.'

Merlin rolled his eyes and called for an assistant. 'What's your shoe size?' he repeated. Lin told him that she was a seven and Achilles was sent upstairs to fetch two pairs of heels, 'the highest you can find, please, try for five inches, in a size seven and a size ten'.

'Do heels exist in a size ten?' I asked.

'I get them from a bloke who used to make shoes for drag

queens,' Merlin explained. 'His dad had a little shop in Islington for years.'

'Do you wear them often? The heels, I mean,' I said, sounding prissy and elderly even to my own ears.

'When I feel like it,' said Merlin. 'Sometimes I try the clothes on myself, and then I put a pair on to get the silhouette right. And sometimes I like wearing them for sex,' he added, looking right into my eyes, enjoying my discomfiture.

Linda hooted with laughter; after a minute, Merlin did too. Achilles reappeared with two pairs of five-inch heels, which he deposited at Merlin's feet like an offering. Merlin and Linny put a pair on each and stood up, he with practised ease, she squealing that she was about to fall over. And that is how Linda became a model.

But I'm getting ahead of myself. Before that, inevitably, Uncle Matthew found out about our visits to Merlinford. We'd gone undetected for so long that we'd become careless. Linda once rode home wearing a gilt and papier-mâché tiara given to her by Merlin; new clothes started appearing and, stupidly, being worn – 'he'll never notice,' Linda said, but of course he eventually did. Even without these giveaway signs that something was afoot, Linda's manner had changed enough to be noticeable, becoming less earnest and more languid, more distracted. Sometimes at mealtimes she seemed almost absent, or would smile to herself in a secretive way, and finally having smelled the rat, Uncle Matthew decided to shoot it.

'Where are you getting these mad fucking clothes from, Lin?' he asked at breakfast one morning after a couple of months of this.

'Oh, they're just old things I found,' said Linda.

'Found where?' said Matthew.

'In the loft,' said Linda. She was a terrible liar, and the lie was already showing across her face. 'And at Sue Ryder.'

'I think they're nice,' said Jassy loyally.

'Sadie,' said Matthew. 'What about these clothes, then? They don't look old to me.'

'I'm not sure,' said Aunt Sadie vaguely. 'But there *are* loads of old things upstairs in the loft, whole rails of them in fact, so I expect . . .'

'Bollocks,' said Uncle Matthew.

'Oh dear,' said Aunt Sadie.

'Ah, crap,' said Jassy.

'Uh-oh,' said Robin.

'I smell,' said Uncle Matthew, 'a neighbouring rat. A SHIT-HEAD WHOM I DO NOT WANT MY CHILD HANGING OUT WITH.'

'Matthew,' said Aunt Sadie, 'calm down. Linda, have you been going to Merlinford?' This was disingenuous of her, as although Aunt Sadie hadn't explicitly stated that she knew of our visits, she gave every indication of turning a blind eye to them.

'Well, maybe once or twice,' said Linda. 'And what's so wrong with that? Franny and I . . .'

'FRANNY!' Uncle Matthew roared. 'I might have known FRANNY would be involved.'

'Darling,' said Aunt Sadie, 'don't blame poor Franny. She's hardly the gateway to vice.'

'IT'S ALWAYS THE QUIET ONES,' shouted Uncle Matthew.

'We just went to tea,' I said. 'We had sandwiches. It was nice.'

'It was nice!' Uncle Matthew repeated in a wheedling voice. 'Nice! There is nothing nice about that, that, that *creature*. You both know perfectly well how I feel about him.'

'We just hang out and chat,' said Linda. 'Nothing bad happens. He gives me clothes. It's fun. He's fun.'

'He's a bloody junkie, is what he is,' said Uncle Matthew. 'He's a bloody junkie shithead twat.'

'I really don't think he is. A junkie, I mean,' I said.

'And you can shut up, you ninny,' said Uncle Matthew. 'Like you'd know a pill-addled freak if you saw one.'

'Are people who are addled by pills technically junkies, though?' mused Jassy.

'I DON'T CARE,' shouted Uncle Matthew, banging the table so hard that the plates leapt about. 'I DO NOT WANT YOU NEAR HIM.'

'Well, it's too late,' said Linda, her eyes filled with tears. 'You can't ban me or us from other human beings. And anyway, we've been going for ages. Months. We like him. I like him more than Franny does, but we like him. He's fun. It's fun there.'

'NO,' said Uncle Matthew. 'He is not FUN. Stop saying he's fun. The beach is fun.'

'Not really,' said Jassy. 'Not when you go every day.'

'The fair is fun,' continued Uncle Matthew. 'The DODGEMS are fun.'

'What fair?' said Linda. 'There isn't a fair.'

'EATING DOUGHNUTS IS FUN,' shouted Uncle Matthew.

'These are really weird examples, Pa,' said Jassy.

'Having sex is fun,' said Aunt Sadie, entering into the spirit of things.

'LINDA RADLETT,' Uncle Matthew now roared. 'ARE YOU HAVING SEX WITH HIM?'

'What?' said Linda. 'Pa, no, of course not.'

'I shouldn't have mentioned sex,' said Aunt Sadie. 'I'm sorry. It's my fault.'

'They are not having sex,' I volunteered.

'Like you'd know, Frances,' snorted Uncle Matthew.

'I would, though,' I said, feeling braver than usual. 'Because I'm there too, Uncle Matthew. There is no sex. We just chat and hang out and Lin tries clothes on.'

'Matthew,' said Aunt Sadie, 'do calm yourself. They've been visiting an interesting neighbour. It's not the end of the world.'

'I AM PERFECTLY CALM,' bellowed Uncle Matthew. 'I DON'T LOSE MY RAG LIKE I USED TO. BUT THIS IS TOO MUCH, LINDA. IT IS TOO MUCH.'

On and on he went. Merlin was not only a narcissist and an unwholesome wanker, but Uncle Matthew wouldn't be surprised if he were also a practising Satanist. He was a torturer of animals (this because of the dyed doves), a manipulator and a depraved human being. He ran 'some sort of harem' at Merlinford – this accusation struck me as exaggerated but plausible – and was not to be trusted further than Matthew could throw him, 'which would be pretty far, let me tell you, fucking thin piece of crap'.

The long and the short of it was that we were banned from ever setting foot near Merlinford again, on pain of death. We were also banned from riding horses or bicycles, or walking. We were, in fact, banned from going anywhere at all. Later that night Linda ran away to Merlinford.

There was tremendous drama the following day, when it turned out Merlin and Linda had gone to London and were at his house in Spitalfields. Uncle Matthew was all for mounting 'a rescue mission', but Aunt Sadie now put her foot down.

'You're behaving as if he'd abducted her,' she said. 'And he hasn't. They've just gone to London, Matty. People go to London all the time. It's fine. She doesn't need rescuing.'

'It is *not* fine,' said Uncle Matthew.

'I wish he'd abduct me,' said Jassy.

'And you can be quiet, Jassy,' said Uncle Matthew. 'Stop talking.'

'No,' said Jassy. 'Stop always telling me to stop talking.'

'You're making very heavy weather of it, Matt,' Aunt Sadie continued. 'She did have a point, you know, about never going anywhere. Annoying of her to take off like that, but I can understand it.'

'I can't,' said Uncle Matthew.

'Of course you can, if you think about it,' said Aunt Sadie. 'She's a young woman, the world is suddenly full of opportunities, and of course she's going to take them.'

Uncle Matthew harrumphed.

'Look, here's Merlin's phone number. I'm going to call him and speak to both of them and reassure myself that everything's OK. Which I'm sure it is. And then we're going to get on with our normal day. And send her some money – maybe Bolts can take it round.'

'They're probably at an orgy high on MDMA,' said Uncle Matthew.

'I wish I was at an orgy high on MDMA,' said Jassy.

'JASSY!' said Uncle Matthew.

Linda came back to Alconleigh for the weekend a fortnight later and laid out her plan: London Fashion Week was coming up and she was going to try her hand at modelling for Merlin, who had taught her how to catwalk in the preceding months; she was going to live in the tiny attic of Merlin's house for a bit; she loved London more than life; and if modelling didn't work out she would get a proper job. Aunt Sadie and Uncle Matthew agreed to the plan – he very much more grudgingly than she – and various London friends and relations were deployed to keep an eye on Linda.

'Now look, Bolter, I'm counting on you,' Uncle Matthew

told my mother on the phone. 'Do you know any of those fashion bastards?'

'I do,' said my mother, 'a bit. From the gays. But darling, I can't make myself responsible for Linda. I couldn't even make myself responsible for Frances,' she added with a little laugh. 'Not even when she was tiny.'

'She can hear you,' said Jassy, rolling her eyes. 'We all can. You're on speaker.'

'Hello, Franny,' said my mother. 'How nice. Well, it's true, isn't it? I don't think I should be in charge of Linda, Matty. Or of anyone. The thing about me is, I do know my limits, darling.'

'I'm not saying *in charge*, Bolter,' said Uncle Matthew. 'I'm saying *keep an eye*. At all the parties and so on.'

'Me no likey,' my mother said in a baby voice. 'But I'll go and say hello if we find ourselves in the same room, of course. Though Linda never seems especially pleased to see me. And I'll tell people I know to do the same. That's the best I can do, Matt.'

'I don't think Auntie Bolts is cut out to be the eyes and ears,' said Jassy.

'Quite right, darling,' said my mother cheerfully. 'I'm more the life and soul.'

I started university in the north of England shortly after this and temporarily rather lost touch with Linda. There were still phone calls, and the odd text, and we'd see each other for high days and holidays at Alconleigh, but our new lives swallowed us up for a while. Mine, at the other end of the country from London, consisted of books, awkward boys and sweaty house parties, hers of metropolitan high glamour, lavish bashes in jaw-dropping venues, small talk and, very quickly, regular appearances in gossip columns and websites. She seemed to be living the kind of existence Uncle Matthew most dreaded, which is to say a version of the existence he himself had lived in his youth: a lot of parties, a lot of being seen out on the town with a lot of different people, wall-to-wall fun and, increasingly, a degree of notoriety.

'The worst thing is that she's becoming famous for doing nothing,' he raged. 'Normal fame is bad enough, and I should know, but that kind of *empty* fame is the pits.'

'It won't be for ever,' said Aunt Sadie soothingly, but I knew from Aunt Emily that she too was becoming anxious about Linda's non-stop partying. She wondered where, or what, it would lead to: 'It's so pointless,' she said, 'and I can't bear the way they always mention who her father is, as though she weren't even a person in her own right.'

Linda's occasional visits to Alconleigh did nothing to alleviate anyone's concerns: she seemed jittery and unfocused for much of the time, slept a lot, or else paced around aimlessly in the middle of the night. Linda had always been my favourite person in the entire world but now she seemed to me to be becoming jaded, cynical, her contagious sense of joy replaced with something heavier and more airless, as though she were a canary and someone had thrown a blanket over the cage. For the first time in my life, I found her unenviable, and the feeling made me terribly sad. Jassy, now an A-level student and hoping to go to art college, saw her more often than I did during this period, and said that beneath her veneer of sophistication and her occasional druggy haze, she was still, reassuringly, the Linda we all knew and loved. 'It's just, the veneer is so awful,' said Jassy. 'And so thick.'

'I think she's lonely,' said Davey when I went down for Aunt Emily's birthday. 'There's nothing worse than being lonely when you're surrounded by people.'

'Tell me about it,' said Uncle Matthew. 'Story of my life, until I met Sadie.'

'Matt once said to me years and years ago that he had fun literally all the time and was never happy for more than a moment,' Aunt Sadie said. 'You know, when he was in Sin. It seems a bit like that with Linda.'

'I was happy all the time at the start,' corrected Uncle Matthew. 'Couldn't believe my luck. Thought I'd won the pools. But I wasn't happy in the middle, and the middle was quite long. What are we going to do? Davey? And where's that freak Merlin in all this, eh? He's supposed to be her friend. Why isn't he looking after her?'

'I think he's probably trying, Matt,' said Davey. 'We all know what Linda is like. She's not malleable once she settles on a course of action.'

'She's like her father,' said Aunt Sadie.

'I'll call Merlin,' said Davey. 'As for what we do – well, I think we do nothing, for now. We all love her and – I'm sorry, Matthew, I'm going to have to say some emetic words now, and I know they will upset you, so brace – we are going to be here for her.'

'Ugh,' said Uncle Matthew, who detested expressions of this kind.

'If she takes too long to come looking for us, we'll make a plan B,' said Davey calmly. 'But if I know Linda, she's more than likely to get bored of it all sooner rather than later.'

Davey was right, as he so often was, but this was not a happy period for the Radletts. However, by the time I graduated Linda, very Linda-ishly, just stopped doing whatever she'd been doing without recourse to rehab or any specialist programme, and in time re-emerged, fresh as a daisy, as though the murk had dissipated overnight. We later found out that Merlin was behind her recovery, in ways neither he nor Linda specified. 'I'm fine now,' was all she said to me, 'but I do need to think of something else to do with myself.'

12

It was at one of Merlin's London parties a year or two later that Linny met Tony Kroesig. It later turned out that Tony hadn't actually been asked to the party at all, just tagged along with a group of drunken people he'd vaguely attached himself to at a members' club earlier in the evening, a telling piece of information that unfortunately came to light too late. Linny had assumed that he was a bona fide guest, maybe even an intimate of the host whom she'd oddly never met, but when she eventually asked Merlin about him, he shrugged and said he had no idea who Tony was at all. Linda was not to know that Tony's social ambitions were such that he thought nothing of not only attaching himself to strangers in bars but begging invitations – from gallerists, film companies, publishers – to events that he felt he should attend because doing so would reflect well on him. He was obsessed with money and status, perhaps because, as Aunt Sadie later pointed out, he was one of those people who are just about clever enough to work out that they aren't a sufficient draw on their own.

Linda was, still, a terrible judge of character and took people entirely at face value. Our overprotected childhood meant that we all did this to an extent, having been so carefully shielded from people who were anything other than benign. Lin was the worst, though, being soft-shelled as well as soft-hearted, with an overabundance of the trusting optimism and friendliness that had been drilled in by Aunt Sadie and that had resurfaced, intact, since she'd cleaned up. 'You must never develop rustic mistrust,' Aunt Sadie would say, rustic mistrust being, according to her, a uniquely rural quality born of isolation, examples of which abounded in Norfolk.

We met rustic mistrusters because sometimes we'd drive to particular farms to buy apple juice or half a side of pork for the freezer from them, and since these were usually impromptu detours on the way from A to B, Aunt Sadie didn't ring ahead. This was fine 98 per cent of the time, but the other 2 per cent consisted of perfect examples of rural mistrust: leathery, frowning women (usually), peering out flintily from beneath eyebrows that were bleached by the sun, their mouths pinched and grim, their suspicion palpable. They'd sidle out from a building and mutter, 'Can I help you?' almost sarcastically, or sometimes just say, 'Yes?' in a way that suggested we had come to murder them. 'Well, no, it's worse than that,' Aunt Sadie once said. 'It's as though you'd come to murder them at a particularly inconvenient time *and* interrupted the very sinister thing they were up to inside.'

Aunt Sadie considered the rustically mistrustful women a personal challenge. Nine times out of ten she would proceed to charm them. She was particularly irritated by their mistrust because our visits to these farms never sprang out of nowhere: their wares were cheerfully signposted – 'Next right for apples' or 'Rare breed pork for sale' – in the active expectation of business, but the mistrusters seemed alarmed and bewildered by the appearance of actual customers. Sometimes they just stood silently, arms crossed, eyes narrowed, glaring at the car, as though they should really be chewing on a cheroot and reaching for their gun.

When Aunt Sadie failed to charm the mistrusters, which was rare, she would decide that they were racist, which may well have been true. Or perhaps the sight of a Range Rover, aged as it was, driven by someone quite glamorous – Aunt Sadie largely went bare-faced but believed very much in sunglasses and lipstick ('The scruffier the clothes, the redder the lipstick,' she would say. 'It's a rule of life') – with a gaggle of unruly children in the back was startling to the mistrusters. Or perhaps they knew who she was – Mrs Radlett, wife of the local rock star, and found it tongue-tying. Regardless, if the mistrusters remained unfriendly – hostile, even, which did happen once or twice – the farm, or nursery, or shop in question would forever be known as Racist Apples, or Racist Pork, or 'No, not the magical nursery with the good ice cream, the Racists, further along on the coast road. Fuck their pelargoniums, frankly.' 'Think I'll go and have a word, Sadie,' Uncle Matthew would say, gnashing his teeth, already on his feet. She usually managed to dissuade him.

Linda met Tony Kroesig, and Linda fell for him hook, line and sinker. He'd been at Oxford, where he'd read Geography at a college within spitting distance of the Kroesig Building and been a rowing Blue; after that, he'd spent some time working for one of his father's companies in the US, which may partly have accounted for his abundance of thrusting confidence. Now twenty-six, Tony was strikingly good-looking, blond, blue-eyed, square-jawed and athletic in a way that seemed more American jock than Englishman about town, as did his fine white teeth. There was a certain springy fleshiness to him, like a cut of prime meat, that carried with it the passing suggestion of a portly middle age. But that was for the future. For now, Tony was, as Davey said, 'a fine physical specimen', and Linny found him both desperately attractive – 'So straightforwardly good-looking in a really basic way, and I love that, don't you?' – and exceptionally amusing, perhaps because his jokes, such as they were, were not sarcastic or world-weary but uncomplicated and undemanding, in marked contrast to the bitchier, snippier humour she'd spent the last few years encountering. But what she liked best of all was his generosity, which was also uncomplicated and straightforward. Linda once mentioned in passing that, in her modelling days, she'd on one occasion been biked a bullwhip, a pair of five-inch heels and two grams of cocaine by a man she'd slept with a couple of times. Tony, by contrast – he had something to do with finance, though exactly what this was was never entirely clear, possibly because none of us ever asked – sent wholesome flowers, cases of vintage champagne and towers of pastel-coloured cupcakes. He wore handmade suits and crisp blue shirts, always looked freshly showered and was absolutely mad about Linda, wooing her as thoroughly and efficiently as a sniper on a mission. As the relationship progressed, the gifts began to include beribboned boxes of expensive silk lingerie ('Fran, look, it has a slit all the way up the back!'), jewellery, more flowers, now with tickets to weekends in Venice or Paris or Barcelona tucked in among the foliage. Linda, raised on hand-me-downs in a family almost pathologically averse to any kind of ostentation and then catapulted into a world where cupcakes and silk underwear, even the vented kind, were considered criminally vanilla, was instantly and completely charmed by Tony's approach.

Tony Kroesig was the only son of a UKIP supporter called Sir Leicester Kroesig, a tall, coarsely good-looking thickset man who'd once made a lot of noise about Europe and immigration in between enriching himself, chiefly through owning a controversial Congolese mining company. He was enormously, conspicuously rich, wore snug double-breasted pinstriped suits that accentuated his heft and was rarely seen without a huge cigar ('Compensating, should think,' Aunt Sadie said, studying the *Daily Mail*, whose diarist had once written a story about how Sir Leicester, who'd got his gong for services to industry, signed himself Leicester, in the manner of a peer of the realm). The family, as evidenced by Tony, were almost performatively well off. They were glossy, neat, taut-skinned, milk-fed, with that patina of wealth that takes dedication and constant maintenance. Months later, having shared a faintly traumatic sauna with them – the steam made it hard to see and there had been unfortunate bumpings – Linda told us with wonderment that they even looked rich naked.

The Kroesigs were the opposite of the Radletts – no tatty old rugs or wine-stained kitchen tables, no bric-a-brac, no dog hair on sofas, no silver bangles, friendship bracelets or wafty dresses in Indian block prints. Linda adored how lavishly, glamorously, carelessly Tony spent money and found the whole set-up fascinating. 'His parents don't have anything old,' she told me. 'They don't see the point. Everything is brand new and pristine and nothing is squishy, it's all sort of *hard*. If something breaks, they throw it away. I said I'd take things to the charity shop for them, but Tony says they're not charity shop sorts of people. What does that even mean? Anyway, it's amazing. You should see their kitchen in London, Franny. Not that they ever use it, but still. It's absolutely massive, like a restaurant kitchen, with this huge professional cooking range with four ovens, and acres of shiny empty worktops. Ma would say it looked like a morgue, which it kind of does, but in such a good way. It almost turns me on. And then you open the enormous fridge looking for a snack and it's just champagne and Lady Kroesig's face creams. Face creams! Can you believe it? And they have staff, and they wear these dinky little uniforms and call Lady K "milady".' Linda hooted with laughter. If she'd been the sort of person to clap her hands in delight, she would have. 'And milady has someone who comes to her house every morning to blow-dry her hair, even though she doesn't have a job and doesn't really go anywhere except to lunch. Isn't it fabulous?'

'She sounds a bit like my mother,' I said.

'Oh no, she's nothing like the Bolter,' Linda replied. 'She'd be appalled by Auntie Bolts – sorry, darling, but it's true. Lady K is not racy. You'll see. And say what you like about Auntie Bolts, but she's not for show. I mean, she does follow her heart, doesn't she? Wherever it may lead, and come what may, poor her.'

A whole year passed; the relationship grew more serious. The Kroesigs spent more time with Linda, who, after an initial flurry of enthusiasm, they now considered bewilderingly bohemian, but whose glamorous parentage meant she could not easily be dismissed. 'They can't make head nor tail of me,' she said cheerfully. 'I don't think they like me much any more, but really, who cares?'

Uncle Matthew and Aunt Sadie had been introduced to Tony over dinner in London. Unless it was his idea, the act of going down to London generally put Uncle Matthew in a foul mood – he remained highly recognizable, and people stared and came up to him asking for selfies in a way that they rarely did in Norfolk, where he could shop in the North Walsham branch of Waitrose unmolested. Then there was the venue, picked by Tony. Uncle Matthew only really liked the Pakistani restaurants in and around Whitechapel, or Hendon or Upton Park if he was venturing further afield for a really good lamb chop. Three or four times a year, he and Aunt Sadie would disappear off for an eating weekend, staying in a crooked old Huguenot house in Spitalfields rented from the Landmark Trust (these trips had long ago given birth to the Radlett expression 'too fat to fuck', which is what happened, Aunt Sadie informed us, when you had an enormous dinner and the mind was willing but the body unable because it just wanted to lie there in peace, digesting. We were repulsed by the phrase as children but all of us use it in adulthood).

There were whole swathes of London that Uncle Matthew refused to set foot in. These were chiefly the neighbourhoods that had been fun, meaning rackety, in his youth, before they had been colonized and sanitized by bankers and their bored wives. Now, he said, they were 'full of wankers with triple basements and panic rooms. I'd bloody panic too if I lived like that. Tools.' He hated everything about these people, whom he still came across occasionally: the fact that they collected horrible art or, worse, paid people to tell them what horrible art to buy because they didn't even have the gumption to trust their own eyes; their overuse of stone or marble floors, which he hoped they'd slip on on the way back from their detestable subterranean swimming pools; the hotel-like aesthetic of their houses ('Imagine being the kind of prick that wants their home to look like a hotel'); their minimalist gardens, full of decking and gravel paths, these being 'an insult to nature, not a blade of grass in sight, let alone a so-called weed'. Given that Tony's house in Holland Park ticked several of these boxes and had a 'Japanese' garden, Linda thought a restaurant might make for a less provoking setting.

Tony had chosen In My Mouth, a fashionable new place in Mayfair that had recently opened in a blare of publicity; its logo, engineered for controversy, was a plump pair of parted female lips. Unfortunately, Mayfair was another no-go zone for Uncle Matthew, with a couple of exceptions around Shepherd Market – Aunt Sadie had long had an account at Heywood Hill, her favourite bookshop, which was around the corner from where the Bolter had her fillers done – but In My Mouth was not on this particular patch. 'I did try for Upton Park,' Linda said, laughing, as she kissed her parents hello, 'but Tony refused to believe me and said no such place existed. And anyway, isn't this fun?'

The meal had not been a success. Uncle Matthew claimed the very act of reading the menu, which included things like kale crackling and prawn sorbet, was making him allergic due to its ponciness. He disliked Tony on sight, initially because he had 'too much hair', men with short quasi-bouffants being another of his bêtes noires, but also, very quickly, for a number of other reasons. Tony was, he reported back to Aunt Emily and Davey, sycophantic, ingratiating, flashy, rude to waiters – he had heinously carried on talking while theirs was listing the daily specials – and laughed loudly at his own bad jokes: 'bloody irritating laugh, as well, like this, hur-hur, hur-hur'. His watch was too big and shiny, his suit was 'spivvy', he looked 'like he lives off Parma ham and cream, like an old woman's bloody cat'. He was boring, hadn't said a single interesting thing throughout dinner and had addressed 90 per cent of his remarks to Uncle Matthew rather than to Aunt Sadie, an unforgivable sin. To cap it all, he had 'manhandled' Linda in a way that Uncle Matthew found intolerable, at least until Uncle Matthew barked at him to stop pawing his daughter. And as if all of that weren't bad enough, Tony had leaned back in his chair and grinned proprietorially as four separate groups of people stopped by and told Uncle Matthew that they loved his music, prompting Uncle Matthew to tell Tony that he didn't know what he, Tony, had to look so pleased about. This was Uncle Matthew on best behaviour, because he could see that Linda looked happy. Aunt Sadie merely said, 'Ghastly restaurant, ghastly people, rubberneckers for miles, food not nearly good enough for those prices, we had to stop for a bagel on the way back, and Tony does love Linda but he is the sort of person who has a great deal to say about things he knows nothing about. Quite a trying evening, but Matthew was very sweet to him, considering.'

Aside from his looks, and the jewels and the vented lingerie, none of us really understood why Linda seemed to like Tony so much. I wondered whether it was the sex, but when I asked her about it, Linda was evasive rather than her usual enthusiastic self.

'It's fine,' she said, smiling brightly. 'It's good. I mean, we have a nice time. Everyone's happy.'

'But?' I said.

'But nothing.' Linda shrugged. I stared at her encouragingly. 'Oh, Fran, stop going on. I mean, it's not my numero uno favourite sex of all time – I think that was probably that man at a party in Westminster, in the bathroom with a queue outside, remember? Anyway, it's not that. But it's fine.'

'Adequate,' I said, which is what Aunt Sadie used to say about egg sandwiches, for which she had an elaborate rating system.

'No, a bit better than that,' she said. 'Adequate plus.'

The other baffling thing was that Linda found Tony intensely amusing – Tony, who by his second drink referred to himself in the third person as the Tonester or the Kroesigator, 'the Gator' for short. He found the wearing of Lacoste polo shirts exquisitely witty. 'Do you see, Linda?' he once guffawed. 'Gator' – pointing at himself – 'and gator', pointing triumphantly at the embroidered insignia on his chest. 'Yes,' Linda replied, with every appearance of delight. 'So, so funny.' 'I've never met anyone like him before,' she'd say, which was true of all of us.

'Tony's an absolute freak,' Jassy said to me after witnessing this particular exchange. 'Linda's lost her mind. She can't seriously think he's Bonting.' Linda, when pressed, had admitted that her love was not Bonting going by the classical definition, but was 'a different kind of Bonting', or Bonting-adjacent. Jassy and I had pointed out that there weren't gradations: either you were Bonting or you weren't. Linda rolled her eyes at us and told us we just didn't know him well enough, and that we'd see how wonderful he was when we did.

Tony was the antithesis of everything Merlin and his crowd liked – fun, froth, wit, beauty, sex – and of everything that Linda had tired of. Instead he incarnated – and it was the right word for his fleshy handsomeness – all that Merlin despised: ploddiness, posturing, dispiriting literal-mindedness and a veneration of money. Tony talked in terms of people 'dropping' any number of Ks on things, which Linda found hilarious, initially at least, mistakenly thinking that this was a Kroesig version of the made-up family language we used among ourselves, and that perhaps the Ks stood for his surname. Poor Linda. She remained, in her way, an innocent. She hadn't paused long enough to examine Tony properly, to hold him up to the light: she'd only thought that if he was a friend of Merlin's, why then, he would be a friend of hers and they'd take it from there. By the time she realized Merlin didn't know him – and, having met him, didn't much care for him either – she'd fallen for him. And now here we were. No one was keen, but she did seem happy.

'Do you think he was a member of one of those drinking societies when he was at Oxford?' asked Jassy. We were all back at Alconleigh for the weekend and Linda was out of the room. 'I bet he was. I can just see it. The Gator, all red, roaring for Veuve and trashing the room with friends called things like Turd. Bit bleak.'

'Man can't hold his drink,' said Uncle Matthew disgustedly. 'He's an absolute arse.'

'He is, a bit – quite a big bit admittedly – but I do wish you'd try, darling,' Aunt Sadie said. 'You can't just go about insulting Linda's boyfriend. I think it's pretty serious, and at least he's sane and well intentioned.'

'Gah,' snorted Uncle Matthew. 'And anyway, facts aren't insults. He *is* an arse.'

'All the same,' said Aunt Sadie.

Tony didn't remain Linda's boyfriend for very much longer: three months later, the couple's engagement was announced in *The Times*. The only person to have really tried to make

Linda see that she was making a mistake was, unexpectedly, Merlin. Having by then spent a number of evenings with Linda and Tony, he'd asked her to dinner and spelled things out for her. 'He is literally the most boring man you or I have ever met,' he said. 'You'd be better off marrying a nice Norfolk farmer. Or not marrying anyone at all. Why do you need to get married? You're not Louisa. How's she doing, by the way? No, actually don't tell me, I don't care. But I care about you, Linda. You're way too young to marry anyone. You're gorgeous. You could do anything.'

'I love him, though, Merly,' Linda said. 'I want to be with him all the time, properly, you know, really together.'

'You don't know a single thing about love,' said Merlin. 'You're a country bumpkin who came to London and went a bit mad with the old recreationals. You've slept with a handful of people and you think that makes you a judge of anything. Sleep with some more! Have some dates! I mean, look at you – you're the flavour of the month. You could be with anyone you wanted.'

'Yes, and I want Tony,' said Linda, growing mutinous. 'You're not me. You have no idea who or what I want.'

'I have a better idea than you,' said Merlin. 'It's a complete waste of you. Are you doing it to spite your parents?'

'How do you mean? No, of course not,' said Linda indignantly. 'How would it be spiting them?'

'He's everything they taught you not to be,' said Merlin. 'But mainly he's *boring*. He doesn't have anything to say and I cringe every time he opens his mouth. If you're so keen on marriage, marry somebody else. Marry me.'

'I hate to break it you, Merl,' said Linda, smiling for the first time, 'but you are massively, massively homosexual.'

'You'd still have more fun married to me for two seconds than in a lifetime of being married to Tony. Is that what you want, to be a nice little wifey for some rich tosser? Bang out nice little babies and throw boring dinners? Linda, look at me. You're a girl who dances on tables. What are you doing?'

'I haven't danced on a table for ages,' Linda said huffily. 'As you well know. That ship has sailed, Merl. And anyway, it had finite appeal.'

'Women who marry men like Tony are looking for security,' said Merlin. 'I should know, I dress loads of them. But you are completely secure. You're not short of money. You're funny and smart and everyone loves you. Lin, what are you doing?'

'I love him,' Linda shouted. 'And you're getting on my nerves. Pipe down, Merlin.'

'You love the idea of love,' said Merlin. 'It isn't the same thing. One day you really will fall in love, and you'll see what an idiot you've been. And you'll come crying to me and I'll say I told you so. Yes, yes, I will make your wedding dress, I know you're about to ask, but I won't make the wedding dress I *could* make.'

'Don't be so mean,' said Linda. 'That is just a cruel thing to say.'

'It'll be spectacular, don't worry. But one day you'll actually get married for love and then I'll make you a dress you will never forget.'

Merlin sent Uncle Matthew a postcard saying, 'Dear Mr Radlett, Tony is awful but I tried my best.' It went unacknowledged, but not unnoticed.

The tabloids had a field day at the irresistible conjoining of rock and roll royalty with household-name industry, and everything that my aunt and uncle had striven so hard for – restraint, relative anonymity, relative normalcy, the absence of regular mentions in gossip columns – evaporated further overnight. The Sunday supplements raked over Uncle Matthew's past outrages yet again. One of them ran extracts from a twenty-year-old book called *Sinner by Name*, the schlockiest and most scandalous of the band's biographies, over two consecutive weeks. To add insult to injury, the decades-old narrative contained therein made Uncle Matthew and his band mates sound like the worst kind of sexist dinosaurs. There were fashion stories and profiles of 'exotic' Aunt Sadie, who sighed wearily and said that she was mixed race, not a bloody macaw. There were features about north Norfolk and who lived there and where, colour pieces about the Wild Radletts, and articles that tried to piece together information about what each of the children was up to. Uncle Matthew was livid.

'This is what happens when you invade your own privacy!' he hollered. 'This absolute rancid nonsense! "Much-married hellraiser", my arse. Sadie and I just sit here eating stew and playing Scrabble.'

'I enjoy it much more now you don't make up words,' said Aunt Sadie. 'That Scrabble dictionary was such a good buy.'

'That Scrabble dictionary is a pain in the arse,' Uncle Matthew said with feeling and without looking up from the newspaper. He jabbed it with his finger. 'And look at this – why does it say Jassy is a sculptor in dung?'

'Because I told a man who hung around outside college looking for me last Wednesday,' said Jassy. 'I said I was a good friend of mine. He's left out the bit about my prodigious intelligence freaking out the other students, who would hate me if I weren't so magnetically charming. Even if I do sometimes reek of my craft.'

'Is that why there's a picture of Lavender Davies captioned "DUNG-GONE: Jassy Radlett"?' said Aunt Sadie.

'Yes, I had a photo of her on my phone so I emailed it to him from a fake address,' said Jassy. 'Probably the most exciting thing that's happened to Lavender in ages.' Times had changed.

Everyone now had a phone, and even occasionally a signal to go with it.

'She's a sweet girl,' said Aunt Sadie. 'I bumped into her in Cromer the other day. She was on her way to a beach litter pick-up, she gave me a leaflet. She said something I didn't quite catch about saving goats. Or possibly boats. Or oats? Are oats endangered? I must ask Davey. Anyway, she's very diligent.'

Linda, meanwhile, was used to the attention and no longer minded it. By now ensconced in premarital bliss in Tony's west London town house, which he called 'my west London town house', she swam about once again in the warm waters of publicity, despite Uncle Matthew's direst pleadings and threats. Unfortunately, the main threat he had at his disposal was cutting her off financially, which would have gone against his every instinct, and would anyway not have made a blind bit of difference.

It was around about then that the Kroesig parents invited the Radletts – the couples had still not met each other – to come to Saplings, their country estate near Guildford, for 'a nice mini-break', as Lady Kroesig put it in an email to Aunt Sadie. 'It will be good to have the chance of a catch-up,' Aunt Sadie read out, 'and perhaps you will enjoy a pampering session in our spa.' She stared blankly at Linda. 'Darling, what does it mean? What spa? And what catch-up, for that matter? We don't know them. We'd have to catch up with each other's entire lives. It would take weeks.'

Uncle Matthew was already in a tailspin of despair. He loathed being a house guest, he loathed mini-breaks – he loathed leaving Alconleigh, really: it was his world and contained all he needed – and he had been felled further by the mention of catch-ups and spas. 'Surrey's not even in the country,' he roared. 'Not properly.'

'Pa gets so hangry,' Jassy observed. 'Have your eggs, Pa. You'll feel much better.'

'Linda, what spa?' asked Aunt Sadie again.

'Oh, they have a spa,' said Linda. 'In their grounds. They converted the chapel.'

'Gosh,' said Aunt Sadie.

'It has frescoes about massage,' said Linda. 'In the Roman style, you know, mosaic people with togas and really sly-looking eyes, and amphoras everywhere. I could tell you how much they cost but you would actually die.'

'Sadie is staring with a wild surmise, like Stout Cortez,' said Jassy.

'Sadie isn't stout,' said Uncle Matthew with a wolfish leer. 'Sadie's bloody sexy.'

'So traumatic for us, when you say things like that,' said Jassy, her mouth full of egg. 'You have no idea. The older we get, the more inappropriate it becomes.'

'I'm a bit stout,' said Aunt Sadie, looking at Uncle Matthew fondly. 'These days. I prefer to think of it as filling out nicely.'

'I bet the Kroesigs have rows and rows of pristine wellies in their pristine boot room, like at that members' club in the Cotswolds,' said Jassy. 'So ersatz and hilair. Can't we all go?'

'They do, actually,' said Linda. 'Wellies, I mean. Pristine Hunters –'

Uncle Matthew snorted.

'– in every size and colour, including gold, imagine. Oh, it's all so incredibly well appointed and comfortable.' She stretched happily, like a cat. 'Everything is lovely and new and unshabby. Toasty too, though I sometimes wonder if it isn't *too* hot.' With the exception of Uncle Matthew, everyone at Alconleigh felt suffocated if they didn't sleep with the windows open all year round, even if it was snowing.

'Could you pass the jam please?' Linda continued. 'They got

that woman to do the house, you know. I say house – I suppose you'd really call it a . . . well, a mansion.' (Imperceptible wince from Aunt Sadie.) 'Oh, what is her name? Davey would know. She buys second-hand books by the metre. She did that hotel where people pay £400 a night to stay in pig arks.'

'God,' said Uncle Matthew. 'I can't bear these fucking fools.'

At this point Aunt Sadie suggested to her husband that perhaps the Kroesigs could come and stay at Alconleigh instead.

'Surrey!' Uncle Matthew repeated. 'Spas!' He spat the last word out. 'I don't mind telling you, Sadie, I don't like it even one tiny bit. Hey, do you remember that spa in Marrakech, with the swingers?' Aunt Sadie did, and they both chuckled. The memory had seemed to perk Uncle Matthew up a bit, because now he shook his head, seemed to compose himself and said, 'Fine, fine. They can leave their estate and come and stay here, with their gold wellies. It won't be quite as bad, will it? It can't be.'

'No swinging, I promise,' said Aunt Sadie, still chuckling. 'I wouldn't fancy it much, would you, Matt? Pants on, I say.'

And so it was decided: Tony, the Kroesigs and their daughter, Blanche – I thought it a sinister name for the offspring of a UKIP supporter – would come for a long weekend, for the sake of Linda. Although: 'They now hate me, you know,' Linda said over aubergine parmigiana the night before they were due to arrive. 'Well, maybe not hate, only Blanche hates me. But they have no idea what to do with me.'

'Don't be ridiculous,' said Uncle Matthew, who loved his children with ferocity and was appalled by anyone who did not.

'Oh, Pa. They're not mean to me or anything. They couldn't be nicer, especially Lady Kroesig, who really tries. But they don't understand anything about me. Not my clothes, or what I think, or anything I say, really. I think I make them feel like there's a joke they aren't getting. I perplex them,' Linda said, distractedly.

'Fuckers,' said Uncle Matthew.

'Matthew!' said Aunt Sadie. 'You're going to have to try to make this weekend pleasant.'

'I don't mind one bit, Pa,' said Linda, laughing. 'It's not them I'm marrying.'

'Oh, darling,' said Aunt Sadie. 'Often with people like that it sort of *is* them you're marrying.'

'Well, I mind!' Uncle Matthew said. 'I bloody mind if those fuckers don't see how lucky their, their fat-bottomed goon of a son . . .'

'Their fucktrumpet,' said Robin delightedly.

'Their fucktrumpet of a son,' Uncle Matthew continued, seizing upon the word, 'their fucktuba, arsetrombone of an offspring, their . . .'

'I'm liking the wind instruments,' said Jassy. 'Their fuckflute . . .'

'That will do,' said Aunt Sadie.

'By the way, don't you think Tony has a really feminine bottom, Linda?' Jassy asked. 'I keep meaning to say. It's just like a woman's. Don't you mind? Don't you mind caressing his woman's buttocks? Do you bump into them by accident?'

'He does not have a woman's buttocks,' said Linda.

'I'm afraid he does, poor thing,' said Aunt Sadie. 'Callipygian, which is unusual in a man. But never mind. He can hardly help it. Besides,' and here she smiled kindly at Linda, 'I always think it must be just lovely to have a great big bottom. So comfortable, like walking around with one's own cushions, or pillows even. No chair too grim. No pew too disagreeable. So clever of Tony!'

'Hardly,' said Jassy. 'He didn't grow his huge bottom, Ma. It was congenital.'

'He must have grown it,' said Sadie. 'I've never seen a huge-bottomed baby. He might have grown it out of greed. To be fair, I can see how that might happen.'

'Hardly a towering achievement, growing an arse like that,' Uncle Matthew said furiously, as though someone had cheated at the village produce show. 'Oh, how lucky he is to have landed you, Linda,' he added, suddenly deflated, all bombast gone. 'Wonderful, kind, beautiful Linda, who is far too good for him, and for them.'

'I'm sure it will be fine,' said Aunt Sadie mild-manneredly. 'Linda loves him, after all.'

'I do,' said Linda serenely. 'Very much. But thanks, Pa, I appreciate it.'

'She can see past his bottom,' said Jassy sadly, flinging her arms out behind her to indicate monumental girth, 'for love is blind.'

13

An invitation to come and stay was duly emailed to the Kroesigs and accepted in seconds, as though Sir Leicester and Lady Kroesig had been crouched over their computers, fingers poised, waiting. Ordinarily any weekend visitors to Alconleigh were instructed to come for cocktails and stay for brunch, which was Aunt Sadie's way of getting people in and out again quickly: Friday night arrival, lots of drinks, big jolly dinner, lie-in the next morning, giant brunch, out again. But this occasion was felt to warrant the full weekend, Friday to Sunday evening. At the last minute, Aunt Sadie panicked and asked Aunt Emily and Davey to come and stay in the house, rather than simply walk across from theirs for meals. 'Safety in numbers,' she said. 'Or at least, a burden shared.' 'What fun,' Davey had said. 'I'll have to bring across a few essentials, of course, to save me ricocheting back and forth – just my new eucalyptus towelettes, to which I have become so very devoted, and hypoallergenic bedding. And perhaps a few small extra treats, say a couple of bottles of celery juice. Do they strike you as kombucha people at all, Sadie?'

We'd all been told to be on best behaviour, and were now awaiting the Kroesigs' arrival anxiously. Linda, pacing, looked beautiful in an old cashmere cardigan that perfectly matched the violet of her eyes. She wore it with a red tweed skirt, brogues and a green velvet ribbon in her dark hair, and managed to make the whole ensemble look ravishingly chic, as only she could: no wonder they were still all so mad about her at Merlinford. Aunt Sadie looked her wafty best in a vintage kaftan thrown over an old silk dress, arms clanking, as ever, with silver bracelets. Uncle Matthew had shaved for the occasion, but was otherwise unchanged, rakish and handsome in his farmer-pirate country uniform of Viyella shirt, Dubarry boots and ancient, second-skin leather trousers from which he had sponged off the worst of the mud.

The arrival of the Kroesigs was not auspicious. At Aunt Sadie's suggestion, Uncle Matthew had very reluctantly gone out to the drive to rake the gravel over the most treacherous potholes, to no avail as the sheeting rain dislodged it again almost immediately. Then every single light in the house went out just as the Kroesigs' maroon Bentley hove into view. Davey had ('I don't have, darling. I *suffer from*') seasonal affective disorder and travelled with a huge daylight simulator as well as a special lightbox under whose golden rays he liked to bask, naked and cheerfully seal-like, in brisk twenty-minute bursts, in, he said, a 'meditative, breath-led' fashion. He had recently upgraded the daylight simulator to a superior American one he'd found online, but something had gone wrong with the voltage converter, and the whole socket fizzed and exploded the moment he plugged the machine in. The lights all fused, the house went dark and the Kroesigs arrived in the pitch blackness, gingerly lighting their own path with the torches from their phones. An agitated Davey could be heard bemoaning the situation from the fuse box in the boot room. 'I'm sorry,' he cried, 'really I am, but if people paid more attention to circadian rhythms – so elemental to well-being – then I wouldn't have to lug this damned machine about with me. Ah, here we are.'

When the lights came back on, everyone looked exactly as one might expect. Sir Leicester was solid, imposing, something about him calling to mind a fat boy in shorts. He was in full tweedy country-house kit, including plus fours, as though he'd come to a shoot in Scotland. Lady Kroesig, in a pastel two-piece, was very much still growing. Tiny and primped and coiffed to fluffy perfection, she was beaming disarmingly and greeted Aunt Sadie by doing namaste. When she spoke, she had a high, girlish, fluttery voice and a strong Glasgow accent. The daughter, Blanche, had the sleek, well-groomed looks and born-again smile of the children of the super-rich – that vacant gloss that makes people say, 'Oh, she is so good to her parents.' Linda loathed her and said it was mutual.

'And this is Angélique,' said Lady Kroesig, bending to pick up a white ball of fluff. 'Say hello, Angélique. She's a shih-poo,' she added.

'Come on,' said Uncle Matthew, who had strong views on dog breeds.

'Hello, Mr Rock Star,' said Lady Kroesig, speaking for Angélique in an English accent. 'I is vewwy happy to meet you.'

'Christ,' Uncle Matthew said. But he didn't want to show Linda up so early on, so after an awkward silence, during which Aunt Sadie glared fixedly at him, he turned to the dog Angélique, nodded at her curtly and said, 'Nice to meet you.' Aunt Sadie beamed, started fussing, gathering all the Kroesigs up and urging them to plonk themselves down by the fire while she went and got the tea things. 'Did you have a good journey?' she said on her return, perching teapots and cups on the coffee table and plates of food on every available surface. 'You must be exhausted. Have a pakora while they're hot. Have a scone. Have some cake.'

'A pakora?' said Lady Kroesig uncertainly. 'At tea?'

'Yes,' Aunt Sadie nodded encouragingly. 'Have one.'

'Thank you, I will,' said Lady Kroesig, helping herself and nestling into the sofa like a little bird. 'This isn't at all what we were expecting, is it, Leicester?'

'No,' said Sir Leicester.

'Is it not?' said Uncle Matthew.

'It's nice, though,' said Lady Kroesig, looking around the room. 'Reminds me a bit of my nana's. Bigger, mind. But she was like you, Mrs Radlett, she loved a knick-knack.'

'How lovely,' said Aunt Sadie.

'Indoor thoughts,' muttered Jassy. Indoor thoughts, as we were always explaining to Robin, were private thoughts that preferred to live inside your head and not find their way outdoors through your mouth.

'And it's great to be here,' continued Lady Kroesig. 'To be honest with you, we were glad to get away. We're having terrible problems with the bison and it's a blessed relief not to have to think about them for a bit.'

'Rampaging all over the place,' said Sir Leicester crossly. 'Bloody waste of money.'

'Bison?' said Aunt Sadie.

'Yes,' sighed Lady Kroesig. 'We read about some people in Sussex who have given over their estate – well, their *castle* – to beasties. It's called rewilding. You make your land scruffy and reintroduce the various species and . . .' She waved her hand about to convey the various species. 'Well, and it's very fashionable. In the end, storks come. You know, the white ones with big beaks. You get grants for it.'

'And it's good for the environment, Mums,' said the daughter, Blanche. 'That's the main point,' she explained. 'We try and do our bit.'

'For bison?' said Jassy.

'Yes,' said Lady Kroesig. 'So we got these bison from a place in Holland – well, I say "we got", it was actually a total rigmarole, at first I wanted aurochs, said we'd pay anything, but it turns out they're extinct. So we got the bison – we had to get a special licence and everything, didn't we, Leicester – and we set them free. At the back,' she added. 'Not in the garden. We've a fair bit of land.'

'But they went and tore everything up and frightened Angélique,' huffed Sir Leicester. 'We didn't realize they'd be so big. They're huge.'

'I thought they'd be cuter, to tell you the truth,' said his wife. 'More cuddly. You don't really get a sense of scale from Google images. But they're quite scary. I don't like their nostrils, or their faces, if I'm honest, and I know it's silly but I keep wondering what would happen if one got into the house and came up the stairs.' She shuddered. 'I mean, I don't think they would, we've got fencing and they're miles away. But I wish we'd got Highland cattle.'

'Goodness me,' said Sadie.

Uncle Matthew had listened to this while spluttering like an old boiler. We feared the worst, but the eruption was more like a leak.

'You might have started smaller,' he now said to Lady Kroesig. 'Beavers, or something.'

'We did think about beavers,' said Sir Leicester, 'but we weren't sure about where to source them from. And we were going for scale, you know, something for Blanche's Instagram and for the papers to get their teeth into. Big fan of your tunes, by the way, old boy.'

Uncle Matthew made a noise.

'I did not like the idea of asking people to come and look at my beavers,' said Lady Kroesig. 'It's not nice, is it?'

'It *is* nice,' said Robin. 'Beavers are amazing.'

'What will happen to the bison?' said Jassy. 'Poor things. Will you get special bison keepers? Like a bison ghillie? Who's with them now?'

'I expect so, eh, Mums,' said Tony, keen to move away from

a topic that clearly vexed him. 'Dads, shall I take these cases up? There's no staff here.'

Sir Leicester looked rather thrown by this, but acquiesced.

'You look after this great big place on your own?' asked Lady Kroesig, agog.

'Oh no, not on my own. The children do their bit and Mrs Hopkirk comes and helps out most days,' said Aunt Sadie. 'But not in a carrying people's bags sense. Now, do go and have a rest before supper. You must be tired, bison or no bison. London is so far away.'

'Surrey,' Sir Leicester corrected.

'Yes,' said Aunt Sadie, smiling at him brightly.

While not catastrophic, the weekend was not an unqualified success. Lady Kroesig was friendly and seemed fascinated by Alconleigh, but Blanche eyed everything and everyone with suspicion. 'She thinks we're slightly dirty, I can tell,' Jassy said. 'Unkempt. I bet she lives in an empty white flat. She wants to spray us with bleach.' Blanche had asked to move rooms because there was a spider. At supper, for which all the Kroesigs had changed into formal evening clothes, Sir Leicester asked Sadie where she was 'really' from, and seemed to find the answer – Highgate, north London – confusing. Lady Kroesig was initially too shy to address Uncle Matthew directly, and so communicated with him largely through the medium of Angélique, whom both Beppe Colombo and Ribston Pippin had repeatedly tried to mount. Sensing his agony, Aunt Sadie moved everyone around between courses. Even Davey, who in our experience could charm anyone, found Sir Leicester challenging, until he stopped trying to make general small talk and reverted to his specialist subject. It turned out that Sir Leicester, a stout man, was an experienced dieter of many years' standing and showed a keen interest in Davey's up-to-date regimes.

'What you must absolutely try, Sir Leicester,' said Davey, 'is eating only white food.'

'He'll like that,' said Jassy, smiling pleasantly.

'Why's that?' Sir Leicester asked Davey, looking interested for the first time that evening.

'It's the Eat Your Politics diet,' murmured Jassy from the other end of the table, earning herself a sharp look from her neighbour Blanche, who hissed, 'Lots of people think Dads is a racist but it's simply not true. He doesn't have a racist bone in his body.' 'Ma says that's what racists always say,' Jassy hissed back. There was something irritatingly self-righteous about Blanche, who now tutted and crossly took a gulp of wine.

'It just works,' said Davey to Sir Leicester. 'So you can eat fish, chicken, yogurt, rice, egg whites, cauliflower – do you love cauliflower? I do – and drink rivers of organic white wine.'

'Davey, have you made this diet up?' asked Aunt Sadie. 'White food tends to be processed and white wine is hardly going to make you thin, it's full of sugar.'

'But not this white food, darling Sadie. We're not doing flour, that's the beauty of it. And then what you do after two weeks,' Davey said, turning back to Sir Leicester, 'is you stop that, and really jolt the body by eating only *brown* food. So the really nourishing grains, your groats, your buckwheat, which is really a pseudo-grain but packed with goodness, your teff, your sorghum. Evacuation becomes an absolute dream, and I do think thorough evacuation is always the goal, don't you?'

'I suppose,' said Sir Leicester uncertainly.

'It is, it is. So your quinoa, your millet, your spelt,' Davey continued, as though he were reciting the rosary. 'Your amaranth, your bulgur. Your einkorn.'

Sir Leicester looked like a man hypnotized.

I found myself sitting next to Uncle Matthew after the main course. He looked so worn out by having to behave that I think he was grateful for my company. 'Here, Fran,' he said. 'Shove in closer so I can talk to you.' I shuffled over. 'What d'you make of all this, then?' he said. 'Fucking nightmare, isn't it?'

We were interrupted by Tony clanging a knife against the side of his glass.

'I've got a new name for him,' whispered Uncle Matthew. 'It's Twats.'

'Uncle Matthew!' I said. 'He's your future son-in-law.'

'Mums, Dads. It's too much. No, he is Twats. He will always be Twats. Now and for evermore. Tony Twats Kroesig. And the dad! He looks like Cook from *Downton Abbey*.'

Tony was on his feet.

'On behalf of the Kroesig family,' he started, 'I would like to thank Matts and Sades for their wonderful hospitality. I think it's fair to say that we haven't been anywhere like this before . . .'

'No, we haven't,' said Lady Kroesig. 'It's so unusual.'

'. . . and we appreciate the opportunity to look round a real slice of rock and roll history. Hopefully Mums and Dads will have you all down to stay at Saplings soon.' He paused and nudged Beppe Colombo's nose away from his crotch. 'But what I really wanted to do tonight was give Linda the second half of her engagement present. I can't wait to marry her. I can't wait for the pitter-patter of tiny Kroesig feet.' Here Uncle Matthew audibly said, 'Ugh,' but I don't think anyone else heard. 'Here you are, my darling. With all my love and gratitude.' He reached into the inner pocket of his country jacket and pulled out a jewellery case.

'Tony!' squealed Linda. 'You shouldn't have! I was so happy with my enormous ring.'

'Well, here's an enormous bracelet to go with it,' Tony said.

There was a small pause, and then the Kroesigs started clapping and whooping, so we all joined in.

'Why couldn't he give it to her in private?' said Uncle Matthew.

'He likes an audience,' I said. 'Like . . . well, like you. You can hardly blame him.'

'Not the same,' said Uncle Matthew. 'This is my house, not Wembley Stadium.'

Tony and Linda were married the following spring. The wedding itself took place in London, where Linda felt she now belonged and where all of her and Tony's friends were based ('His friends *are* quite dull, but they're devoted to me,' Linda said. 'Like puppies with a new toy. Well, the men are. The women are not especially friendly, except for one called Laura who won't flush'). Despite neither the bride nor the groom being devout, there was a religious ceremony at a grand central London church and lunch and dancing for 500 people in the Art Deco ballroom of a smart hotel. The wedding made the front page of the *Evening Standard*, who declared it the wedding of the year despite it only being May. In the photograph, the bride is resplendent in a couture, honey-coloured gown by Merlin Berners and the groom is punching the air in a made-to-measure morning suit. The short accompanying article made much of the 'amusing' contrast between the bride's and groom's respective sides of the church, which it said pitted 'haute bohemia against the staider worlds of industry and finance'. Uncle Matthew started crying in the car on the way to the church, cried as he walked Linda down the aisle and carried on crying solidly throughout the ceremony, with the odd pause to glare murderously at Tony's front-pew friends and relatives as they spotted his tears, nudged each other and went, 'Aah, he's crying,' a sentence that could have been expressly designed to make Uncle Matthew insane with rage. On their way out of the church,

Merlin, passing by, silently gave his shoulder a squeeze. Afterwards the Radlett children and I threw slightly browning apple blossom from Alconleigh at Tony and Lino as they stood on the steps. A small crowd of passers-by had gathered on the pavement to stare at the wedding party, many of them taking pictures with their phones. 'I can't believe she married Twats,' Jassy said to me despondently towards the end of the party. And off Linda went into married life.

14

The honeymoon was three weeks in Mustique – ever mindful of privacy, Uncle Matthew had arranged for the happy couple to borrow Uncle Jimmy's house, Mon Péché, Uncle Jimmy being Sin's lead guitarist. Lino said Mustique was lovely, boiling hot and with wonderful swimming and really interesting fish, but that three weeks was rather a long time and that the mosquito situation on the island meant she'd spent the first week looking like a blister. She was pleased to be back in London and keen to set up home properly. She and Tony had decided against buying a new house – Uncle Matthew had offered – but Tony had given her carte blanche to redecorate, being mindful that his house, all pale wood, minimal, angular furniture and pointless electronics that could turn the lighting blue or green at the stroke of an app, was more bachelor pad than family home. Every single one of the walls was painted grey. 'But they're all very slightly different,' Tony had explained with a seductive wink when he first met Linda, 'so you could say there were fifty shades, eh? Eh, Linda?'

There were four sofas in the enormous open-plan sitting room but, Lin complained, nowhere to really sit comfortably. 'I'd just like one really squishy sofa,' she told Sadie, 'to read and splodge about on.' Having triumphantly acquired exactly such a sofa in the George Smith sale, she was dismayed to find that the lone comfortable item of furniture in the room now looked alien and disconsolate in its chilly setting, 'like a gentle old hen surrounded by mean rats', so she got three more and sold Tony's rock-hard Italian 'seating system' on Gumtree.

'But then,' she told me when I went round for lunch, 'the whole room looked so odd and unbalanced. I'm going to have to redo it completely.'

A month or so later, Davey was duly summoned and charged down to London, suitcase, scrapbooks, supplements and drinking vinegars in tow. Linda fell on him, hugged him tightly and said she'd never been so happy to see anyone in her life, which struck Davey as rather an extreme thing for a newlywed to say. There was no point in doing just one room, he said – they might as well redecorate the whole thing. 'Do you think dear Tony might like to go and stay with his parents for a few days? Or with friends? Does he *have* friends?' he asked on the second night after a stilted dinner. 'I'm not being rude, darling, it's just that, as your ma always says, lots of men tend not to. But we could get so much done and it'll be much nicer for him not to come home every night to a bomb site, especially when the wallpapering gets going.' Tony, who found Davey unsettling, readily agreed to the plan, and went to hole up in Richmond with his friend Timmo and his American wife, Pixie. Pixie and Timmo had something they called a cabaña in the grounds of their gated property, and since Timmo was a colleague – 'one of the boys,' Tony said, 'a proper lad' – they commuted to work together.

Linda felt bad about the George Smith sofas and told Davey that they must keep the cost of the renovation down. 'I know just the look we should go for,' was Davey's reply. 'Something much looser and more comfortable, young, creative, playful, but original, not too east London, you know, with some classic elements. And pretty. This is all so *ugly*, darling, forgive me for saying, but really, one can't help having eyes. Here, look, I've got some tear sheets,' he said, opening up one of his many scrapbooks.

'I love it,' said Linda. 'All of it.'

'I thought you might. I'm just going to nip out for a couple of hours – there's a wonderful spa three streets down, do you know it? Full of women with minuscule dogs. My chi feels blocked, I think it's this space, so oppressive, and of course this savage lighting. And no bookshelves! So peculiar. But we'll soon get it sorted. Now, I made some calls, people might deliver things while I'm out. Rugs and so on. Non-hideous light bulbs. Some lamps too, I think.' He left the room, and came back in almost immediately. 'I forgot to ask, Linda darling. That little room on the half-landing – should we think about turning it into a nursery? Or into something sweet that could become a nursery eventually?'

'No thank you,' said Linda. 'I was thinking maybe a dressing room for me?'

'Righto,' said Davey. 'Understood. I really am off now. See you later.'

While Davey took care of redecorating the sitting room from top to bottom, Linda set to work on the kitchen, which she had identified as an area she could save money on. Tony's anodyne cabinets – 'What would you call this colour? Ash? Cinder?' 'Doom,' said Linda – were now covered in shells and old wine corks, painstakingly glued on by Linda and Jassy, who drove down from Norfolk laden with bits and bobs from Alconleigh. The empty walls were repainted and soon filled with family photographs and old paintings in wooden frames, purloined in part from Aunt Sadie's own stash. A battered farmhouse table was procured from a shop on Golborne Road and installed in the dining part of the kitchen; Tony's high-backed metal chairs went to the charity shop and were replaced by mismatched upholstered ones, 'so much comfier,' cried Linda. 'Those other chairs hurt my bottom.' 'Of course Tony wouldn't even notice, butt-wise,' noted Jassy.

Tony called and texted Linda all the time and sent flowers

twice, but had agreed to stay away for another ten days, during which time Linda hired a mini-digger and, with the help of a friend of Davey's who worked at Clifton Nurseries, turned much of the so-called Japanese garden into a vegetable patch, had the rest laid with wild-flower turf, planted three mature fruit trees and two rambling roses, and created a charming pergolaed dining area out of reclaimed wood. The marital bedroom, vast and grey, with an emperor-sized bed that Linda and Jassy happily shared for a fortnight, chatting away until the early hours (sometimes with Davey cheerfully ensconced in the middle), was painted a puttyish pink shade; the blinds were replaced by washed-linen curtains made in double-quick time by one of Davey's ever-summonable elves, and an order was placed for reclaimed wood flooring. Years later, Linda would remember this time as being one of the happiest in her London life: 'It was such a simple thing, sitting eating spaghetti in bed with Jassy,' she said, 'with Davey fussing about making colour schemes and talking about pranic healing. We laughed so much. Thinking about it now, I wouldn't have minded that much if Tony hadn't ever come back.'

But he did come back, by which time the house was entirely unrecognizable. 'Very nice,' he said flatly as an excited Linda showed him what she'd done. 'Very nice. Different. It's different, isn't it? Very different. Reminds me a bit of your parents'.'

'I know,' Linda said happily. 'Me too. But with our own imprint on it, darling, and without twenty-odd years' worth of clutter. I feel so much more comfortable. I think I'm maybe a bit homesick for Alconleigh.'

According to Linda, Tony 'went white' when he saw the kitchen. He leaned back against the worktops – once sparkling black granite, now flat Belgian bluestone – and said, 'Oh my God,' twice, before pointing out that the original kitchen had cost £50,000.

'Yes, and for what?' said Linda triumphantly. 'So it could look like a soulless show home for people with no taste. The absolute shameful waste. We had everything we couldn't reuse collected by a charity. They were so pleased – they said they'd use every last scrap of it, so everybody wins. And look at it now! I love it so much.' Here she leaned over and kissed not her husband but a particularly pretty pattern of shells on a cabinet door.

Tony seemed most affected by the disappearance of the dining room, which was now a small library.

'But you literally never used it!' said Linda. 'Not in all the time I've known you. And there was nowhere for my books. And anyway, the table in the kitchen is huge, it easily seats twelve.'

'We're hardly going to have dinner parties in the kitchen, are we?' said Tony.

'Oh God, are we going to have dinner parties?' said Linda in a despairing voice, before collecting herself and saying, 'Kitchens are so much friendlier, anyway. If you want to have dinner parties, we could have lovely ones in there. So cosy.'

'I wasn't after cosy,' said Tony. 'I'm not going to ask my boss, or, or, Timmo and Pixie to dinner in the kitchen, am I?' But Linda didn't see why not, and pointed out that Tony's boss was his dad.

At supper that night – she had made dal, rice, and aubergine and pea curry – Linda said, 'You don't like it, do you? The house, not the food, though come to think of it I'm not sure you like the food either.'

'The food is fine,' said Tony. 'Bit spicy. I don't mind it, it's just I prefer English food. Can't go wrong with a nice British banger. Nice bit of sausage, hur-hur. The house is . . . well, it's not really my taste. I'm sure I'll get used to it. I like neat things.'

'It's not unneat,' said Linda. 'It's just got a bit of life in it. Our life.'

'Your life,' said Tony dispassionately. 'But I guess it'll be a talking point. When people come round. It's not like any of their houses, not the ones I've been to. It'll be . . . a talking point,' he repeated. 'God, I wonder what Mums and Blanchie will make of it.'

Lady Kroesig and Blanche weren't keen. They were the kinds of people who use the word 'funny' when they really meant 'weird' or 'repellent', and now availed themselves of it lavishly. Lady Kroesig mourned the beautiful designer space that she and Sir Leicester had loved so much. 'It was pristine,' she kept saying. '*Pristine*. Everything new. And so tidy, like in a magazine.' Blanche concurred. Linda took umbrage, and said that excessive tidiness was anal, and that anyway Davey was not only an expert when it came to decoration but an actual world-class genius, and worth twenty naff designers who charged tens of thousands of pounds to make nice old houses ugly and soulless. Tony stared helplessly at his wife, mother and sister, like someone watching a three-way tennis match, and tried to lighten the mood by announcing that he'd got everyone dinner reservations at Gullet, yet another fashionable new restaurant.

'I've been dying to go there,' said Blanche, who had no interest in food whatsoever and was permanently on a rigorous diet, but liked posting pictures of her dinner on her social media.

'Tony is so well connected, he can get a table anywhere,' Lady Kroesig said, cheering up. The remark had been directed at Linda, who shrugged. 'I wanted to say he was well connected because he was married to *me*,' she told me the following day on the phone, 'but by that time the atmosphere was so strained that I bit my lip. Honestly, though. It's not because of the great wondrousness of Tony that we get asked everywhere. The boredom is he always wants to go, Fran, and I hardly ever do. Those places are all the same, and we see the same people, round and round, just in different settings, all pretending to have fun, all staring at each other to make themselves feel like they're the cool gang (they are so not the cool gang. They're not even the second or third cool gang, poor them). He swaggers about like the cat who got the cream, a bit like the party or opening or restaurant was all for him, when really he's just my plus one.'

'But are you unhappy, Lin?' I asked. 'Because it doesn't sound great.'

'Not *really* unhappy, no,' Linda said. 'You know when you order a thing and it's not quite right, and you could easily get a refund but you'd have to find a box and some bubble wrap and sticky tape, and then go to the post office miles away and queue, and then probably discover you'd left your wallet at home, so you end up thinking, "Oh, never mind, I'll just wear it, it's not like it's horrendous"? It's a bit like that. I mostly hang out with other people, to be honest. Merlin and his lot, mostly.'

'Are you still sleeping with him?'

'With Tony? God, yes, all the time, it's exhausting. I can't seem to be friendly to him in any other way. If I try to be friendly in words, it comes out all wrong and we have a row. He says I'm belittling and always finding fault. But it's so hard not to, Franny. He *is* quite faulty and I expect I am too, but you mind your own faults less, don't you? I almost like mine, I'm sorry to say. The other thing is that I'm dying of boredom, faffing about doing nothing all day. It's embarrassing. I need to get a job. I met a woman the other day and as far as I can see all she does is swan around wearing necklaces and getting tattoos, but she calls herself a curator. I could do that. But Tony says there's no need for me to get a job, so we fight about that too.'

Linda was by nature keen to please, and for a little while she tried her best. But she had found herself in a world that, while superficially recognizable, was in reality so unfamiliar to her that it might as well have been the moon. It had by now become limpidly clear that the Kroesigs were not merely interested in money but obsessed with it, and that this presented a potentially insurmountable difficulty. Linda had been brought up with money but shielded from its complexities. Money was never discussed at Alconleigh other than in the context of Mrs Hopkirk tutting at the price of heating oil or Aunt Sadie extolling the virtues of slow-cooking the cheaper cuts of meat. Linda knew, of course, that her father was very rich and very famous, and she was aware of the style and comfort in which the Radletts lived, even as she moaned about hand-me-down clothes and saggy mattresses. It wasn't that she took her financial circumstance for granted – 'I'm not quite that bad,' she said shamefacedly – but the cost of things, whether they were a kitchen stool or Louisa's wedding, was simply never mentioned. Either on grounds of distaste or on grounds of cushioning the children from their monumental good fortune – probably a combination of both – no one at Alconleigh ever said, 'Cor, that must be worth a bit,' or talked about Ks or how things might be 'good investments'. If a new painting or side table appeared, nobody trumpeted its price. Uncle Matthew and Aunt Sadie kept their finances entirely between themselves and their accountant. If Aunt Sadie turned up in a new dress, it wouldn't in a thousand years have occurred to her to name the brand and broadcast its price tag, unless she'd found a particular bargain at one of the charity shops in Cromer (Aunt Sadie's wardrobe was a mixture of extremely expensive hippy-luxe clothes and cherished finds that cost under £30, these sourced from places referred to in abbreviated form as, for instance, Sue, Salvy and Canse, for Cancer Research). Once a year, Uncle

Matthew would violently hurl the *Sunday Times* Rich List across the room, shouting about the wankers who wanted to read this shit, which was meaningless, prurient toss that appealed to people's BASEST INSTINCTS. The Kroesigs, by contrast, sat down with metaphorical, and for all I know literal, highlighter pens and forensically studied every last word of the List. It was the most reading they did all year. They could tell you how much someone was worth at the drop of a hat, filled with approval and a sort of pride, as though all the rich people in the world were their intimate friends.

The Radletts valued creativity; the Kroesigs worshipped hard cash. It wasn't simply a passing interest – a matter-of-fact need to keep on top of their various businesses and investments – but their consuming, indeed their only, passion. They didn't believe that anyone unrich could possibly be as interesting as someone who was: in their eyes, the very fact of having money made a person fascinating, and having none made someone a loser who hadn't tried hard enough. Such people weren't even worth looking at properly; the Kroesig eyes glazed over and moved on. Holding on to, and exponentially increasing, their vast fortune was the Kroesigs' life's purpose. Money defined them. They also saw it as a remedy to all their insecurities: if they lived in the right place, in the right way, wore the right clothes, shopped at the right shops and ate in the right restaurants, then they would be liked, admired and envied. This theory was only partially successful: they weren't admired enough, they felt, by the right kind of people, and were only envied by those so contemptibly beneath their radar as to be invisible.

Linda was, despite having made quite a lot of money herself in her modelling days, not sophisticated when it came to finances. When Sir Leicester gave her a large cheque as a wedding present, she delightedly spent all of it on a tiny Dutch still life of two lemons and a knife. He was horrified: he had meant for her to invest the money in stocks and shares, not a painting on which the chances of a return were slim. 'But I don't want a return,' said a genuinely perplexed Linda. 'It's not like I'm going to give it back. I just really love this painting, it was so unbelievably generous and kind of you, look at the way the light falls on the blade, right here, and at that incredible leaf. Look at the pittedness of the lemon skin! I can practically smell it, can't you? Have a hearty sniff, Sir L.' Sir Leicester could not smell the lemons, declined a sniff, said that the dish the lemons sat on looked dirty, but that at least he supposed the painting, being 'old', might hold its value better than modern rubbish by men in dresses.

Despite their wealth and their belief in its all-conquering abilities, it niggled the Kroesigs that the circles they moved in were not, in their opinion, quite up to snuff. Other people often seemed to be having more fun than them, at events they were not invited to, hosted by people they didn't know. The Kroesigs would dutifully turn up to Covent Garden, for instance, to endure an interminable opera they didn't really care for, and in the interval someone would trot over and say, in passing, 'Oh, we missed you at the Jacksons'! Such a fun night. They really know how to throw a party, those Jacksons, you should have been there.' That they hadn't been there, because they hadn't been asked, ruined the entire second half for Sir Leicester and his wife, who would poke at their umbrage all the way home, until it turned into an open sore and they went to bed wounded and dispirited. This sort of situation was the issue, the lone fly in the pale, smooth Kroesig ointment. Enter Linda. With the melding, as the newspapers had put it at the time of the wedding, of bohemia and industry, it was entirely expected that the Kroesig lives might take on a little added artsy glamour – a famous musician here, a model there, the odd painter or writer, even a Jackson, scattered like fresh green herbs over the dull stodge of Tony's social circle. Sir Leicester and Lady Kroesig wanted to say, in a breezy, jaunty way, that they weren't surprised to see clever Percival Botty on the Booker shortlist, because they'd read *The Beaks Peck Loud Inside My Head* in proof form – 'Great friend of Tony's, you know, they're very close'; or 'No wonder Lee won the Palme d'Or. We were at a private screening of *CUNT* late last year, actually. A stunning work, though –' and here they might insert a knowing chuckle – 'it's strong meat. Not for everyone! Dear Lee.' This increasingly bothersome lacuna lay behind Lady Kroesig's fixation with the dinner parties Linda and Tony would throw, and Tony's great dismay at the dismantling of the dining room.

Linda tried, in the wrong way. All she had to do was open her address book, phone up the caterers and ask people to drinks. Instead, she took herself off to an intensive course at Ballymaloe cookery school, in Ireland. She'd always liked pottering about in the kitchen, but now, to her delight, she found that she had an aptitude that went beyond home cooking. She was interested in the nitty-gritty of why and how a recipe worked and she adored everything about the course, from its location to the teachers and her fellow students ('so warm and kind and normal'), who came from all over the world and sat down every evening in their shared cottages to cook, eat and chat long into the night. She felt more at home there than she did in London, she said, what with the school being on a working farm and within striking distance of a couple of beaches – 'All I need is a horse, really,' she said on the phone. 'And you and Jassy. I feel more like myself than I have in a long time. Even the tea is delicious here, Barry's, do you know it? Nectar.' When the week-long general course ended, she inveigled her way on to another one and learned how to make bread; when the baking course ended, she found there was a space on the short course about the basics of running a cafe. By this point Tony was becoming antsy – she was originally only going to be away for a week – and so Linda reluctantly came back, radiant and well fed, full of ideas and keen to cook up a storm. If Tony wanted dinner parties, he would get dinner parties, and the food would be fantastic. She would be a better wife, less critical and more placatory. 'Might have had a tiny shag with a potter in Shanagarry,' she said to me in passing. 'Just to sort of reset myself. It always works. Lovely man. Beautiful skin. Beard, would you believe. Surprisingly unitchy. Marvellous sex, Fran. You forget, don't you, how good sex can be. Anyhow, I'm raring to go.'

Now she asked Merlin to dinner again – he had refused half a dozen invitations, saying, 'I love you, Linny, but you know I can't bear him. Can't we go out, just the two of us, and have a laugh?' – but this time he accepted, finally persuaded by the desperation in her voice. 'Promise to behave,' Linda said, 'because I think it might be quite grim.' She also asked me, a woman called Serena to whom she'd taken a shine at yoga because they were the only people who laughed when someone farted, and her very beautiful Ukrainian friend Oksana, whom she knew from her modelling days. The rest of the party would be made up of Tony, Tony's boss Michael Cash, Sir Leicester and Pooper Carmody, a rich American Tony's firm were trying to woo. 'At least Lady K and Blanche are away shrinking at some place where you pay thousands of pounds to be starved,' said Linda. 'Not my idea of a good time. Anyway, the relief, because Sir L isn't too bad solo provided I flirt with him slightly. I know, revolting, don't make that face, needs must. I'm going to make delicious food, though, so that's something. Make sure you're really hungry, Franny. Arrive starving. And come early.'

Tony was in a state of high alert about the dinner party for days beforehand. What was Linda going to cook? It wasn't going to be weird, was it? And not too spicy? He liked plain food, the plainer the better. Why couldn't they get caterers in? What about canapés? Flowers? What about staff? Would it look strange not to have staff? What would he wear? What would she?

'It's dinner for eight people, Tony. Ma did it every night of my childhood. Why would anyone need staff?'

'I just wondered whether Pooper Carmody might be more, well, impressed, if things were more formal and English, and . . . well, splendid. We really want his business, Linda. This dinner is super-important for me and Dads. I want to put on the best possible show.'

'Stop fretting,' Linda said. 'It's all in hand. Now please go away while I sort out my menu.'

15

Things got off to an awkward start because Serena, the woman from yoga, said, 'Sorry, what?' when she was introduced to Pooper Carmody, and then started giggling helplessly to herself with the abandon of a child, if children took cocaine. Pooper Carmody would, you'd think, be used to this sort of response, but he looked most put out. He explained, with a pained expression, that Pooper was a nickname he'd acquired at university – 'I was at Yale' – following an incident involving a drinking society and – 'Well, I think we can guess,' interrupted Linda, with a dazzling smile. 'Have a cocktail. It's called a Sunbeam. Like your presence. Welcome, Pooper!' In the kitchen, she said, 'I used to think Pa's prejudices were all mad, but actually he does have a point about grown men who define themselves by where they went to school or university. Imagine using your nickname for the rest of your life.'

'You have to have incredible confidence to go through life calling yourself Pooper,' I said, 'and to get annoyed when people start laughing. A really particular kind of entitlement.'

'Vagina Radlett,' Linda said, very stiffly, holding out her hand. 'How do you do. Yah, they called me it at Oxford following an incident with a rigid penis, but I rather liked it, so it stuck, as it were. And who are you?'

'Pisser Logan,' I said. 'Following an incident with a toilet lid when I was at Harvard. How nice to meet you. Sherry?'

'Yes please, Pisser,' Linda managed to say in a strangulated voice that turned into yelps of laughter, which in turn made me splutter, and then we started laughing – really laughing, as though we hadn't laughed in weeks – which unfortunately was the exact moment Tony came into the kitchen, not looking that amused.

'Merlin's arrived,' he said furiously. 'He seems to be wearing some sort of a dress thing except with a crotch and he's sitting on the sofa looking at his phone and giggling. Fuck's sake, Linda. It's like a zoo in there, with your stupid friend – she's completely out of it, by the way – still sniggering away to herself every time she looks at Pooper. What are you doing? Your mascara is all over your face. Michael doesn't know who to talk to. Sort yourself out, Linda, for God's sake, and come and butter him up. Where are the fucking canapés? I knew we should have got caterers.'

'We were just laughing at Pooper Carmody,' Linda said.

'Not unreasonably,' I added.

'He was indignant,' Linda said. 'Fran said she was Pisser Logan.' This set us off again.

'You're like a pair of idiot schoolgirls,' Tony said, very staccato, through gritted teeth. 'Idiot *babies*.'

'If you don't want people to be babyish,' Linda said, 'you shouldn't have friends with babyish names.'

After Tony had huffed out, she said, 'Butter him up! I could probably make myself bang him, at a push, if I got really wasted. Do you think it would help Tony's prospects? Perhaps it's my wifely duty. Ugh, he's so awful sometimes. Let's quickly have another drink.'

When we came out of the kitchen, Sir Leicester was saying, 'It was a bear week for me, all right. Had my eyes on this cheeky small cap minerals opportunity. Africa. Coup attempt, bigger slide than a Florida waterpark. Bit risky, but grabbed it fast near the floor. Had a top tip, you see; coup over, all well, back into bull territory, cashed in, something for tipper's back pocket.'

'Woohoo! That's Dads for you!' Tony said triumphantly, raising his right fist and rotating it and his forearm in the air.

'I literally don't understand a single word they're saying,' said Linda. 'Apart from *a* and *the*. Do you?'

'Not a clue,' I said, truthfully.

'It's like this every time they talk,' she sighed. 'At least with foreign languages you can usually make an informed guess.'

Michael Cash was saying something about sitting tight and taking the dividend, and how the margin didn't warrant the sale anyway. Serena was reading Merlin's aura and looking troubled. Then Oksana arrived.

Oksana was startlingly good-looking, like a beautiful alien cat, all sharp angles and elongated eyes, with a mane of tawny hair pinned up into a vague chignon. Her long, sinewy limbs were tanned and glossy. Her breast implants were high and larger than was fashionable. She looked like an extraordinary sex robot, all planes and edges apart from her soft, oversized mouth. She was wearing a long, tight black T-shirt dress, no apparent underwear, and a very high pair of heeled sandals that laced up her calves and made her about six foot four. Pooper Carmody was staring at her, his jaw slightly slack, which made a tiny bit of his tongue stick out, like a tired puppy. Tony, his boss Michael Cash and Sir Leicester had all gathered around her. She peered down at them non-committally. Oksana had a heavy accent and talked in a sombre monotone. She was not a smiler.

'Lin,' she cried – in as much as a person can cry with no expression – when we came back into the room. 'I am so happy to see you.'

'It's been ages,' said Linda, kissing her fondly. 'I'm happy too. You look fabulous.'

'Eh,' shrugged Oksana. 'I know.'

The men laughed.

'You remember last time, Linny?' said Oksana, her imperious face finally breaking into the merest suggestion of a grin. 'Naughty naughty.'

'I sure do,' said Linda cheerfully. 'Here, have a canapé. And maybe spare everyone the details, Oxo.'

'Only caviar or thin ham,' said Oksana. 'You have thin ham? Or maybe salami. Otherwise I get fat. Oh, hello, Merlin.'

'There's some in the fridge, I think,' said Linda. 'I'll get it for you in a sec.'

'Hi, Oxy,' said Merlin. 'Looking good, babe.'

Oksana nodded briskly once, acknowledging facts. 'Always,' she said. 'You know this.'

'What was naughty naughty?' said Sir Leicester.

'I've been wondering that too,' said Tony with a hostly, avuncular chuckle.

'We all have,' said Pooper Carmody, whose pupils were suddenly so dilated that his eyes looked black.

'Just a party,' said Linda. 'Who wants a spiced nut? I made them myself, and they sound boring but they're amazing. Merlin? Open wide.' Merlin, who was still on the sofa, obediently opened his mouth and Linda started lobbing nuts across the room, laughing, as he angled his head to catch them, like a seal. 'Tony?' said Linda. 'Nut, darling. Open your beak.'

'No thanks,' said Tony stiffly.

'Go on,' said Linda. 'Just the one nut. For me, your one true love.' Tony demurred with a tight smile, but she threw the nut at him anyway, deliberately missing the target and forcing him to stand with his mouth open, gormlessly. Linda laughed unkindly and refilled her glass. 'Anyone else?' she asked. 'Nut, Pooper Carmody?'

'So, you girls were saying you last met at a party,' said Sir Leicester.

'Ya, just a party,' said Oksana, winking at Linda. She downed her cocktail in one. 'Again,' she said to Michael Cash, holding out her glass.

'Fashion party, you know,' said Linda. But of course nobody did, apart from Merlin, who had closed his mouth, put his phone down and was now following the conversation with a look of pure delight on his face. 'Well, after-party, strictly speaking. Was it Paris, Oxy? Bit messy.'

'South of France. Bit *fun*,' said Oksana, her voice deepening by about an octave on the word. She edged away angrily from Sir Leicester, who had been snaking his hand around her waist. 'No! Dirty man!' she shouted at his face.

'I'll have a nut,' said Pooper Carmody, opening his mouth wide.

'Merl!' said Linda. 'Have you given Pooper Carmody whatever you're on? He looks so silly.'

'Linda, can I have a word?' Tony said. 'In the kitchen.'

'No,' Linda said.

'Oh Lord,' said Sir Leicester, rubbing his right hand back and forth across the top of his left. 'Oh Lord.'

'Rude not to share,' Merlin shrugged. 'Right, Pooper?'

Pooper Carmody sniggered randomly, then resumed opening his mouth.

'Oh, you might as well know,' said Linda wearily, throwing nuts rather haphazardly at Pooper Carmody. 'Oxy and I last saw each other in the context of a threesome.'

'Linda,' said Tony.

'Where?' said Michael.

'What a funny question,' said Linda. 'Near Cannes, I think.'

'I see,' said Michael.

'Oh good,' said Linda. 'Glad we're geographically on the same page, as you would say. Anyway, the thing about Oxy is that she fucks like an absolute machine, so once the man was out of the scenario, which was very early on – she basically broke him –'

'LINDA,' said Tony, but Michael Cash shushed him.

'I ride like horse,' said Oksana. 'Hard, you know. Then he, the man, quickly finish.' Here she made a terrible expressive grunt. 'Then he rest.' She made a slack-mouthed face, as though she'd had a stroke. Linda let out a bark of laughter, then quickly put her hand up to her mouth and cleared her throat.

'But I am not finished,' said Oksana. 'So then . . .'

'. . . so then it was just the two of us,' Linda said briskly. 'Amazing night. Well, morning, technically.'

'Two days,' Oksana said. 'Two sex days.'

'Two days. So there we are. Could you all come through to the kitchen please, it's starters and artichokes do *not* like sitting about.'

16

By September of the following year, it had become piercingly clear to everyone including Linda and Tony that the marriage had been a disastrous idea. He was spending more and more time at Timmo and Pixie's, and Linda, like a homing pigeon, was back at Alconleigh most weekends. Davey said that she started moaning about having to go back down to London ten minutes after she arrived and that by the time she had to leave she was 'deeply depressed'. In between flits to Norfolk she often stayed with me – I was by now living in a long, narrow house in Stepney with my boyfriend (and eventually husband), Alfie Wincham. The relationship with the Kroesig parents had broken down entirely once it became obvious that the dreamed-of injection of bohemian glamour bore no earthly resemblance to anything they'd imagined, or could cope with. There had been a mere handful of dinner parties. The Jacksons had not been produced, although, enragingly, it turned out that Lin had known their son Theo intimately for years. It was very like Linda to casually inform the Kroesigs of this several months later.

Merlin was abroad for the various Fashion Weeks, and although Linda knew dozens if not hundreds of people by now, Merlin remained her only close friend from outside the family. 'I don't really know what other people are *like*,' she once said. 'People who aren't us, I mean. I can talk to them superficially, but I don't really understand them, and they don't really understand me. It's such a strange feeling. Does it ever go away? Do you remember how I always used to say that we were utter freaks when we were little? It was so true. And Pa's *so* famous. I don't think I really understood that either, not properly, not in Norfolk. When I first came to London I thought the photographers and the gossip pages were to do with modelling, and with running about with Merlin's crowd. But that wasn't really it.'

'Daughter of reformed hellraiser,' I recited. 'Rock legend's wayward gal.'

'I don't mind,' said Linda, 'but it's a bit weird. I get why Pa doesn't like to leave home.'

Now she missed, she said, the constant chatter of Alconleigh, the sisterly squabbles and teases, the life and warmth; she missed Uncle Matthew and Aunt Sadie, Aunt Emily and Davey, the animals, the comfort and security of the house itself – all of it. She had a key to our house, which irritated Alfie – he was one of those rare men who never quite fell for her charms. He liked her well enough, but he thought she was spoilt, indulged and exasperating, though she *was* very good at making him laugh. 'She takes nothing seriously,' Alfie said. 'Or rather, she treats tiny little things as if they were international catastrophes and international catastrophes as if they were tiny little things. It's a crazy way of looking at the world.'

On this particular day Alfie was out – he was then teaching history at Queen Mary, part of the University of London – and I was, as usual, working from home. I had a job researching patterns for a big fashion house, which that autumn involved sourcing old plaid patterns from vintage American checked shirts and sending them to the designer to modify minutely and pass off as their own. The internet was a rich hunting ground. The job, finicky but surprisingly well paid ('Lucky you went to school,' Uncle Matthew had said, 'and got that degree'), had come via Merlin, whom I found much less scary these days, if still a bit unsettling. I was in the middle of an email exchange with a thrift-store owner in Arizona when Linda let herself in.

'Fran, stop doing what you're doing and listen to my terrible news,' she said, plonking herself down on the sofa horizontally, as if it was a therapist's couch. 'I am pregnant. I am in pig. In lamb. In calf. A baby is coming.'

'Oh,' I said. 'But *is* it terrible news? I think it's lovely. I want to congratulate you!'

'I'd be happy if it was someone else's,' Linda said. 'But the terrible thing is that it's definitely Tony's, and I was hoping Tony and I were done. It's a Kroesig.' She glared furiously at her stomach. 'In me. An internal Kroesig.'

'Well, and an internal Radlett,' I said. 'I bet your genes win out over his.'

'You'd think so, wouldn't you? I was thinking the other day that the reason Tony is theoretically good-looking is that he doesn't really have any interesting features at all. He is completely bland and inoffensive,' said Linda with a tiny shudder, 'as though he'd bought his face from John Lewis. It works as a face, but there's nothing curious or beguiling about it. Merlin says that all the best faces have at least something curious and beguiling, and it's really true. Anyway, I bet my genes sink without trace. They'll be swamped by the great Tony blanket of blandness. I just sense the Kroesig-ness, Fran, I really do. This is not a Radlett baby.'

'You're being ridiculous,' I said. 'Of course it's a Radlett baby – it's yours.'

'You'll see when it comes out,' Linda said gloomily. 'I know I'm right.'

'What are you going to do?' I asked. 'I mean, if you're really as unexcited as you seem to be, you do have options.'

'That's the thing – unfortunately not. Tony caught me puking twice on Saturday morning. I've stupidly been moaning about my tits hurting – I thought it was just my period coming – but he was more on the ball than me. He ran out to get a test, and obviously it was positive, and now he's delighted and apparently we can make everything work and isn't it wonderful, we must tell Mums and Dads. He rang them that second, obviously.' She made a horrible face. 'They nee-naw nee-nawed round straight away. You can imagine. Joy unconfined. Blanket even hugged me.' Blanket was one of Linda's unaffectionate nicknames for Blanche. 'I mean, I hate them by this point, all of them, but I'm not going to be the one who gets rid of their child and grandchild and nephew or niece. You should have seen them. They practically carried me aloft singing hymns of praise, they were so pleased. All my sins forgiven. Ugh.'

'It's your body,' I said. 'You can do what you like. Not that I'm saying you should, because I don't think that at all . . .'

'Oh, I know, I know, but imagine the drama. No, I might as well have it. I wish it was an egg, though, that I could just lay.' She screwed up her face and delicately lifted her left buttock an inch off the sofa. 'Like that. So much easier. From the *back* bottom. Do you have any cheese? I'm starving.'

Linda looked radiantly beautiful throughout her pregnancy – radiant if very bad-tempered. She was sick all the time, she hated going to antenatal classes with Tony, saying that 'literally everyone in the room is happier than us, even the single parents and even the poor woman who cries all the time'. She said more than once that she wished she'd had an abortion after all, including once in the middle of a row, to a horrified Tony. 'I know I should be happier,' she said to me. 'But I just keep thinking about how I'm going to be stuck with Tony and his doppelgänger square-jawed baby and his parents in my life for evermore even if I do manage to get away from him, and if I start thinking about it for too long I feel like I can't breathe. And I miss my dressing room.'

The Kroesigs, noting – you couldn't not – the distinct lack of enthusiasm from Linda, had taken it upon themselves to convert Linda's dressing room into a nursery. They'd hired Vole Pippings, whose upmarket company, Pippings' Poppets, specialized in creating 'magical spaces for magical kids'. Linda hated Vole at first sight – 'She came sort of *skipping* in,' she said disgustedly, 'like a giant baby, with a giant smile and a giant box of muffins for "Mummy". She's one of those women who are so relentlessly upbeat and sugary that you just know they have a really dark secret. It's anal depravity all over again.' This was a reference to an occasion when Uncle Matthew had gone to New York to promote a remastered compilation album called *Sin: Circles of Hell*. Aunt Sadie had him on speakerphone in the kitchen while she made supper. They were chatting companionably away about this and that when, scrolling through the news channels from his bed, Uncle Matthew had suddenly remarked that American pundits were so nauseatingly squeaky clean on screen that he expected they liked nothing more than 'anal depravity' in private ('Speaking in code, Sades, in case the kids are around'). Jassy had quietly been doing her homework at one end of the kitchen table and 'anal depravity' was quickly adopted by everyone to denote anything suspiciously saccharine, from movies to Lavender Davies.

'Ugh,' Linda now said. 'In the end I just left her and Lady K and Blanche to their hysterical squealing and came here. It's going to be hideous, I just know it.'

'The dressing room or the baby?'

'Both, I should think,' Linda said disinterestedly. 'This cheese is unbelievably delicious.'

Linda gave birth in June. She was unwell with pre-eclampsia before the birth, which didn't help morale. The baby was a girl, who at the insistence of the Kroesigs was named Moira, after

Lady Kroesig's mother. Linda didn't put up a fight about the name, other than murmuring that it would be well suited for a geriatric lady murderess. As Linda had predicted and as she now took little pleasure in pointing out, Moira was the spitting image of Tony, pale-skinned and fair-haired with no trace in her of Linda, who may as well not have been involved in her conception, except for the shape of her eyes.

Linda looked after Moira beautifully, dutifully, but she remained unmoved, semi-detached. She said that she felt perfectly fine, wished the baby well and found her sweet, but didn't really feel the great rush of emotion and love that other people talked about and that she was sure would eventually follow. When a sceptical and concerned Aunt Sadie raised the possibility of post-natal depression, it was instantly dismissed by Linda ('I think I'd know, don't you?'); looking back, I wonder if that had been the right call and whether we shouldn't have pursued that further, or at least persuaded her to speak to a doctor.

'Do you remember those people, the Fanshawes?' Uncle Matthew had interjected loyally. 'Really *terrible* babies, both times. Judgemental-looking. Never cracked a smile. Gave babies a bad name. Some babies *are* awful. I'm afraid those Fanshawe babies just got worse with age. Don't look at me like that, Sades. Say it isn't true.'

'Well, it's a tiny bit true,' conceded Sadie, 'and they had such funny little pointy teeth, but the Fanshawes loved them. Love them.'

'So they claim,' said Uncle Matthew.

'And Moira is adorable,' said Aunt Sadie. 'She's just a baby.'

The Kroesigs had hired a maternity nurse, a full-time nanny and a weekend nanny too, so Moira – whom Merlin called Moiré, he sent a tiny emerald bracelet, which Lady Kroesig immediately had valued – was wonderfully well looked after.

Tony doted on the baby already, as did the grandparents. Linda called her Momo, or Mohammed when she especially wanted to annoy the Kroesigs.

Aunt Emily, when I relayed all this, said that Linda was much too young to have a baby, and that older mothers were often more interested in their children – 'They're much more grateful for them.'

'She's a baby herself,' said Davey sadly.

Any suggestion that a baby would paper over the crevasses of Linda and Tony's marriage proved unfounded. If anything, Moira's arrival made things worse, Linda's by-rote care in constant and stark contrast to her husband's passionate adoration of the child. Moira, Tony and the weekend nanny spent every weekend at Saplings, his parents' house in Surrey, which Linda, who had once swooned at the lavishly appointed interiors, comfortable mattresses and spa, now only ever referred to as Toad Hall. With Linda at Alconleigh more often than not, the London house was empty every weekend, and when I went to visit during the week I started to notice that, the cheerful nursery aside, it had taken on a chilly, unloved atmosphere, as though it were a holiday rental rather than a place where people lived, laughed and loved, as the large framed poster above the cooker in Blanche's flat proclaimed, according to Linda ('Can you imagine? Aside from anything else, what kinds of people advertise the fact that they need to be visually reminded to be alive?').

The marriage plodded on for a while longer, until Linda noticed that when Moira and Tony returned from Saplings on Sunday evenings, the baby's hair often smelled of Pixie's distinctive and insistent tuberose scent, which particularly annoyed Linda 'as one of the things I really like about Momo is the smell of her head'. On a hunch, Linda asked Tony how Pixie and

Timmo were doing; under persistent questioning, he eventually admitted that they had begun a trial separation.

'*Well*,' Linda said to me. 'Name me a single trial separation that ends with the people getting back together.'

'I can't personally think of one, but I'm sure they must exist.'

'No,' said Linda. 'They're just a way of making things less upsetting for people who can't face the truth, but I think they're a bad idea. You want to yank the plaster off in one go and be done with it, as Ma always used to say, instead of peeling off a little bit and then having it just hang there, getting messier and grubbier, knowing you'll have to do the horrible yanking eventually. You want to expose the wound to give it a chance to heal quickly, not keep it half covered up getting all soggy. Anyway, clearly Pixie spends weekends at Saplings, putting her nauseating scent on Momo and all over Tony too, I expect, except he washes off the evidence.'

A further inquisition confirmed that this was indeed the case: Tony said that poor Pixie had taken the break very badly and needed cheering up. He did not reply to Linda's, 'With your penis?', choosing instead to huff out of the room, but the game was up. 'I'm thrilled, obviously,' said a delighted Linda, 'though it does seem a bit hard on Timmo, who was Tony's friend. I've sent him a note. Well, a text. Why would you sleep with your friend's wife when there are millions of other women whose husbands aren't pretty much your only pal? It's quite low, isn't it? Tony says they were "helplessly" attracted to each other and powerless to resist. Apparently it all started when he stayed in their whatsit, cabaña, in Richmond. Anyway, I'm off, hurrah.'

'Shouldn't he be the one who's off?' I asked.

'God, Fran, no, don't be ridiculous! It's not his fault that he got together with Pixie, not really. We were on our last legs, and it's not like I mind in the least. And I tried my best with that house but I still don't really like it, and anyway, it was his long before I came along. And it's Momo's home.'

'Wait, what? You're leaving Moira?' I was aghast.

'Not leaving, I'll see her every day. She won't miss me – she much prefers Tony and she loves the nannies. I'm going to look at flats later, will you come with me? I want to get out as soon as possible, and then Pixie can move in and everyone can be happy.'

'But . . . don't you want to take Momo with you?' I asked, struggling to keep the disapproval out of my voice. 'Come on, Linda. You can't just abandon her.'

'I'm not abandoning her!' Linda cried. 'Abandoning her would be removing her from everything she knows and loves – her home, her daddy, her grandparents, the lovely nannies, even Pixie. I'm the odd one out in that scenario. And for what – to live in a flat all alone with me? I have to give it to Tony, the whole thing is very civilized. I'll see her every day, or as good as, and she can come and stay with me, and I'll take her with me to Alconleigh whenever I go, Ma made me swear, and anyway I want to.'

'It's seriously weird, Linda,' I said.

'No, it isn't. It's a perfect plan,' she said happily. 'Tony says Pixie *adores* Momo, and that Momo adores her, and I believe him. She'll be a brilliant stepmother, much nicer than me.'

'Hm,' I said, still not entirely convinced. 'I suppose that's something.'

'It's like "for the sake of the children" in reverse. One thing I've learned from all this,' Linda continued, 'this whole chunk of my life, is that lots of women don't especially like their children or their husbands. I'm not saying I don't love Momo – I do love her – but Ma and Pa give us all the wrong impression. We think it's normal to hop upstairs for sex in the middle of the afternoon even when you've been together for ever and are really old, or to still die laughing over a stupid old unfunny joke, but it's so not. It's extremely *un*usual, so unusual as to be downright weird. Most people don't want to hop upstairs for sex even a few years in and most people cringe at old jokes. But they can't do anything about it – they get stuck and trapped and they don't have enough money to make a clean break, so they heroically just get on with it and accept it as their lot. I mean, hats off, truly. But I *do* have enough money, Fran. I'm short of a lot of things, but I'm not short of that. And I want to live my life. Please don't be judgy about it.'

'I'm not being judgy. But aren't you scared of being lonely?' I asked. 'I would be, I think. It's another reason why people stay together and I sort of understand it.'

'No,' laughed Linda. 'Of course I'm not. I find myself heavenly company. Why would I be lonely? It's not like I'm horrible or unpresentable. And anyway, at long bloody last I can get a job – a proper job, I mean. I can stop stagnating and being spoilt and I can maybe do something useful with myself. I can't wait, Fran. Anyway – flats this afternoon? Please say yes.'

17

Two years and a couple of rentals later, Linda was living in a large house in Dalston, which she had bought with help from Uncle Matthew, and of which she occupied the top two floors. Jassy, having completed her interminable art course and started to work part-time creating specialist paint effects for interiors, had moved in and lived on the middle floor, with the pair sharing the street-level kitchen and sitting room. The lower part of the house, a conversion occupying a corner plot, had previously been a restaurant. Now the basement was in the process of being turned into a small, twenty-seater cafe, complete with an extra three tables in the garden. Since leaving Tony and eventually setting up home in east London, Linda's love of cookery – and her very real talent for it, honed by a residential refresher course at her beloved Ballymaloe – had eventually led to her running a series of popular, oversubscribed monthly supper clubs. The customers may have been reeled in by her famous name, but they came back again and again because of her delicious food and the comfort and prettiness of the setting. 'It's unbelievably hard work,' said Jassy, Linda's co-host, 'but quite clever, because our friends come, and then they tell their friends, and so the other people who turn up are interesting and nice and we all hang out afterwards, usually. So although it's arse-breaking, it's fun too.' Now Linda felt the time had come to cautiously expand: 'If it doesn't work, it doesn't work,' she said, 'and I'll think of something else, but it's going to be fun trying. Merlin's lent me his accountant and she seems to think it's doable.' Uncle Matthew and Aunt Sadie came to visit, pronouncing themselves astounded at the trans-formation both of the area – 'Used to come here and buy drugs,' said Uncle Matthew, 'off a skinny bloke who smelled of coley' – and of Linda herself. 'She's properly back, isn't she?' Aunt Sadie said. 'She's herself again, thank God.'

Linda was visibly contented. Aunt Sadie was full of enthusi-astic tips and ideas from her time running Peas and Paneer decades previously; Davey appeared with scrapbooks bulging with his 'design vision' for the cafe space; and living relatively nearby, I spent as much time as I could in Dalston, helping out in what already felt like a blissfully familiar setting. We'd sit in the embryonic cafe late into the night, sampling recipes and drinking red wine; Uncle Matthew, radiating good humour for once, said that the whole 'vibe' reminded him of the 1980s, which we took as a compliment.

People say that houses don't matter – that they're only bricks and mortar, and that it is the energy of the people within that makes them what they are, and this was never truer than with the various flats and houses Linda occupied. She could trans-form even the most unpromising space, and it never took her very long – a couple of days to make a room feel like it had been there, chic and original but ridiculously comfortable, for ever. It was a real skill, and one which she laughed off, but when, later, people moved into any property she'd lived in, they found themselves surprised that the thing they'd bought the house for – the almost seductively charming feel of the place, the magic of it – was gone, just like that, never to be recaptured, as though someone had come in the night and swept away all the glitter.

Linda was happy, full of hope and possibilities, and her mood was contagious. We all had the sense that we were col-laborating on making something worthwhile and exciting out of the cafe, which was to be called the Sausage. It didn't hurt that Linda had recreated something of the free, generous spirit of Alconleigh in miniature, with three rescue hens scratching about the pretty, tiny garden and interiors that felt like old friends: despite the densely urban location, both the Sausage and the house had something almost rural about them. 'I love living here,' she said. 'There are no bankers' wives and I can wear any old thing I like without being stared at. And the people are so friendly, apart from the ones who want to rob you, though even they seem quite sweet – less organized, you know, more sort of spontaneous than in Holland Park, where they turn up in masks and blacked-out vans.'

'Do they?' Aunt Sadie asked, looking alarmed.

'Oh yes,' said Linda. 'All the time.'

'She likes it because there are actual poor people living here,' said Jassy.

'Don't be nasty,' said Linda, laughing. 'And anyway, there are poor people living about two inches away from Holland Park. That's what makes the whole thing so obscene.'

Moira, now nearly three, came to stay every weekend, delivered by a nanny and accompanied by a small wheelie suitcase full of the food she liked. 'Mostly potatoes,' said Linda. 'And biscuits. "Nothing spicy", like her pa. I keep saying that there are potatoes and biscuits in the house, but they send them anyway.' Moira was a chipper child, stout and solid, who travelled everywhere with her toy llama, Llama, and chatted away happily to her mother from the moment she arrived until it was time for bed. She called Linda Linda. 'Fine by me,' said Linda breezily, but I wondered if this was quite true: presumably Moira called Linda Linda because she called somebody else Mummy. She had an extravagantly expensive wardrobe – tiny cardigans with rabbit-fur collars, butter-soft shoes in palest pink, little velvet coats with pearl buttons – in stark contrast to her mother's more bohemian wardrobe or her aunt Jassy's paint-splattered

Birkenstocks, and didn't like getting messy. 'She says it isn't nice,' said Linda. 'And she's frightened of the hens. Imagine being frightened of a hen! We're working on that, though. She did collect the eggs earlier, so that's something.'

'Lots of people are frightened of hens,' said Jassy. 'We see only beauty and love and feathery goodness, but they have cruel eyes.'

'Still,' said Linda. 'Bit weedy. Apart from that, though, she *is* rather sweet.'

18

Why did Linda fall for Christian Talbot? I think her growing guilt at the extent of her privilege explained a great deal. Christian abhorred privilege, and she felt that he could lead her out of the golden labyrinth of her own good fortune and towards something grittier and more egalitarian. Or perhaps it was initially because he was from another world, one that was as far removed from Merlin's shallow and glamorous orbit as it was from Tony's aggressively capitalist idea of a life well lived. It wasn't that the people Merlin surrounded himself with were stupid, exactly, but that their interests were so narrow and so unrelated that it was sometimes difficult to navigate a conversational channel. You'd find yourself chatting to someone wearing see-through pants who had an enviable familiarity with the Greek myths, for instance, or to a man who knew everything there was to know about Haile Selassie despite being white and not Rastafarian, or to a woman who was a fount of knowledge on Dior's New Look. But when you tried to talk to them about anything else, particularly anything current, they would look instantly bored and their eyes would suddenly go blank, like a fish at the moment of death.

Usually it would turn out that the interest was based on aesthetics – 'What I love about Haile was the divine braiding. That man redefined epaulettes' – or the perceived sexual freedoms of the period in question – 'Well, of course the ancient Greeks . . .' (there was a lot of 'well, of course the ancient Greeks', particularly at the Dionysian end of things; one of Merlin's early collections had been called Satyr) – and to their credit Merlin's friends fully immersed themselves in their passions, but rather to the exclusion of everything else. This cultural tourism had its limitations, and like ordinary tourism could often feel as if the person was showing you too many holiday photographs long after you'd stopped caring.

Nevertheless, the pick and mix approach had much in common with Linda's own erratic education. Aunt Sadie would often pause and linger on whatever side shoot of a topic particularly grabbed us, so that we knew more about bonnets and carriage types, having spent hours drawing dozens of our own invention and staging various Regency 'fashion shows' in the barn, than about the intricacies of Jane Austen's literary style, although when I said this to Linda, she replied, 'Don't be silly, Fran, I know all about Jane Austen's style. It's clever and sarcastic. Snarky. That's all you need to know. Do you remember that sweet bonnet I designed, with harvest mice all around the brim?' (I did remember the bonnet, and the argument we'd had when I'd said it was impractical as there would be no way of keeping the mice compliant and still unless they were stuffed, which had made Linda cry with indignation. The harvest mice would want to stay still, she'd said, out of devotion to the wearer – Linda – and because of the supply of nutritious seeds provided within the bonnet. 'They'd be too full to wriggle so they'd just go to sleep, framing my face. That's the whole point. Honestly, Fran, you have no imagination.')

Despite, or perhaps thanks to, the home schooling, Linda had hinterland. She was not self-invented for effect but fully formed, wholly and undeviatingly true to herself. It's only now, as an adult, that I understand how rare that is. With no one to impress as a child, no one's cool gang to join – there was only one gang at Alconleigh and we were all in it out of desperation – no notion other than her own of what was and wasn't desirable or hip, she ploughed her own furrow and never felt the need to swerve away from it. She was not interested in being pleasing; the fact that so many people found her captivating was, to her, an unsought but agreeable side effect, and not something she thought about at any length.

The long hours, days, weeks, months, years of boredom that marked our childhood had yielded, it now became clear, some benefits, in particular Linda's voracious reading of any material that came her way, from the daily newspapers to Aunt Sadie's full set of the Everyman Library to the dentist's *Grazia*s, from opera librettos to Davey's vast collection of back issues of *World of Interiors* to the weekly delivery of *Country Life* magazine, from John Deere tractor catalogues to the parcels packed full of contemporary fiction that made their way to the house a few times a year, when various literary long- and shortlists were delivered to Aunt Emily courtesy of Heywood Hill. 'You could just read, couldn't you?' Linda once said. 'You don't really need school at all, unless you want to know about parabolas and where countries are.' When I'd primly replied that most people did want to know those things, she said she bet they didn't, not really, and that anyway she knew all the flags, which was easily as good.

She was also musically literate – we all were, to a greater or lesser extent, because you couldn't not be, living at Alconleigh, where Uncle Matthew's eclectic choices were always on in the background, from death metal to Mozart to Ethiopian jazz. He liked and collected vinyl, which meant the album covers often had sleeve notes and lyrics, but it was only Linda who would study these for hours, lying on her stomach on the fattest, shaggiest rug in the sitting room, snoozing dogs at her side, with the intensity she applied to everything from Baudelaire – 'He sounds so dangerous and sexy but he looked like a potato in real life, poor him' – to Aunt Sadie's old Jilly Coopers (there was a full set of the 'name' novels – *Emily*, *Bella*, *Harriet*, *Octavia*, *Imogen* and

Prudence – in each of the guest bedrooms at Alconleigh, on the basis that there was nothing anyone sensible would rather read in the bath). Linda had an unusual ability for remembering song lyrics, the older the better – we were both puzzled and annoyed by how more modern lyrics often made no sense and told no interesting stories. Once, in bed with Tony, Marvin Gaye's 'Sexual Healing' came on and Linda told him that the lyrics reminded her of him, which pleased him until she added, 'Well, actually they remind me more of someone else, but a bit of you too.'

While Linda's friendship with Merlin himself was unshakeable, he had moved to Paris the previous year as designer in chief to a grand, long-established fashion house. She'd been growing tired of his ever-changing entourage and social circle for a while – 'It's Groundhog Day,' she said. 'I was weary of it even before I met Tony, and now here I am again. Same people, same jokes – not particularly funny ones either, but people look so hurt if you don't laugh. Same parties, give or take. Same chat. Everyone always slightly out of it in one way or another. Endless name-dropping. You just glaze over. A lot of it is about how hot you look and how gossipy you can be, or how bitchy.' Linda, child of a rock star, hated the gossip that had followed her family around for her entire lifetime, and by extension hated gossip generally: 'I do think Ma's right, it's provincial, for boring people who don't have enough going on in their lives to talk about. Also, why should I be interested if someone I don't know is sleeping with someone else or has left their wife or become a drunk? I don't care. Good luck to them.'

She'd made a point of seeking out new people during this time, befriending cafe customers and random strangers she met at various social events. It was a move that was only partially successful because she often found, to her dismay, that the new friend liked her more than she liked them, and that they were often preternaturally curious about her background and upbringing. 'You know how some people want to sort of eat you up?' she asked me. 'I don't like it.' The new friends would text endlessly, often at epic and overly intimate length, or mention her too much on their social media feeds and laugh when she told them that she was a private person and would much rather they didn't. 'They think I'm joking. But I am a private person! I am completely private. Do you know, in my ideal world I wouldn't really have friends – well, maybe one or two – but really I'd be fine with just you and Jassy and even poor old Louisa, and Robin of course, especially when he's a bit older and we can stop talking about games consoles and trainers. And then one person to really passionately love. All I need is one person. That's why I married stupid Tony – honestly, Fran, you might have said he was awful, everyone knew it, Ma says he gave her hives, I don't consider it an act of friendship for you all to have kept so quiet about it. No, I would have listened. Maybe. Eventually. You should have persisted. At least he was quite good in bed, ish, even though he had a signature move, can you imagine.' Here we both paused to laugh like drains. Linda made me laugh more than anyone else. 'Do you know, I used to think he was so good-looking, and now I can't see it at all any more. The John Lewis face was one thing, but when Momo was born, so identically like him, I went home afterwards and looked at Tony and all I could see was a giant six-foot baby, Momo magnified to grotesque proportions. And after that I couldn't unsee it – he was just a humongous Momo walking about with his great big baby Momo face, talk about creepy.'

'Linda!'

'It's true. You wouldn't like Alfie to look like a massive baby either, Fran, so don't pretend you would. How do you think other women do it? I suppose they must love their husbands, or maybe they just don't notice. The point is, I am not what

Davey would call a social creature. I mean, I know lots of people, but I don't really like any of them enough. I like them for about an hour, or maybe for lunch, but then I get bored. You're so lucky, having Alfie. You're like two hedgehogs in their mossy nest. Do you ever get bored?'

I told her that I did, but that I didn't mind the boredom. 'That's the thing,' Linda said knowingly. 'Companionable boredom. I think that's when you know you're with the right person, when you can sit there together, really quite bored but completely happy.' She sighed. 'I don't actually know anyone like that who I'm not related to.' Another sigh. 'I'd settle for being interested all the time. I wish someone would say something new.'

In the winter of that year, a particularly insistent recently acquired friend called Cass, whom Linda had got to know because she worked in the local bookshop – 'except now she will not stop texting and I have to go to the other, much less good bookshop, talk about annoying' – asked Linda to supper for what must have been the fourth or fifth time. She called the supper a dinner party – 'Christ, not again,' said Linda doomily, sounding a bit like Uncle Matthew – and now dangled a trophy guest as bait, this being a literary novelist – 'published!' Cass had said, voice trembly with excitement – called Christian Talbot, whom she had met when he did a reading at her bookshop, In Other Words. Linda had not heard of him, but Cass assured her that she should have, that Christian Talbot was 'a genius' and also 'an extraordinary person', and in the event Linda, aware of the cumulative rudeness of always turning Cass down, had nothing much better to do that night. She thought that perhaps going to supper at Cass's once meant she would never have to go to supper there again and that anyway it had to be more fun than yet another gallery opening with people she was tired of, so she said yes and then moaned to me about it for a whole week. 'I don't even know what to wear to that kind of dinner party. Do you think I should read this Christian person's book? Oh, I wish I'd said no. I can't cancel, Cass would be too upset. I think she fancies him. Probably just asked me to make up the numbers.' Typically, it didn't occur to Linda that she might also in fact be the trophy guest, the lure.

Christian Talbot was deeply charming; it didn't hurt that he was handsome too. Brown-haired, brown-eyed, lightly bearded and fine-boned, he looked not unlike that famous photograph of the young Stalin. When we got to know him, Alfie and I thought there was a whisper of the confidence trickster in the ease with which he shape-shifted to become whatever his inter-locutor required. It was only later, when she came across him telling an amusing anecdote out loud in front of the bathroom mirror, complete with pauses, facial expressions and wry smiles, that Linda realized how much of the easy charm was literally rehearsed. But that was in the future. For now, Chris-tian dazzled her, and she fancied him like mad. Cass's dreaded dinner party turned into the most fun she'd had in months, even though every place setting had a copy of *Fish with the Worm*, Christian's slim hardback novel, lying thoughtfully in the middle of the plate, 'which did make me want to laugh, Franny, admit the funniness. I'd have died but he didn't mind at all, in fact he looked quite pleased, except when Cass said, "Six more sales, woohoo!" He immediately offered to sign them all. The other guests were sort of groupie-ish, isn't it strange? A bit like when middle-aged blokes meet Pa and look like they're going to cry, or come, or something, both probably – isn't it awful when people do that? I always want to laugh. So nice of him to take the trouble, Christian, I mean, Pa would only mut-ter rudely and try and get away as quickly as he could. He had an old-fashioned fountain pen in his top pocket, like a don. I suppose you travel prepared when you're a famous writer.' *Fish with the Worm* had been published six months before to some acclaim and been shortlisted for a couple of small literary prizes.

'Is it about angling?' Linda had enquired.

Christian had smiled indulgently at her ('lovely teeth, never a given'). 'It's not about angling,' he said.

'Or then is it from *Hamlet*, that bit about the worm that ends up on a fishing hook having eaten the remains of a king, circle of life sort of thing – do you love *The Lion King*? I do.'

Christian had looked mildly surprised at this, but then told her that yes, it was 'indeed' a quote from *Hamlet*, which he proceeded to recite.

'*A man may fish with the worm that hath eat of a king, and eat of the fish that hath fed of that worm,*' he said, sonorously. He had a beautiful, richly modulated voice.

'Oh, bravo,' said Cass, and clapped her hands together three times.

'That's right,' said Linda. 'And somewhere in that scene there's a line that says, "your worm is your only emperor," which I always thought sounded so sweet. I know the sweetness isn't the point, in fact the opposite of the point, but still, bless the worm-emperor, with his tiny worm regalia.'

'You're a dark horse,' said Cass to Linda. 'Quoting *Hamlet*.'

'Hardly,' laughed Linda. 'Everyone knows that worm quote.' Turning to Christian, she explained, 'People think I'm thicker than I am because I'm pretty.'

'Now *you're* fishing,' Christian said, and Linda laughed again and said that she wasn't, only stating a fact, before turning the conversation back to *The Lion King* and asking Cass if she'd ever fancied Mufasa. But Cass didn't answer and said she had to get on with the salad dressing.

⋆

Christian lived in a garret on one of the roads that led directly to Hampstead Heath, or at least that was how he described his one-bedroom flat. 'Welcome to all the patch of world a poor, penniless writer can afford,' he'd said to Linda when she went over for supper a few days later, though as Linda said in our phone debrief, a one-bedroom flat in Hampstead, practically on the Heath, cost the same as a whole house elsewhere. 'But he's a wild romantic,' she said approvingly over breakfast when we all met up at Alconleigh that weekend, 'and that area has so many inspiring associations, apparently. Loads of writers and artists live there. He's among his people.'

'Hampstead?' said Uncle Matthew. 'All tarts and oligarchs these days, Lino. Fat blokes with thin birds. No writers or artists for a long time. Not struggling ones anyway, but maybe their managers. Is he rich, this Christian? He must be.'

'Oh no,' said Linda happily. 'He's quite poor. He wears shabby clothes and eats out of tins – we had the most disgusting dinner – and he has a horrible toothbrush despite his marvellous teeth.'

'A flat in Hampstead isn't poor,' said Uncle Matthew.

'All right, Zoopla,' said Jassy. 'Maybe his granny left it to him, or something.'

'He's working class,' said Linda. 'He had the heating on full blast even though it wasn't at all cold.' This sealed it. Aunt Sadie said that you could always tell someone's social background by their relationship to central heating, even someone who'd gone from poor to rich – 'these things are bred in the bone' – and that she and Uncle Matthew were the living proof. Working-class people loved heat – Uncle Matthew's old London house had been so disgustingly hot, she said, that you had to change into summer clothes if you were going to spend any amount of time in it and not swelter to the point of suffocation. Upper-class people loathed nothing more than a too-warm room and slept with open windows in all weathers. If we were cold as children, Aunt Sadie would never turn up the heating. She might light a fire if our teeth were actually chattering, but otherwise she'd tell us not to be so feeble and to put on a jumper. Uncle Matthew, meanwhile, would be toasty as anything, shoeless and T-shirted in his oven-like study. 'Your mother thinks heating is common,' he said fondly. 'Poshos are fucking nuts.' 'It *is* slightly common,' said Aunt Sadie. 'Nothing wrong with that. A lot of common things are wonderful, like Wotsits or old bingo halls or that tinned mango drink. Or you.' Uncle Matthew flushed pink with pleasure before shaking his head and fondly muttering, 'mad bint'.

'Back to me, please,' said Linda. 'Where's Davey, by the way?'

'On a silent retreat in Croatia,' said Aunt Sadie. 'Though *I* think he's having a thread lift.'

'Thinks he's got jowls,' said Uncle Matthew. 'Bolter recommended someone.' We'd long ago given up being surprised at Uncle Matthew's tolerance of Davey's quirks. Anyone else having pointless cosmetic work – quite aside from the fact that pin-thin Davey did not have jowls – would have triggered a tirade.

'I wonder who he sees,' said Linda. 'Very discreet work. He does look young, doesn't he? Boyish, almost. He needs to be careful he doesn't start looking too smooth. Nothing worse. A friend of Merlin's overdid it and now her face looks like an ostrich egg. Anyway, as I was saying, Christian –'

'Do you call him Chris?' asked Jassy.

'No, he prefers Christian,' said Linda. 'He was quite emphatic about that.'

'Has anyone actually read the fella's book?' asked Uncle Matthew. 'Sadie?'

'I have, as a matter of fact,' said Aunt Sadie. 'For research. I'm halfway through. Have you read it, Linda?'

Linda flushed. 'Yes, nearly.'

'What's it about?' said Uncle Matthew. 'Any animals in it?'

'No,' said Aunt Sadie. Uncle Matthew made a lugubrious sound and went back to his crossword, which he continued to fill in every morning over breakfast, convinced that this daily exercise made Alzheimer's a physiological impossibility.

'No, but Pa, Christian does this amazing animal charity work,' Linda said. 'He's involved with some people who rescue animals from circuses and zoos abroad.'

Uncle Matthew looked up. 'Well, I'm all for that,' he said.

'Me too,' said Linda.

'And me,' said Jassy.

'And me, obviously,' said Aunt Sadie. 'But back to his book, Linda. What did you think, darling? It's quite dense, isn't it?'

'Well, yes,' said Linda. 'But that's because he's so incredibly clever. You have to work at it – he wants you to. He doesn't want to spoon-feed you pap, he says. It took me ages to get into it and . . .'

'You don't sound that into it,' said Jassy. 'Or you'd have finished it in one day.'

'I am into it,' said Linda. 'It's just really tightly packed, like a tin of anchovy fillets, and it's a bit, well – a bit . . . opaque. In places.'

'I'd move house for a really *good* anchovy,' mused Aunt Sadie.

'Why do you have to work at it?' said Uncle Matthew. 'Stupid idea. People should just write stories that other people are into from the off. Like, you write tunes that people love. Not tunes that feel like sodding homework.'

'Not until at least the third album,' said Jassy.

'Same principle, though,' said Uncle Matthew. 'That's what's so brilliant about James Bowen.'

'Not every book can be *A Street Cat Named Bob*,' Aunt Sadie said conciliatorily.

'More's the pity,' Uncle Matthew said. He was starting to bristle. 'Opaque, my arse. Opaque is for tights. It sounds more like poncy showing-off.' Poncy showing-off was a crime of the very first order, perhaps even the worst crime.

'Yes, well. It's actually about a boy's grim childhood,' said Aunt Sadie.

'Bummed by the monks?' asked Jassy through a mouthful of toast.

'No, not bummed by anyone thus far, which is something at least,' said Aunt Sadie thoughtfully. 'No, he's just miserably unhappy. Unhelpful family, you know. Bleak domestic situation. Addiction issues.'

'Tell him to go to AA,' said Uncle Matthew. 'Or NA. Any of the As.'

'I can't, Matty, he's in a book. Anyway, it's set in the countryside but some of the details are way off, like the wheat harvest is in late October and the swifts arrive in February – well, quite – and anyway, going by his description the swifts are actually house martins. Which is a strange mistake, because the boy is supposed to really love birds.'

'Man's an idiot,' said Uncle Matthew, loudly. 'Go to AA and get a birding guide.'

'Pa!' cried Linda. 'You are banned from being horrible about Christian.'

'Sounds great,' said Jassy. 'Is it autobiographical, Lino?'

'I did ask,' said Linda, 'but he didn't really answer, just looked out of the window for quite a long time, so I'm guessing yes, poor him.'

'What else is good about him?' asked Jassy. 'I'm not really getting a proper sense of the goodness. Do you want to jump his bones all day, as Pa would disgustingly say?'

'Heh,' said Uncle Matthew, winking at Aunt Sadie.

'He is dazzlingly good-looking,' said Linda, beaming happily.

'And it's sort of tripled because he's so confident. He's the most confident person I've ever met. It shines out of him in beams. And the cleverest, by miles. He is so clever. I love listening to him. I love his voice. And so he's very attractive in more than one respect.'

'Would I think he was attractive?' asked Jassy.

'Yes,' said Linda. 'But you'd say something horrible about his keffiyeh.'

'Does he have hair?' asked Jassy. 'Is he fat or thin? Pass the book, Ma, I want to look at the author photo. Oh, how annoying, there isn't one. Let me google him, pass your phone, Linda. Oh, for God's sake, is the broadband down again?'

'Yes, sorry,' said Aunt Sadie. 'That storm last week did something to the box.'

'He has tons of hair,' said Linda.

'Ugh,' said Uncle Matthew. 'Not again.'

'And he is thinnish. I'm absolutely mad about him. He has the most terrific social conscience, you know. Did I tell you he also writes poetry?'

19

Linda had wanted a new social circle and within a few weeks, as Christian's girlfriend, she got one that was comprised of people unlike any she'd come across before. Christian's close friends were mainly unpublished authors, fellow poets and writers of essays for small online journals. They had day jobs that they mostly hated, and came to life at night, when they gathered in each other's flats after work, several times a week, to discuss the arts generally and their own writings in particular. There were readings. Since Linda came on to the scene, they mostly gathered at the Sausage after hours. 'They're divinely unglamorous and basic,' Linda said delightedly over lunch at Alconleigh. 'Awful clothes. And they're all obsessed about being ignored by a magazine called the *London Review of Books*,' she added. 'They talk about it for hours sometimes, getting crosser and crosser. The other night I said that perhaps the *London Review of Books* wasn't so much ignoring them as unaware of their very existence, but Christian said not to be silly and that that wasn't it at all. He got quite cross, actually.'

Jassy started to laugh.

'Shush, Jassy,' Linda continued. 'Christian said if they hadn't heard of him even though *Fish with the Worm* is nominated for the Popotin Prize, then it just showed how out of touch they were with the young intelligentsia, and that just showed they weren't doing their job properly and had become complacent and bloated. Anyway, I said, why not ring them up and have a cheerful chat and say, "I have written a 15,000-word essay on the role of cheese in the work of Dickens," and see what happens, but apparently you can't do that. I don't see why not, do you?'

'No,' said Aunt Sadie. 'Of course not. Worst thing they can say is no thank you.' This approach to life was what caused Aunt Sadie to often ask workmen if they'd mind quickly rehanging a picture – she moved pictures around on a weekly basis – on the understanding that anyone with any kind of tool kit – plumbing, building, electrical – was bound to know what they were doing. She would pay them extra for this, and encourage them on to worktops or wonky chairs by patting the surfaces encouragingly and saying, 'Up you pop! Uppety-up tup tup!' in a cheery voice.

'Cass would say that was our privilege talking,' Linda explained. 'Because we're so entitled. Which we are. We'd just pick up the phone and say, "Oh hello, I don't suppose I could interest you in a tiny little essay about cheese," without thinking twice about it, because that's the sort of people we are. Cass says she just couldn't do it because she doesn't have unshakeable bourgeois confidence. Cass has very much fallen out of love with me, by the way, thank goodness.' It was just like Linda not to mind this at all. 'But she does have a point.'

'There's nothing privileged about taking a punt,' Aunt Sadie said mildly, adding, 'I'd 100 per cent read a 15,000-word essay on cheese in Dickens. *Is* there much cheese in Dickens?'

'I don't know,' said Linda. 'I made it up as an example. The real examples are a lot less fun. But also you couldn't have Dickens in the first place because he was mean to his wife, according to Christian, so that's out – they can't write about anyone who did anything mean by today's standards, even if they did the mean thing hundreds of years ago, when the mean thing wasn't considered mean. Or even if it was. Time heals no wounds, that's what they say, Cass sells a T-shirt saying it, it's got a picture of Philip Roth as the background, with his crazy eyebrows, you'd think someone who loved him might have introduced him to tweezers at some point, wouldn't you? Also Christian's friends are all mostly vegan, so the cheese thing was a poor example.'

'There's cashew cheese, I suppose,' said Aunt Sadie doubtfully.

'But how can they be sure the person did a mean thing hundreds of years ago?' I asked.

'They either know from biographies or they suspect. They're very clever.'

'Most people who do mean things do them on the sly,' Jassy pointed out. 'They don't usually get found out.'

'Yes, but you can still suspect,' said Linda. 'You can *extrapolate*. I know, it doesn't make a huge amount of sense to me either, but then I didn't really go to school. I have a lot to learn.'

'Yes you did!' cried Aunt Sadie indignantly. 'Your education may not have been absolutely classical but it was wide-ranging. And I taught you to cook. Well, I started you off.'

'Christian says you taught us the wrong books,' said Linda, 'but that it wasn't your fault. You are a product of your social class and generation and so am I, but he's educating me. He's mad about my cooking, though, they all are, so thank you for that, Ma. I've never known people eat so much, even though they despise what Morag – she's Scottish, very fierce – calls "the domestic arts", you get no brownie points for those at all, you should see the way they look at my house. And Morag picks up the plate and sniffs at it, which I can't say I care for in a human. It's different with dogs, obviously.'

'Fucking rude,' said Uncle Matthew with tremendous disgust. 'Sniffing plates. I won't have it.'

'Yes, well. After the sniffing she practically licks it clean. I did that toffeed peaches thing the other night, Ma, you know, with nut butter and brown sugar, and they fell on it like animals. Oh!

That reminds me. Where's my handbag? I must have left it in the hall, wait there, I want to show you something.'

'Lin's taste in men is a catastrophe,' Jassy said when Linda was out of the room. 'It's perfectly obvious even without meeting him. And why haven't I met him? I'm out a lot but I swear she waits until I'm gone to have them all over. Why? Rhetorical question. It's because she knows I'd hate him.'

'Don't be unkind, darling,' said Aunt Sadie.

'I don't like the sound of him,' said Jassy. 'She's started going on and on about atoning for her privilege and of course she's right – we should all atone – but it's like a fixation and it's all coming from him.'

'He can't be as ghastly as Tony,' said Aunt Sadie. 'And that's not nothing. And he's handsome, she says. Mind you, so was poor Tony.'

'Here,' said Linda, coming back into the kitchen. 'Listen to this. It's a poem Christian wrote for me. It's *so* beautiful, I'm going to frame it. It's called "Kernel", the toffee peaches reminded me. Ready?' She cleared her throat. 'He said he'd never written a poem for a woman before, so I was extremely pleased.'

'What, never? Weird,' said Jassy. 'For a poet.'

'His main poems are political,' Linda said. 'And quite sweary. He feels injustice so deeply.' She cleared her throat again. 'Right, so. "Kernel. For Linda by Christian Talbot, in his hand, 23 January, Hampstead, NW London." Shut up, Jassy.'

'I didn't say anything!' protested Jassy.

'I know you were about to,' said Linda. 'Because of "in his hand". He wrote it out, you see. Longhand. It's not a printout. It's in ink.'

'Magical,' said Jassy.

'Do you want to hear it or not?'

We all said that we did, very much, apart from Uncle Matthew, who said 'No' and went off to walk the dogs.

Linda rolled her eyes, paused and then began:

> 'opulent fruit
> languid flesh
> but holy o holy
> at the intersection of desire and hunger
> marmoreal but dark
> o dark
> she has a kernel
> ridged
> hard as wood of tree
> pitted as heart of man
> fatal eros stalks.

'Well! Isn't it wonderful?' she asked, looking around the table bright-eyed.

'What's he on about, kernels at intersections?' asked Jassy. She put down her coffee cup and looked thoughtful for a moment. 'Wait, is it about your bum? Pass it over, would you? Oh my God, Linda, it's about your bum!'

'Or your vagina,' said Aunt Sadie. 'But then why "ridged", like a walnut? I'm sorry, darling, I'm not really laughing.'

'You are,' said Linda furiously. 'You're wheezing and there are tears in your eyes. For God's sake, Ma! Ma! Stop!'

Aunt Sadie, unable to speak, appeared to be weeping silently and waved Linda away with a strangled yelp. Jassy started reading the poem aloud again in a deep, gloomy voice, but Linda snatched it away.

'I don't even know what to say,' said Jassy. 'This poem is just so terrible.'

'Then say nothing,' snapped Linda. 'Philistine.' Until the age of fifteen or so, we used to think that 'philistine' was a person, Philip Stein, because we'd heard Uncle Matthew talking about a famous record label boss called Seymour Stein and it had made sense for him to have a brother.

I wanted to say something neutral, so I asked if there was punctuation, because from the way she'd read it out it wasn't clear.

'Only at the end,' Linda explained. 'Where it says fatal Eros is stalking. It's to make the line even more powerful. A real gut-punch. Kapow! You don't think it's bad, do you, Franny?'

'Franny,' implored Jassy. 'Come on, man.'

'I do think it's quite bad, but I don't know much about contemporary poetry. The main thing is that you like it,' I said. I was poised somewhere between horror and trying not to join in with Aunt Sadie's giggling, and I was also trying to understand why Linda herself wasn't rolling around the floor crying with mirth and derision. 'Lovely to have a poem written about you, though,' I added weakly.

'Or your bum,' said Jassy.

'It's not about bums, Jassy, you absolute moron, it's about hearts. The pitted hearts of men,' said Linda.

'Ridged,' said Aunt Sadie.

'. . . redeemed through love. Or lust, or something else nice. And anyway, I don't see famous writers writing you poems.'

'He's not famous,' said Jassy. 'You'd never heard of him either.'

'How long did it take him to compose, do we know?' asked Aunt Sadie, who had wiped her eyes on her napkin and regained a tiny degree of composure.

'Ages,' said Linda. 'He said he'd been working on it for weeks as a special gift to me. Couldn't get the scansion right.'

'No,' said Aunt Sadie. 'I can see that. I have to leave the table now,' she added, rising suddenly, her lips pressed together against another laughter fit. 'I'm happy you're happy, darling. You have that bloom about you again, it's lovely to see. Bring him to meet us soon, with or without his circus animals. Can you all clear up, please?'

'This family!' said Linda.

Later that day Davey wandered in to say hello and mentioned in passing that he knew a Christian Talbot – 'Davey knows everyone! Everyone!' Uncle Matthew roared approvingly – or rather that he'd known his late mother. 'Etonian, wasn't he, your Christian?' he mused. Linda laughed and said that she really didn't think he'd been to public school, reiterating her point about central heating and the autobiographical nature of *Fish with the Worm*, which was set on a housing estate in Doncaster. 'Mmm,' said Davey. 'You'll have to ask him. It's an unusual name. My Christian Talbot's mother was called Candida Rowse. She married someone military. He'd be about the right age.'

20

Jassy went back to London with Linda the following day and was later that week finally introduced to Christian. It was quickly established that he was indeed the son of Candida Rowse – 'Small world,' he'd grimaced. Christian had been displeased to have his public school career brought up – there was no mention of it in his self-penned Wikipedia entry or in any of his publisher's publicity material, and the impression he convincingly projected was bracingly proletarian. 'The thing is,' he'd smoothly told Jassy and Linda upon being busted, 'that from a socialist perspective, the advantage of having attended a private school such as Eton is that people like me, ex-insiders – ex-*cons*, really – can critique the injustice of the system properly, you know? We've walked the walk. We've *survived*.' Christian was, therefore, central to the anti-capitalist revolution, he said, adding that he'd nevertheless be grateful for their discretion, and that now he had to leave for a meeting. Even Linda had blinked rapidly at the 'central to the revolution' bit. Jassy said ugh, and that he was a total shyster, though she granted easy on the eye, but Linda said that people couldn't help where their parents sent them to school, and that at least he wasn't insanely right wing, like Tony, and made Jassy tell her which bit of Christian's face she most admired (Jassy said this was far from the point but probably his nose).

Unlike Jassy, I liked Christian, when I eventually met him too. He really did look like the young Stalin and had unusually pool-like, soulful, thickly lashed brown eyes. Jassy said he had dogs' eyes in a human face and that it was creepy, and reminded Linda that she, Linda, had always hated men with calf eyes, these being eyes that were overly moony and, crucially, too kind and too gentle. During our endless teenage discussions concerning the desirability or otherwise of certain physical traits, both Linda and Jassy had been unwaveringly emphatic about overly kind eyes, decreeing that they were exactly what you wanted in a nice fat grandma, and by extension categorically not the sorts of eyes that you wanted in a lover. Mean eyes, by contrast – eyes you couldn't entirely trust, perhaps slightly narrow, ideally green – were intensely sexy. 'I don't know what you're doing with someone with giant chocolate buttons for eyes,' Jassy said. 'It's disgustingly unhot.' Linda had replied that Jassy was not required to find Christian hot, which Jassy said was just as well, considering the eye situation, and then after a bit Linda said that Jassy had no taste because it was obvious to anyone that Christian was in fact scorching hot. Jassy said that if he was that hot, his eyes would melt, which made Linda laugh despite herself and throw a cushion at Jassy's head.

Christian was intensely, almost unsettlingly, charming. He was the sort of person who makes you feel understood, appreciated, somehow more than the sum of your parts, even if you've only exchanged three sentences. There was a thrum of energy about him – 'I know!' Linda said when I mentioned it, 'and it's not even coke!' – that was osmotically invigorating and that made the world seem vivid and full of possibilities. He said 'we' a lot: you'd say, making small talk, that you wanted to go to visit a particular National Trust garden in the spring (Alfie and I had moved to Oxford earlier in the year and I had developed a keen interest in horticulture), and Christian would reply that 'we' must all make the trip to see it, despite having no interest in gardens whatsoever and, you suspected, despising the very existence of the National Trust and its egregious colonial legacies. You knew all this perfectly well and yet, in that moment, you believed with all your heart that gardens were his life, that you were close friends, that you were part of his gang and that it would be fun. It was a neat trick. The trip would, of course, never materialize, the notion genuinely having evaporated from Christian's head the moment his words had done their job. He had no interest in ordinary life, or in the ordinary ins and outs of people's days, or in how people felt about subjects that weren't politics, mistreated animals or Christian Talbot.

It would have been too babyish and whiny to remind him of the plans he'd made – 'But you said', 'But you promised', 'Weren't we supposed to . . . ' – and besides, we all had lives to be getting on with. We also knew from Linda that Christian's 'gang', such as it was, was neither appealing nor fun-sounding and that we had no desire to be part of it. But, in the dazzle of the moment, all that was forgotten, whitewashed by the vivid pictures he painted and by the spontaneity he seemed to embody ('Road trip!' 'Group swim!' 'To the Odeon!'). The real Christian vanished, replaced by whatever Christian you wanted him to be. Really, he operated like an old-fashioned seducer, a 1950s Riviera gigolo with all the sex and criminality removed – 'Yeah, all the fun bits,' said Jassy. Instead of running away with your jewels in the night, all he wanted to steal, and perhaps try on in private, were your esteem and your admiration. It would be too glib to say he wanted to be loved, because it went far beyond that.

But when he turned on the full beam of his charm, as he often did in those early days, it was hard to imagine that Christian was the person who wrote impenetrable books and terrible poetry, the man who read aloud from his own work at the drop of a hat, and easy to see how Linda had fallen for him.

Christian, for all his desire to be liked, admired, envied – whether by connivance or accident, his previously non-existent public profile had taken an upward turn since hooking up with Linda – lived almost entirely inside his own head. His chief concern was himself and his own work. His second concern were the causes he tirelessly and admirably campaigned for. He had only very superficial feelings about anything else. He liked his group of friends well enough, but largely because his fellow writers served as a useful yardstick to measure himself against; later, when he became better known and a couple of them found their way to their own publishing deals, he would remain intimately acquainted, in part to monitor their progress, their finances, their media coverage, and compare theirs to his. And Linda? He liked her well enough too. He told her, infrequently, that he loved her, he wrote her occasional poems, and when they had sex, often in front of a mirror so that he could maintain eye contact with himself, he would mumble endearments that she found lyrical and poetic and a pleasing change from what she described as the usual porn chat – 'Though sometimes what you want is porn chat, don't you think, Fran? But he's not into it and I can hardly porn-soliloquize all by myself. Never mind.' Linda said that sex was the least important aspect of her relationship with Christian and that really she loved him best because he educated her, which was so unlike her as to sound downright peculiar. But she was in love with him, she said, and her happiness and contentment shone clear to see; the restlessness that often characterized her had gone. She poured everything she had into him: her own considerable charm, her jokes, which fell on deaf ears as Christian had no sense of humour whatsoever, her cleverness and wit, her beauty, and now also her desire to remake herself in his image, or at least in an image that he would find more pleasing – less privileged, more sober, more serious, more like him.

Her wardrobe changed for about six months. Linda had never

dressed like anybody else and had, from childhood – Alconleigh had a particularly well-stocked dressing-up box – always been able to put clothes together with the kind of wit and panache that eluded the rest of us. She was able to do this without any obvious effort, and it had quickly become second nature. But the jewel colours she liked to wear, the reds and pinks and greens I had associated with her for as long as I could remember, were now replaced with utilitarian browns and greys. Her vintage necklaces, her elaborate earrings, the grandma brooches she was so good at digging out at car-boot sales, were confined to a drawer. Linda was unavoidably Linda, and the androgynous denim boiler suits and itchy-looking sweaters she'd taken to wearing were well sourced and better cut than most. Her sack dresses were cinched in at the waist. But the change in her appearance was notable. She looked diluted, somehow, fainter, like a faded photograph of herself.

Christian was deeply politically committed to the far Left, she said, or at least politically committed enough to have 'issues' with her golden life of great good fortune and frivolity. Of his, there was no mention. He was reshaping her, she explained cheerfully. That it never occurred to Christian that Linda's life was, unlike his, not without its troubles – that she was, for a start, a young woman with a divorce behind her and a child who lived elsewhere – went unremarked. Her work at the cafe, where she cooked and served all day before feeding his friends at night, was never discussed. Christian loved her because he could mould her into the ideal woman for him, and, to general incredulity, Linda became pliant, eager to please, hungry to learn. For the first time in her life, she found herself wanting. As a child and young woman, she'd often said, 'The good thing is, no matter what happens, at least I'm me,' or variants thereon ('How awful to be other people, Fran, aren't you glad we're us?'). But the certainties that had seen her through were now in question, and she liked it. She seemed energized. The odd thing about all this was that Christian also clearly liked the glamour that clung to her even as she tried to get rid of it, and enjoyed the attention that came with it even as he decried her frivolity. They made a beautiful couple.

Nobody was especially surprised, or especially pleased, when Linda and Christian got married the following year. In contrast to her lavish wedding to Tony, the ceremony took place at Hackney Town Hall, with only two dozen or so guests and stout little Moira, now five, as the sole bridesmaid. Aunt Sadie's eyes filled with tears within moments of taking her seat and explained that it had nothing to do with Linda but was rather because town hall wedding ceremonies were so desperately depressing and thin, and one's soul yearned for more. Davey, wearing a made-to-measure pearl-grey morning suit, square-cut antique emerald cufflinks and jauntily angled top hat, had agreed and said that he knew for a fact that God wouldn't be so petty as to mind if people pretended to believe in him for a day so that they could get married in a beautiful church with ravishing music and majestic vows. 'One doesn't like to think of Him as prim,' he said, before taking out a miniature jar of Manuka honey – 'nectar for the throat' – and a tiny silver spoon to prepare himself for his reading, this being a new poem of Christian's called 'Conjugal Bond'.

Christian had been against the institution of marriage, which he blithely likened to indentured slavery (Jassy had pointed out that this was in itself a monstrously privileged comparison to make, but Linda, in her joy, ignored her). He claimed he'd proposed purely to make Linda happy, as though it were a philanthropic act of great generosity and goodness, and there was no denying that she was. The groom wore jeans, Converse and an ironic, 1970s formal shirt with ruffles; if the intention had been to suggest rock and roll insouciance, it wasn't quite conveyed. The bride was, once again, in couture Merlin Berners. Merlin, having observed Linda's short-lived conversion to linen and flax and having been told by Linda that Christian had said he'd hoped she wouldn't be wearing anything 'too flash', had outdone himself with the splendour and luxuriousness of the gown, which somehow managed to be both demure and provocative, and which caused the *Daily Mail* to run a two-page spread on how to copy Linda's enviable hi-lo style. (Christian, who said he despised the mainstream media generally and the *Daily Mail* in particular, bought six copies of that particular issue.) Uncle Matthew gave Linda away again – stony-faced rather than weeping, this time – and I was struck afresh by the contrast between Uncle Matthew and normal men. You tended to forget about it in the familiar context of Alconleigh, but it stopped you in your tracks in the outside world. He looked like some sort of demigod even standing near handsome Christian, towering over him, radiating charisma and bad temper.

Like Jassy and Merlin, Uncle Matthew had proved resistant to, and suspicious of, Christian's charm. Uncle Matthew had glared at Christian the moment the latter arrived for a weekend at Alconleigh a few months previously, wearing a pair of workman's dungarees over a chunky sweater. Linda had filled me in.

'Good grief,' Uncle Matthew had said. 'Have you come from the 1940s to mend the boiler?'

'I couldn't be happier to meet you, Matt,' Christian said, pumping Uncle Matthew's hand. 'Always happy to assist with any honest work,' he added with a smile.

'My wife calls me Matt,' Uncle Matthew said. 'You can call me Matthew. Or Mr Radlett. Sadie!' he bellowed in the general direction of the kitchen. 'Linda's here with her fella.' He looked Christian up and down and continued, still shouting, 'Sades!

Where are you? Hurry up! It's the Posh Trot. He's carrying a spanner.' This wasn't in fact true. He chuckled to himself. 'Eh, Trotty? Eh?'

'For heaven's sake, Matt,' Aunt Sadie said, finally emerging with both arms extended in welcome. 'Hello, Christian. How lovely to meet you. Linda's told us so much about you. Ignore Matty. Matty, don't call him Trotty.'

'It sounds like a pig,' observed Linda, extricating herself from Uncle Matthew's embrace. 'Mr Trotty, the champion hog.'

'Yes, it does. A really *fat* hog. Come and have a cup of tea,' said Aunt Sadie. 'I made a cake.'

'Trotty, this is my wife,' Uncle Matthew said. 'Sadie. Mrs Radlett. Sadie, this is Trotty.'

'I know who it is, Matt,' said Aunt Sadie with a sharp look. 'It's Christian.'

Christian, to his credit, remained wholly unflustered by Uncle Matthew saying Trotty every two seconds. 'I can see where Linda gets her looks from,' he said smoothly to Aunt Sadie, smiling a charming smile. 'And I would love a piece of home-made cake. Linda tells me you don't employ staff, which I find commendable.'

'You do, do you,' said Uncle Matthew. It wasn't a question, but it got an answer.

'The exploitation of the working class by the gentry . . .'

'I'm not the gentry,' said Uncle Matthew.

'Nevertheless, the centuries-old exploitation of the workers by the capitalist class . . .'

'Oh God,' said Uncle Matthew, very loudly. 'I'm not into it either, just so we're clear. But nor do I need a lecture about it.' He muttered something we didn't quite catch about 'synthetic cochineal' as he marched off into the kitchen.

'We try not to exploit the workers,' Aunt Sadie said from the larder as we all sat down. 'Though I'd like to see anyone try to exploit Mrs Hopkirk.'

'Mrs Hopkirk comes to help out,' explained Linda. 'You'll meet her, she's heaven. She is married to Mr Hopkirk, the estate manager.'

'I see,' said Christian.

'He went to Cirencester,' Aunt Sadie said. 'It's an agricultural college. He's also a local councillor. Just to help you situate the Hopkirks, Christian. I'm afraid they don't especially keep the red flag flying.'

'Well, Norfolk is a true blue county,' said Christian. 'Alas.'

'Apart from Norwich,' said Uncle Matthew. 'Which is true red.'

'But let's not talk about politics,' said Christian. 'Though I am glad to find myself among fellow travellers.' He silently raised a clenched fist.

'Not quite,' said Aunt Sadie, though she politely raised her fist too. 'But each to their own. Tea?'

'Yes please,' said Christian. 'Oh, orange pekoe, my favourite. Now, Matt – I can't tell you what a thrill it is to meet you. I'm a long-standing fan. I had a poster of Sin in my room for years.'

'At Eton?' Aunt Sadie asked.

'Uh, yes, and thereafter,' said Christian. 'I loved the band, the energy, the boldness. And the brutal efficacy of your lyrics, of course,' he added.

'Speak English, man,' said Uncle Matthew.

Christian took a delicate sip of his tea and cleared his throat. ' "I would go / Deeper into Hades / I would run / Towards the flames / Deeper into Hades / Deeper / Way deeper / With you," ' he intoned. 'I mean, that's very powerful, before you even get to the melody.'

'Thanks,' said Uncle Matthew.

'Or,' said Christian, 'what you do with "Gonna Blow". The

yearning candour of the line "Give it to me give it to me give it to me hooooo/Give it to me there." And that pounding bass. There's a marvellous directness to the lyric, a true exposition of masculinity at its rawest and most feral.'

'Well, yeah,' said Uncle Matthew. 'Because it's about wanting a shag. That's why you feel the bass in your crotch.'

'Indeed,' said Christian, putting his cup down on the kitchen table and helping himself to another slice of Sadie's lemon polenta cake; he had wolfed down the first one extraordinarily quickly. His voice became sombre. 'Of course, the music was very much of its time. You could hardly accuse it of mirroring current mores and attitudes.'

'Different times,' said Uncle Matthew. 'We were who we were, and now we're different people. Well, most of us are.'

'I mean, where to start?' continued Christian in the same sepulchral tones. 'The objectification of women and girls. The machismo. The fetishization of capital in all those videos where you're on yachts or private jets.'

'Ever watch hip-hop videos, Trotty?' Uncle Matthew asked.

'Don't clutch at straws, Matty,' said Aunt Sadie. 'You're quite right, Christian, though Matt is well aware of . . .'

'Hip-hop videos are hardly the same thing,' Christian continued, as if Aunt Sadie hadn't spoken. 'You can't blame people who have been downtrodden for centuries for celebrating in the more obvious ways when they finally do make some money. The same is not true of, for instance, "Put It in Your Mouth",' he added, 'which is about cis white men exercising their gender privilege.'

'Well, we stopped playing that one live fairly sharpish,' Uncle Matthew acknowledged. 'Even I thought it was a bit much, after Sadie explained. But point taken, even though you talk like you swallowed a book.'

'Christian talks in whole paragraphs,' Linda said adoringly.

'Have you noticed? It's so wonderful. Makes you realize how badly most people speak, with their ums and ahs and repetitions. God, Pa, aren't you glad you didn't marry a sixteen-year-old?'

'That was only my thing when I was sixteen myself,' said Uncle Matthew.

The point about much of Sin's back catalogue had, of course, been made to Uncle Matthew hundreds of times before, not least by his wife and daughters. There had been a whole period where the members of the band just sat about waiting to be denounced, shamed and then cancelled for evermore. But, curiously, nothing had happened. The topic nevertheless continued to make Uncle Matthew deeply uncomfortable, and I could tell that he wouldn't thank Christian for bringing it up over tea.

The conversation perked up once it moved on to rescuing animals from cruel circuses abroad. Trunk Stop, the organization Christian worked with, did excellent work, and Christian was not dismissed out of hand when he asked Uncle Matthew whether he might consider turning some of his land into a temporary sanctuary for the beasts, should the need ever arise.

'We rehome them in the country we find them in,' he explained, 'but it sometimes takes a while, so every now and then we ask people with the right set-up if they could have them to stay for a bit.'

'Christian's so committed,' Linda said approvingly. 'He's always trying to make people store his elephants.'

'Well, not elephants,' said Christian. 'Although we have successfully rescued a few in our time. I'm talking about more transportable animals. Ones less likely to find the journey traumatic.'

'Seals?' said Aunt Sadie. 'We'd love a seal or two, wouldn't we, Matthew?'

'S'pose so,' said Uncle Matthew. 'Wouldn't say no. Plenty of friends for it around here.'

Christian, puzzled, looked about the kitchen, and then out of the window.

'Pa means the local seal colonies,' explained Linda. 'Like at Blakeney Point.'

'Circus seals are usually sea lions,' he said. 'Not actual seals.'

'Whatever,' said Uncle Matthew magnanimously. 'Put us down for a dozen, Trotty.'

Things were going well until the conversation moved on and Christian brandished a copy of *Fish with the Worm*. 'I've signed it for you,' he said, and told a rapidly cooling Uncle Matthew that he would be reading aloud from it after dinner. Uncle Matthew started chewing furiously on a cheese scone and glaring at Linda.

But Christian – and it took an impressive kind of courage – had laughed off the palpable hostility, persisted with his plan and read an entire chapter out that night, having first tapped his glass with his knife and repeated, 'Quiet, please, everybody,' twice, earning himself unenthusiastic stares from more than just Uncle Matthew. He read in a Northern accent, in a slow, hoarse voice quite unlike his mellifluous speaking one, making and maintaining eye contact with various startled family members once every paragraph or so, and stopping only because Aunt Sadie, flushed and damp-eyed with the effort of not laughing, started clattering about clearing plates and shooing everyone into the sitting room for coffee. 'I'm not laughing because it's bad,' she explained to Linda, who was helping her to clear up. 'Necessarily. I'm laughing because he's so intense.' Linda said that it was OK, and that Christian never noticed things like that anyway when he was 'performing'.

The following day, after what he called a hike and everyone else called a forty-minute walk, Christian had been moved to write a poem about the landscape and to recite it at supper that night – 'antediluvian flint, Grimalkin-grey,' it began, and went on to encompass 'savage ponies with the face of God'. Uncle Matthew pointed out that there weren't any ponies – 'It's Norfolk, not bloody Exmoor' – and that the animals in question were pet donkeys. 'Such *kind* faces,' said Aunt Sadie reprovingly.

Circus rescues aside, the visit was not a success, though the Radletts did get to the bottom of the Hampstead flat, which had indeed, it turned out, been left to Christian by a great-aunt. When Davey had very politely asked how Christian squared owning a prime slice of London property with his political opinions, Christian told him, rather impatiently, that while all property was obviously theft, he 'implicitly' refused to take part in the corrupt capitalist mortgage merry-go-round, and saw his ownership of the flat as an essential revolutionary protest against the forces of capital. When he went up to bed, Uncle Matthew said that Trotty was a pompous posho windbag in disguise, that he'd never met anyone less aware of anything, but that the man knew his seals, he'd give him that. Linda said that she didn't care what anyone thought and rolled her eyes. But she never took Christian to Alconleigh again.

21

Linda came to see me in Oxford six months or so after the wedding. Jassy was holding the fort at the cafe for the day and Christian was on his way back from a writing retreat in Yorkshire, where he had been working on his new novel, *Butterkin* – 'Which is not about a rabbit, such a shame because Butterkin is the perfect rabbit name,' Linda sighed. 'What a waste of it. But he was going to call his new book *The Torpid Heart Doth Twist and Sicken* – isn't it funny how so many authors make up lines that sound like they're from the sort of poem you'd really hate to read? – and at least Butterkin sounds quite jolly. Though I'm afraid,' she added, 'it isn't jolly at all.'

She looked as beautiful as ever, but tired and too thin, and when I told her she said that it was because she was quite knackered. A foodie website in the US had put the Sausage on its list of London hot spots, praising the simple but excellent food. 'The vibe at this small but perfectly formed cafe is eccentric, relaxed, deeply English,' they wrote, noting, 'It's not every day your turmeric latte is served with a smile by a rock star's daughter, in this case former model and socialite Linda Talbot, née Radlett. Yes, as in.' As a result, a steady stream of eager tourists were finding their way to the depths of Dalston. 'They're usually very sweet and enthusiastic, but they photograph every single thing, from their food to the hens to the cutlery to me, and they always want to chat for hours.' She was, she said, thinking of instigating a booking system, even though this went against the entire point of the relaxed, drop-in, neighbourhood feel of the cafe. Still, the Sausage was packed all day, every day, and had started turning a profit. It was taking up more and more of Linda's time and less and less of Jassy's, who had moved to her own flat in Bethnal Green, using the proceeds of her Running Away Fund, just before the wedding. Jassy was in the process of training part-time to become a florist as well as an artist – 'Everyone needs a side-hustle,' she said – having decided that there was a gap in the market for the artfully unkempt bunches of wild, meadow-style flowers that she made for the Sausage and that people were always asking to buy. The cafe had other staff but Linda was obsessively hands-on. She knew she was part of the draw, and besides she enjoyed both the cooking and most of the interactions. 'And anyway,' she said, 'I live one floor up – it's impossible to ignore what's going on downstairs.'

Living with Christian was much harder work than living with Tony, she told me, 'even though with Tony I was almost immediately unhappy and had a baby to look after. Isn't it funny? But Christian say's it's immoral to have a cleaning lady, so I do all of that too. God, Fran, housework is so exhausting if you do it properly, it makes me want to lie down and have a nap, and no one ever notices or says thank you, let alone brings you a cup of tea or gives you a massage because your back hurts.' She quickly corrected herself. 'Not that I would exploit people by making them massage me. But still – housework doesn't count as work in anyone's eyes, even though it is such *hard* work. Christian says that it's honest work and that there is nobility in it, and I agree, sort of, except it takes for ever and I am the only one being honest and noble because he can't help. He's far too busy typing and living the, um, the life of the mind and being political. And saving the animals, of course, which I love him for. Where was I? Oh yes, housework. I don't think Christian even knows how to load a dishwasher. You know these cerebral types!' She laughed, and then frowned. 'Though *un*loading a dishwasher isn't complicated and he doesn't do that either.'

I said that I was pleased about the animals, and that I did know these cerebral types – I was surrounded by them here in Oxford and many of our friends were, like Alfie, academics at the university – and that as far as I knew even the most cerebral rolled up their sleeves and got a mop out every now and then. 'Do they?' said Linda. 'Well, Christian doesn't. He says he doesn't mind dirt or mess, barely registers it, and that if I want to be anal and bourgeois about it and poke about with a noisy Hoover that breaks his concentration all morning, it's my look-out. I wouldn't call picking up dirty plates and changing the bed sheets bourgeois or anal, would you?' She sighed. 'What's maddening is that when the house is absolutely sparkling clean – I know it's very unevolved but I do find it really intensely satisfying, I could write rhapsodies about stain removers – he genuinely doesn't notice. I have to point it out, and then I hear myself sounding quite naggy. Though *is* it naggy, I wonder, to want someone to be pleased that the rooms they live in look beautiful and are nice to be in? I'm starting to think that there's actually no such thing as nagging, only lazy men pretending to be deaf. Nagging is a stupid word, like "temptress", which is really another way of saying, "I want to shag her and it's her fault." One of Christian's poems is called "Temptress" ("Temptrex", actually, with an X so it's not so gendered) and I find it quite annoying. It's about how a temptrex – me, presumably – is always getting in the way of his important busy thoughts.' She sighed again – it was the third sigh in under ten minutes – and briefly fell silent. Linda had always been talkative, but she had recently taken to these great stream-of-consciousness gushes of speech, like a bottle that had suddenly been uncorked and was spilling out everywhere. I could have listened to her for hours, but it did give the impression that she perhaps didn't have anyone to chat away to, in the way that she so much enjoyed, in everyday life. Jassy had noticed the same thing since moving out, and Aunt Sadie had delightedly remarked that, having once been impossible to get hold of, Linda was now impossible to get off the phone.

'Not that I'm saying Christian's lazy,' Linda added after a while. 'Though he is, a bit. And he gets really cross if he's out of clean shirts. Anyway, sorry, I'm rambling on and on, but it is so nice to see you. Tell me about you. Oh, Fran, I wish you still lived in London.'

'There isn't much to report, really,' I said. 'We're happy, the baby is due in three months, Alfie's work is going great guns, he loads the dishwasher, tidies up and does his own laundry, I've made some nice friends, I'm still very into gardening . . . I am completely boring, Linny. I'm delighted to have moved out of London, but I wish Oxford weren't so far from Norfolk. It takes the best part of an afternoon to get to Alconleigh. Have you been going lots?' I went up at least twice a month, either solo or with Alfie, of whom Aunt Emily was very fond, and was planning to ensconce myself at the cottage for a few weeks once the new baby was born. Aunt Sadie and Aunt Emily both loved babies and had suggested it, saying they'd help with nights so I could get some sleep. Aunt Sadie really looked forward to Moira's frequent visits.

'No, hardly ever, though I was there last weekend with Momo,' Linda now said. She did not work at weekends, deputizing to Jassy or two of the young chefs she'd hired so that she could spend time with Moira. 'It's not much fun for her in Dalston because Christian needs quiet and starts banging on about the pram in the hall. She's not really on his radar. He's perfectly nice to her – he's friendly – but not really present.' She shook her head incredulously and then let out a sigh.

'Anyway, Momo and Ma made brownies *and* blondies.

Christian says it's abnormal to be so attached to your family and that I'm like a homing pigeon. Homing to Ma and Pa, I mean,' she added. 'Not homing to Momo so much, though I had a nice time teaching her to ride. Tony and Pixie are moving to New York for a year, did I tell you? Not right away, but at some point in the next couple of years. He's got a temporary transfer and of course she has family there too. Momo's excited about it. She's going to come back and stay with me for half the school holidays.'

'God, Linda, you never said. How do you feel about it? I mean, I know you don't live in the same place as her now, but a whole other continent . . .'

'It'll be fine,' said Linda, 'provided the school holidays thing works out. It's not for ages and anyway, it'll only be for a year. I know you disapprove, Fran, but Momo really is happy with them. She loves Pixie, apparently they brush each other's hair for hours and have manicures and film themselves doing dance routines, and she loves her father and all the Kroesigs and she loves her life with them.'

'But don't you mind that she is so Kroesigish because of that?' I asked.

'Actually she's not nearly as Kroesigish as she was,' Linda said. 'And anyway, the Kroesigs may not be my cup of tea, but they're not bad people. Tony really does dote on her, you know, and Lady K is besotted.'

'Being surrounded by doting people isn't necessarily brilliant either,' I said. 'She needs someone who doesn't just say yes to everything and call it love.'

'Yes, well, that would be me. I don't quite dote in that way, so it counters it,' Linda said. There was some truth in this. 'I think New York will be very good, actually, whenever it happens. It'll expose her to all sorts of people, with any luck. Think how much we'd have loved it when we were her age – we'd have died of joy. Now, can we go to that delicious Lebanese place on the Cowley Road that you keep talking about for lunch?' she added, sidling up to me on the sofa and patting my bump fondly. 'Wouldn't it be nice if we could give birth to animals instead of babies? Imagine having a puppy, or a foal. Even a piglet. Or a little baby goat with tiny hooves. Hello in there,' she shouted, putting her lips to my stomach. 'I'm your Aunt Lino. I might be more designed to be an aunt than a mother, you know, Fran. Just like I sometimes think that I might be more designed to be a mistress than a wife.'

'Linda!'

'Don't. I wouldn't say it to anybody else, and I'm not even sure I really think it, and anyway I think I probably mean girlfriend rather than mistress. I'd never nick someone's spouse if I could help it, it's so unbelievably grotty. It's just that being someone's wife sometimes seems a bit of a slog. Wouldn't it be more fun to lie around in your pants eating bonbons and waiting for hot dates? More relaxing, at any rate. Tell you what I do quite like, though.'

'What's that?'

'I like it that Christian doesn't really pay me any attention whatsoever, until suddenly he does, almost as if he'd remembered I was there. It's much better than somebody being constantly in your face, like Tony was, sending you stupid orchids all day long and always trying to touch you.'

'Do you mean he ignores you?' I asked, hating the notion.

'Not exactly ignores, no. He's just not that bothered, which means that when he *is* bothered, it's a bit like a horse you've never met suddenly trotting over for a hug. Or like someone switching all the lights on – you know how charming he can be, Fran, it's really a superpower. Normally with me people are bothered all the time, you know? Or they were, when I saw those sorts of people.' She frowned tinily. 'Anyway, it makes a change.'

Linda publicly took the view that Christian was disengaged because he was so busy shaping the cultural discourse, and while that was arguably true, I thought that he also sounded self-obsessed and deluded when it came to his sense of his own importance in the world. I could not understand how his great love of humanity failed to extend to his own wife, or to even a passing interest in her little daughter. It was clear that he treated Linda carelessly, and she was a person who required care. She wanted to love and to be loved, loudly, wholly and steadfastly, and the fact that Christian seemed to love his various projects and causes – the end of capitalism, the eradication of poverty, the empowerment of minorities, the rectifying of historical wrongs, the freeing of circus animals, the ascent of Christian Talbot – more than he loved or had time for Linda concerned me.

In addition to *Butterkin*, Christian and three of his friends were launching their own literary journal. The assistant editor would be Morag, who disapproved of Linda's wonderfully comfortable interiors but sprawled about in them most days anyway, stuffing her pale, round face while looking around her with a half-sneer. Morag was fey and self-consciously quirky, and considered herself trenchantly humorous, though the humour seemed to consist largely of reading things she disapproved of out loud before saying, 'Aye, right,' in a sarcastic way and looking triumphant (she had even said this about a blameless new jute rug when Linda had, truthfully, told her it had been made by a women's collective in Bangladesh). Christian's deputy editor was to be a permanently furious man called Brian, who lived with his mother and always had crumbs in the corners of his mouth, and who wrote incandescent J' accuse-style pieces for a political website: 'If something happens, anything at all, anywhere in the world, Brian is absolutely full honko livid about it,' said Linda. 'You have to admire it, in a way. He's like a ball of rage. I can't have Radio 4 on when he's around because he starts arguing with the presenter or the guest or both. Doesn't even matter what the programme is.' The third founder, and the magazine's publisher, was Stuart. Stuart had written a bestselling book about his own depression, and had sought Christian out at a literary festival in Wales to express his admiration for *Fish with the Worm*, thereby earning himself a partial exemption from Christian's implacable and spittle-flecked disdain for 'commercial' writers. Stuart flirted with Linda and had long yellow teeth, but he was the friendliest of the group. The journal was to be called *Notus*.

'He's the Greek god of the south wind,' Linda explained, 'and the bringer of summer storms. I said that the south wind reminds me of holidays in Provence and lunch at La Colombe d'Or – do you remember when Ma and Pa took us and Robin fell in the pool and it turned out he knew how to swim? – and that I couldn't really see why that would work for an edgy, leftist London literary magazine, but they ignored me and said that they were disrupters and so the bringing of storms worked perfectly. Anyway, there's lots going on, what with setting up *Notus* and the cafe and the house, and then our social life of course, which is the exact opposite of my old social life.' Gone were the private views, the launches, the dinners in newly opened restaurants, the nightclubs and glamorous parties. Linda's social life still consisted, as far as I could see, of Linda cooking vast amounts of delicious food and serving it to Christian's friends while they gossiped about other, more successful, writers, read their work out loud to each other at interminable length and ranted until the early hours about politics. The last time I'd been to London to see Linda, I'd accidentally barged in on one of their meetings while looking for something. Christian had been in full flow: 'It's far more important to keep socialism alive in opposition than it is to compromise it in government,' he was saying. 'That's why, in a very real sense, we actually won the last election.' I'd mouthed 'oops, sorry' and closed the door behind me.

'I am not an expert, as they keep telling me, but what I don't really understand,' Linda now said, 'is that they seem to hold what they call The People in absolute contempt, because The People keep voting the wrong way at general elections. So really they're saying that The People are too stupid to know what's good for them, which I don't call comradely, do you? I asked Christian, who is after all a creative person who writes books, whether he found it so difficult to imagine that sometimes The People might want nice things that cost money, but he said not in their hearts, only because they had been brainwashed and corrupted by capitalism. Which to me sounds like another way of saying they're stupid. Really by The People he and the group mean people exactly like them.'

I sighed and said I didn't have anything constructive to say. Christian's politics seemed jejune to me, and shot through with the sense of entitlement that he spent so much of his time decrying, especially in relation to Linda. But I agreed with Linda that at least he didn't share any of Tony's more dubious views. 'Don't you mind all the endless cooking?' I asked.

'Not really,' she said, adding, 'I still love the act of cooking. Except, I know it's bourgeois to mind about manners, but I do wish they'd say thank you occasionally. Stuart does sometimes, to be fair, and he brings vaguely decent wine. Did I tell you about Stuart? It's too funny but don't tell anyone, it's a secret, only the group know. So you know he wrote this memoir, *Slam Down an Empty Glass*, all about how he was depressed, which he absolutely was, it was awful by the sound of things, poor him, and how he eventually crawled out of this black hole and reached a state where he could function more or less normally?

You must have seen it, he's practically a cult, Netflix optioned it and everything. It made him lots of money, and so now he's the main backer of *Notus* – well, the only backer so far, I think, Pa said no quite rudely, even by Pa's standards. Anyway, Stuart found that all the money and acclaim and fame really cheered him up. He'd been having therapy as well, obviously, but it all sort of came together.'

'Well, that's good,' I said.

'Yes, it's great, he's as cheerful as anything, always making awful puns and laughing at them for ages afterwards, it's quite endearing. But do you see the problem? He made all his money and success being depressed, so now he can hardly go yay, I am the cheerfullest man alive, hurrah for me, here's my new book about how I feel fucking fabulous. He has to write another book about his demons, except that they've skedaddled without trace.' She started laughing. 'And depression is literally his brand. So now he has to pretend to be miserable all the time, for ever, including on his hugely successful podcast every week. His social media avatar is him looking like he needs an intervention, and his posts are all these not very good aphorisms about suffering and despair and the need for kindness that are liked by hundreds of thousands of people, and meanwhile he's partying and having a lovely time without a care in the world. He's basically the jolliest man around. Do admit, Fran. He goes to all these book festivals and talks about how he fights every day to stay in control of his precarious mental state and at this stage it's completely made up. He says it's exhausting, but nobody in the group is at all sympathetic because he's so successful and rich.'

She stopped laughing and looked at her phone. 'I have to go, darling, what a bore but I said I'd be back in time for supper, we have an American novelist coming – do you know, I'd almost rather Pooper Carmody. God, doesn't that seem like a lifetime ago? – and I haven't seen Christian for two weeks. Please come and see me in London soon. Love to Alfie. You *are* lucky, having Alfie. Bye, Franny.' She hugged me tightly and blew my bump a kiss, then she hugged me again. 'Bye, darling. You'll come and see me, won't you? Soon?' I promised that I would, and reminded Linda that Merlin was back from Paris, where he had been heading up a fashion house for the past three years. I said that I thought she should give him a ring, catch up, go and do something fun with him, something inane. She sighed. 'Easier said than done. Christian really hates the idea of Merlin, even though he doesn't know him. But yes. I'll try. I miss him.'

22

Merlin hated Christian too. He said he was a fraud and claimed, wholly without foundation, that he smelled of armpits when you got up close. He said that Linda needed to be saved from herself because despite everything she was fundamentally a ninny who grew up in a field and who took people at face value, like a beautiful idiot, even though she was so clever about other things, and who only realized that they were awful when it was too late and she was too involved. 'And by people, I mean men,' he said. 'She can read women's characters perfectly well, or maybe she's just not that interested in reading them in the first place because she's got her sisters and you, or whatever. But she is completely blind when it comes to men. Blind. It didn't matter when we used to hang out years ago, because I used to warn her and weed the really bad ones out, and anyway she was only having sex with them, not bloody marrying them. But first Tony and now this one! This one makes Tony look like a prize catch. Well, no, he doesn't, but you know what I mean.'

I had been summoned to lunch at the Ritz, of all places, near Merlin's magnificent headquarters in Mayfair. He had the best table in the restaurant on standing order, reserved on Wednesdays at one p.m. Today he wore an impeccably cut, skin-tight two-piece suit made out of some kind of mysteriously bulkless tweed, a small black codpiece, an eighteenth-century woman's shirt made out of Belgian lace and, in a nod to the restaurant's dress code, an Hermès foulard loosely knotted into a tie. His short, floppy hair was dyed a luminous silver – 'D'you like it? Very Edie, no? Don't look so blank, Franny' – and his fingers clanked with jewellery, including a poisoner's ring from the 1600s that he had collected from Sotheby's that morning and was particularly delighted with. He could have looked absurd but with his fine-boned face and enviably elegant long limbs, he was magnificent. I had stopped being quite so intimidated by Merlin over the past few years, though there was still something suggestive of the profane about him that I found mildly disconcerting. But being away from the ploddy, contented domesticity of my Oxford life and ensconced in the Ritz with Merlin and his jewels, eating delicious turbot in the middle of an ordinary working day while people craned discreetly to take a better look at him and the rain fell in sheets outside, felt like a proper treat, and I told him so.

'Well, I don't suppose you get out much,' he said. 'But bless you.'

'Do you ever wear, you know, jogging bottoms and an old T-shirt? When you're at home, I mean. To watch telly.'

'Fran, you're so weird. No.'

'But what do you wear to watch telly?'

'I watch it in bed, so nothing. Or nothing you'd want to know about.' This was an old game, Merlin knowing that I was unnerved by him and finding it amusing to do nothing to alleviate my discomfort. 'Is that dress from a pregnancy line, or . . . ?'

'No, why? Is there something wrong with it?' I asked, suddenly certain that there was. The ankle-grazing navy-blue knitted dress that had seemed fashionable, unfrumpy, even chic when I'd looked approvingly at myself in the mirror this morning now felt suburban and dowdy. I gazed in shame at my box-fresh trainers, which had seemed such a practical yet modern way to finish off my outfit when I'd put them on at home and which now looked like paws.

'You look very sweet,' Merlin said, quite kindly. 'And anyway, you're preggers – it's good to be comfortable. But text me next time you want to buy trainers. And here –' he scrolled through his phone with a ruby-ringed thumb – 'I'm sending you Johnnie's number. Hairdresser. Tell him I sent you, he'll make space for you, maybe even this afternoon. He's only round the corner.'

'I want to say thank you but I also feel slightly humiliated,' I said.

'Don't be so silly. We're old friends. It's just a couple of tiny tweaks, that's all. You look . . . fine. And anyway, it's not like you're Linda, or any of the women in this room. You need your clothes to work for your life.'

'Doesn't everyone?'

'Very much not, no. For some people it's largely adornment. It's not required to have any other purpose.'

'Oh.'

'At this point I normally have two puddings,' said Merlin, who had eaten a dozen oysters and a dish of creamed spinach.

'Just the one for me, please,' I said.

'Suit yourself. Anyway, what are we going to do about Lino? That whole scene is –' Here he delicately mimed retching. 'What I really don't like about it, apart from him, the husband, and his friends, and the whole set-up that means she thinks she's a terrible person who needs to skivvy herself into something she's not, is that she is running herself ragged. She works the whole day at the cafe and then she basically does another shift just for him and his lazy mates, and none of them acknowledge it, not even him. He thinks she's a rich girl with a little hobby. Now, I happen to love a rich girl with a little hobby, some of my best clients etc., etc., but that's really not where she is now. That place is turning into a little goldmine. She works her arse off.'

'I know,' I said.

'We went out,' he said, 'last week. Did she tell you?' But I hadn't spoken to Linda for a few days. 'Right, well, listen to this. So I haven't seen her properly in ages, what with me being in Paris and her with her new friends and her new husband and her new so-called life. I flew in for two of the dress fittings for the wedding – didn't she look divine by the way, I saw all the pics, there's just something about her body in my clothes – but then I flew straight back out again. Anyway, with one thing and another we hadn't caught up for about eighteen months, not really, not a proper chinwag, not even at Merlinford. Matthew Radlett says she hasn't been at Alconleigh recently.'

'You talk to Uncle Matthew?' I asked, amazed. Merlin's shirt made me think of duels, Merlin and Uncle Matthew and pistols at dawn.

'You'd be surprised. Anyway,' he continued. 'So I think, right, let's make a night of it, and I tootle down to Dalston in my new sports car because I know it will annoy the husband, which it does. Linda opens the door and looks amazing, so at least there's that, do you remember when she went through that phase of dressing like a serf? She's almost back to normal now. Anyway, I go in with my case of chilled Veuve –'

'Because you know it'll annoy Christian.'

'Which it does.' Merlin nods. 'Though not as much as these heavenly 1930s diamond earrings I give her for a late wedding present. Which she of course dies for and immediately puts on while he shuffles about looking sour. Well, not immediately, she asked their provenance first, said she couldn't wear blood diamonds, fair enough. Anyway. We drink half a bottle of champagne, he trundles off in his old slippers to go and masturbate about poor people or whatever it is he does all day – seriously, what does he do all day?'

'Writes his book, I guess. Edits his magazine. He's really nice to circus animals.'

'I've just written a book,' Merlin says. 'Memoir sort of thing. Took three weeks. And I've lived a lot of life.'

'Did you tell him that?'

'Duh, obviously,' says Merlin, rolling his eyes and smiling his wicked smile. 'And about the bidding war and the size of my advance.' He scooped at a blob of vanilla Chantilly with his finger and absent-mindedly licked it off. 'Might accidentally have added a zero.'

'Right, so you antagonize Christian as much as you possibly can, and then you and Linda go off, and then what?'

'And then I've got two cocktail parties for us to go to and three tables booked at various places for dinner, and this new members' club in mind for nightcaps, and do you know what she says?'

'What?'

'She says, can we just go to yours and get into bed and chat.'

'And did you?'

'I made her go for dinner first. Thought it might be nice for her to eat something that someone else had cooked, for a change. Then we went to mine and got into bed with some drinks and we talked for hours, until she fell asleep. She ended up staying over. But here comes the good bit,' he said, tapping his fingers on the table. 'I took her back to Dalston in the morning, and Christian went mental. She'd texted him before midnight to say she was staying over.'

'Oh. So what was the problem?'

'The problem,' Merlin said, 'was first that she was going back to her old ways by having dinner with people who reek of capitalist excess, meaning me who was standing right there and me who went to the local comp, by the way, not bloody Eton, and second that there hadn't been anything for "the group" to eat for their dinner. Seriously – it's like she's their servant. That's how he thinks of her. He'd have her sleep under the kitchen table if he could. That man doesn't need a wife, he needs a, what's it called, a handmaiden.'

'Don't exaggerate.' I sighed. 'But apart from the horribleness, that house is full of food. All they had to do was go down to the kitchen.'

'And it's surrounded by restaurants. And hello, just pick up the phone and order in, you tightwad. But it doesn't count unless she makes it and serves it up to them, clearly. Anyway, she told him to fuck off – literally, she said fuck off – which was good, and that she was still tired and going back to bed. He did look surprised when she said to fuck off, which is something I suppose. So then I had a little chat with him. I said Linda was one of my oldest friends and that if she wasn't happy, I wasn't happy either, and to sort out his own dinner arrangements in future.'

'Merlin! And what did he say?'

'He said, "Get back in your box, old boy," like he was the king of England. He's such a fraud. Hey, isn't that your mother over there, in the tiny hat?'

Maybe Merlin's outburst did have an impact after all, because a couple of months after this, the offices of *Notus*, which had previously occupied Jassy's vacated living quarters, decamped to Christian's old flat in Hampstead. That was the good news. The bad news was that the group had decided to start a weekly literary salon in what had been Jassy's bedroom. 'I said it was a brilliant idea,' said Linda, 'because what's one tiny night a week compared to having them in there all the bloody time? And at least it won't be just them reading their work out to each other – there are going to be guest writers, and a paying audience, which has got to be more fun, don't you think?' On top of this, Linda had bumped into our old Norfolk acquaintance Lavender Davies while out buying baklava from a shop on Green Lanes. It was only the third-best baklava on the lane, but the owner was exceptionally handsome and Linda said he made her rethink everything she'd ever held to be true about moustaches. Norfolk's Dullest Girl – head of school, hockey enthusiast, pony club stalwart – whom we had used as an excuse when we first snuck out to Merlinford all those years ago, was unchanged, Linda reported, 'like a little guinea pig sort of person, you know, compact, snuffling about slightly anxiously, but really capable'. It turned out Lavender was looking for work, having recently lost her job as a personal assistant at a left-leaning NGO. Lavender, unrufflable and placid to a fault, had been competent and organized even as a child, and nothing about her now suggested she'd changed. Linda had an idea there and then: she would hire Lavender as an assistant for *Notus*, with particular responsibility for helping with the salon. 'It was my best brainwave in ages,' she said. 'They're all chaotic at *Notus*, nothing gets done, emails are unanswered, they take ages reading submissions – Lavender is exactly what they need. And then on Thursdays once the salon starts she can take that over too, book guests, organize tickets, send out mailers, hire the chairs and the sound system and sort out the drinks. Which means I won't have to do it, which is a great relief to me, Franny, because even the idea of it makes me want to cry.'

Christian did not demur when presented with the fact of Lavender; he may even have been grateful. In those days he took off for weeks at a time, either for research purposes or to write in various rented holiday lets, claiming that the house was too noisy and that he couldn't concentrate in it, even though it had four storeys and his study was right at the summit, facing away from the street, practically among the treetops. These prolonged absences always threw *Notus* into a spin: Christian had a clear idea of how he wanted the magazine to feel and read – choleric, punchy, agenda-setting – and would fly into rages if Morag or Brian accidentally commissioned, in his absence, something or someone he newly disapproved of, or if a piece of copy was insufficiently provocative. Neither of his deputies had ever edited anything before, Morag couldn't spell, there were no subeditors, and although at this stage *Notus* was an online-only publication, the logistics of getting things to look professional, correctly laid out, thoroughly edited and free of typing errors were proving challenging. Stuart, despite his deep pockets, was no help: he'd recently had his teeth veneered and was enjoying swiping right. When he was in London, Christian spent most of his time at *Notus*, often sleeping overnight on his old sofa. Linda reported all of this blandly, not seeming to mind, or even much register, Christian's absences or his strange detachment. 'It's just how he is, Fran,' she told me. 'If I love him, which I must do, I suppose, I just have to accept it.'

Lavender turned out, as anticipated, to be an organizational powerhouse, so quietly efficient and pleasingly self-effacing that even Morag and Brian approved, especially when she persuaded her parents to temporarily house two former circus horses on their land.

Despite their best endeavours, the salon, when it launched, was not the instant success the group had believed it would be. The guest authors were obscure, partly because the group wanted protégés rather than competitors, and partly because of their violent antipathy towards anyone 'commercial', meaning successful, or at least possessed of some sort of an audience. Despite a small and loyal hard core of a dozen or so of Christian's friends and acquaintances, the salon was sparsely attended. 'It's such a shame,' said Morag, 'because once we get people here, they'll love it and bring all their mates. I can't think of a better night out in the whole of London.' Christian privately told Linda he suspected that hosting a successful literary salon required an aptitude for brown-nosing that he did not possess and was unwilling to fake, and that he would delegate the networking side of things to Lavender. Happily, the salon had two strands and the political meetings were more successful. Morag had herself been a guest at the first one, reading from her doctoral project, 'Tony Blair: Genocidaire' ('Aye, right,' noted Jassy, who was slightly obsessed with the awfulness of Morag and made Linda tell her every detail of anything she ever said). After that Christian made a shortlist of political figures he was interested in meeting, Lavender contacted them and, nine times out of ten, they agreed to come and give a talk or be interviewed 'on stage' – a grand name for what had been the raised area where Jassy's dressing table once sat – by one of the group. The talks had titles like 'War on Structuralism Deniers', or 'Crash! Why Economic Contraction Can Save the Environment', and were relatively well attended, once even drawing a crowd of thirty-two people ('Deconstructing New Labour Fascism: A Workshop'). Linda stayed away from the salon events after she'd been to one – 'Mansplaining Marx: Some Pitfalls' – with Aunt Sadie, only to find the audience staring at them with, she felt, hostility. 'I wasn't even wearing anything nice,' she said, 'and Ma came in her car-boot disguise, you know, with the gilet, when she thinks she looks ordinary, but they all hate the idea of money, and although I get a slight pass because Pa isn't Sir Leicester, he's still a very rich landowner. But they can't properly hate him because they love his music and his Pa-ness, I suppose, so the hatred fast-forwards to me. Also Ma just starts laughing for no reason – well no, not for no reason, I do *see* why she starts laughing – but she's so terrible at controlling herself, she just sits there covering her mouth with her hand, thinking nobody can see her shoulders shake. It's hopeless.'

23

It took another year for Linda to realize that Lavender Davies had fallen in love with Christian and that he, inasmuch as he was capable of loving any individual human, loved her back. Merlin had been right when he'd said at the Ritz that Christian wanted a handmaiden, a shiny-eyed Labrador eager for the tiniest crumbs of his attention, longing to sit at his feet and wag their tail as he read aloud from what he called his oeuvre. If *Notus* hadn't quite turned into the overnight succès de scandale that the group had anticipated, then it hadn't failed spectacularly either, having been saved from capsizing more than once by Lavender's calm, considered interventions. She, in her quiet but stealthy way, was responsible for the fact that the magazine was now professionally designed. It had a logo, a formal-looking masthead, a social media presence, a visual identity, coherent typography, a recognizable, easily navigable format and regular contributors. That its content was somewhat one-note clearly didn't bother its small but growing army of paid subscribers. And Lavender didn't mind when Christian took all the credit at *Notus*'s second birthday party, which took place at Caxton Hall and where the assembled guests, which included a smattering of politicians, sang the Internationale as well as 'Happy Birthday'. She clapped and whooped, gazed at Christian adoringly (much to the amusement of Linda, who was always joking about the size of Lavender's crush), and if she was saddened by having her sizeable contribution to *Notus*'s success wiped from the annals of its history, she didn't say so.

Christian's star was now on the rise, and Lavender's focused efficiency played a part in this too. He'd acquired a brand-new agent at her urging. Christian, whose idea of the daily shape of a writer's life bore no resemblance to the reality of even the lives of the grand old men of letters, would often drop in on this new agent, a woman called Aurora Taylor, who had signed him up after meeting him at a book party in Covent Garden. Christian, aware of who she was and in desperate want of an agent from a grand agency, doubled up on the charm, kept pouring the white wine, took her to lunch the following week and charmed her some more, and mock-shyly pushed a few typewritten – no laptops for Christian – sheets of 'my little work in progress' across the table at her. Aurora, who represented several literary big hitters, liked the work. She believed in Christian and had patiently steered *Butterkin* from two-page outline to reality without ever letting him know how arduous and challenging the process had been. Christian, meanwhile, thrilled to share representation with some of his literary heroes, none of them living, was in love with the idea of having a well-known agent, much as someone else might be in love with the idea of having a Jermyn Street tailor, and genuinely seemed to believe that his visits to the small, busy offices of Gainsford & Taylor were a treat for Aurora, a thing that would cause her to leap out of bed in the morning and, Linda said, 'howl like a wolf with raw excitement'. At first the visits were brief – Christian would appear because he was in the neighbourhood, just to say hi, or because he was on his way to somewhere with ten minutes to kill, or for the specific purpose of dropping something off. But soon the visits became more leisurely and open-ended. Now, Linda reported (she'd gone along once but found the experience too embarrassing to repeat), Christian came to discuss himself, at length, often stretched out on Aurora's cream sofa. He would read to her from his new work, even as her landline rang and her emails pinged and her mobile beeped, even as her assistant said, 'New York on line one again, I think it's quite urgent,' even as her colleagues stuck their heads round the door and said, 'Sorry, I didn't realize you still had Christian with you,' and even as fatally polite Aurora started to glaze over. On and on Christian read, his intonation solemn, his hand rising any time Aurora cleared her throat or started saying, 'Actually, Christian, I really need to . . .' The only time he stopped reading was when the material was supposed to be funny and Aurora hadn't laughed, at which point he'd say, 'I was particularly pleased with that joke.'

Linda called Aurora the Saint. She was by this point no longer under any illusions about Christian: she had discovered for herself what had been apparent to the rest of us for a long time – that he was selfish, careless of her needs, self-involved and vain, and that he had no discernible sense of humour, a small tragedy for someone bought up in a house where every other sentence was playful. But she had soldiered on regardless. She believed, as she always had, that he was a rare bird, that rare birds behave in rare ways, and that loving such a bird wasn't supposed to be an easy task. Or perhaps, these days, she forced herself to believe it. I think she sometimes glossed over the reality of her daily life; there were moments she cast herself more as the wife of a genius, whose job it was to ease the great man's path through life, to steer him away from having to deal with the boring everyday tasks that lesser men took in their stride, and to make his time easeful. From the outside, this easing seemed largely maternal, because really she mothered him: she fed him, made sure he had clean things to wear, tidied after him, entertained his friends with the adult equivalent of someone baking fairy cakes for play dates, fought his corner, always put him first and endured his long absences without complaint. She gave no obvious signs of being especially troubled by this odd dynamic, in which there were so few rewards for her; on the occasions when we discussed the vague cloud of dissatisfaction that would sometimes descend, she would sigh and say that all marriages went through phases (didn't they?) and that she supposed this bit was the 'ordinary' part (wasn't it?) where the rose-tinted spectacles got sat on or left behind in a cab, and everyone had to adjust to looking at their spouse with 'normal eyes'. 'I'm more used to really nice sunglasses,' she said, 'but that's because I'm so spoilt.' I think she knew that her marriage was not a success, and that she was treading water with no hope of ever getting out to the kind of dazzling azure sea she had envisioned when she married Christian. But, she explained in so many words, nor was the marriage a catastrophe, and at least there was water to tread. She'd learned a great deal about herself from him, she said, and she was still learning, and it was good for her, like taking daily medicine. This last sentiment was not Linda-like, and I saw trouble ahead.

It came later that year. Linda had, unusually for her, been at home on a Thursday evening, these being salon nights; normally she got the food ready, leaving the reheating to Lavender, and skedaddled. It was a poetry evening, which Christian had opened by reading from his current work in progress, *Elegy for the Now*, a loose cycle of twelve (thus far) 'protest sonnets' written to be performed rather than read, angrily and with much gesticulating, somewhat in the style of a very white, very middle-class rap battle. This Christian had done, causing Linda to turn to Lavender Davies and whisper that sometimes all one yearned for was a nice limerick. Lavender didn't laugh, or even smile, and instead shushed Linda reproachfully. Christian's reading was followed by a somewhat limp performance poet waving her arms about like seaweed as she recited a prose poem about mental illness in a stonkingly mockney accent. 'You'd never think she went to Bedales,' said Linda, earning herself another, smaller tut from Lavender. There came a smattering of applause before the stage was taken by a rather intense woman called Verity who wrote in ancient Greek. She accompanied her reading of her poem – nobody knew what it was about – with piercing shrieks and stricken, mask-like facial grimaces which she held for seconds at a time, presumably on grounds of theatrical authenticity. When Linda turned to Lavender to ask why nobody was laughing, Lavender wasn't there any more. A quick scan revealed that Christian had left the room too, and, Linda said later, temporarily ensconced on my sofa with a glass of brandy, 'suddenly I knew exactly where they were.'

She found them on the marital bed, 'with Lavender doing all the hard work, as per'. Linda opened the door, observed the scene and closed the door again. She stood on the landing for a few moments. Then she opened the door again – 'I had to make sure I wasn't imagining it' – and marched in for a closer look. Unfortunately, the clattering-heel noise she had cinematically anticipated making as she headed for the bed was muffled by the rugs, so that Lavender and Christian remained unaware of her presence. 'So then I was just standing there watching them fuck,' Linda told me indignantly, 'and they were so involved that they didn't even sense me. Lavender has huge feet, like flippers, I'd never noticed, had you? Anyway, I don't know what I meant to say when I opened my mouth but all that came out was "LAVENDER DAVIES!" in a really loud, angry sergeant major voice, which made her jump and which also wasn't really fair because it's hardly as if he wasn't there – isn't it odd how the instinct is always to blame the woman? She's not the one married to someone else. Anyway, then they stopped – thank God – and Christian just sort of said, "Linda," in a flat voice but looking at Lavvy, and Lavvy literally went puce and said, "Oh no, oh no," and I said, "Don't let me stop you," and then I left and drove here. Can I have a glass of water?'

When I came back with one, and a small brandy on the side, she said, 'How funny of you to have brandy, Fran, like an old lady. Anyway – I wish I'd told him to give her one from me, just because it would have freaked her out, though not as much as if I'd stood there and carried on watching, but I was quite keen to get out. Of my own house!' She shook her head. 'So then I drove here and called Jassy from the car – she's going to move in and look after the Sausage for a few days and make sure Christian properly self-ejects, which she'll enjoy because now she hates him even more than she did before – and now I am hoping I can stay here with you for a bit.'

'Everything about this is awful and I am so, so sorry, and yes, of course you can stay here for as long as you like, but Linda, slow down. You need to talk to him. You can't just run away!'

'I'm not running away, Franny, I'm right here. He hasn't even texted to say sorry, let alone, I don't know, haring down the street after me begging me not to go and crying every-where.' She paused. 'Do you know, though, after I'd finished sobbing all the way to the M40, I started wondering whether I really wanted him to chase after me. I mean, yes, obviously, for my ego. It would have been nice if he'd crawled on his knees and rent his garments. But I wondered if I'd have gone back. Because if I'm absolutely honest with myself, it was a horrible shock – I mean, I'm still shocked, I'm going to be shocked for months, it's horrible and humiliating – but it wasn't really a surprise. We haven't had much to do with each other since – well, for a long time, really.'

'From the off, possibly,' I said, more to myself than to her. Louder, I said, 'But you were crying, you've just said.'

'Rage-crying, mostly,' said Linda. 'It's not the same thing.

I just needed a little shove in the right direction,' she continued, 'to make me jump. And here it is. The universe has provided, or rather Christian and Lavender have, in this odd way. We're done. Not because he's been unfaithful, but because we were going to be done sooner or later anyway. I was just sitting in limbo, wondering what to do about it (I need to stop doing that – it happened with Tony too). So I can't be in London because I don't want to be around to watch him pack, and I don't want to go to Alconleigh – well, I do, I want to go home just like the pigeon he says I am, but I don't want to have those conversations with Ma and Pa yet, can you imagine, it's going to be awful – so I'm hoping for your spare room. Would that be OK? Merlin is at Merlinford at the moment, which is too close to Alconleigh, and anyway he'd just say I told you so.'

'The spare room is yours,' I said. 'Of course. But Linda, you're going too fast. Rewind. You need to stop and think. You need to talk to him,' I repeated. 'To Christian, I mean. He's your husband! You can probably fix it.'

'Yes, I know, but I've just said, Franny – I don't think I do want to fix it. I'll only be here for a few days, so I can catch my breath and clear my head and, I don't know, wander the banks of the Isis or something. As for talking, I realized on the drive up that I don't have anything to say, and clearly neither does he or I'd have heard from him by now.' She swiped her screen and waggled her phone at me: no missed calls, no texts, just a locked screen with an old picture of Linda laughing with a dachshund puppy balanced on her head. 'I don't mind so much that he fucked someone else – beams and motes, though I was always faithful to him – but I really do mind the way he was looking at her. The way he's looked at her for a while, actually, now that I have hindsight. It wasn't just sex. He's in love with her, inasmuch as he can love anyone, which he can't, but anyway. She'll find out. When I shouted at her, he took her hand in his and held it. He wouldn't look at me, and it wasn't because he didn't dare or anything like that. It was because he was too busy looking at her. He was more concerned about how she was feeling. I don't think he's ever been that concerned about how I feel. I'm not even sure he thinks I *have* feelings. And at a certain level I knew it all along. I forgave it. And now I don't. So, you see . . . The only thing is, I don't have any clothes. Can you lend me some?'

'Well yes, of course. But think things through properly before making rash decisions. Sleep on it. I'll make us an omelette, or some cheese on toast, and we can sit and talk. Or not talk. Whatever you like,' I said. 'Alfie's out at a college dinner, he'll be ages. I've got all night.'

'Cheese on toast, please,' said Linda. 'I'll go and get us some wine from the shop.' But she didn't immediately move. She stayed on the sofa, slumped sideways into me while I stroked her hair. Eventually she said, in a small voice, 'God, though, imagine preferring her to me.'

24

After a long sleep and a hearty breakfast – 'I was as hungry as a hog' – Linda said that she had not changed her mind. There had been no communication from Christian, and she said she was grateful that at least he understood that there was no useful conversation to be had. Another woman might have taken exception to her husband's lack of explanation or apology, but Linda was glad not to have to rake over any of the detail, 'because what would be the point? He wants a sort of nanny-secretary he can sleep with when he feels like it, and he's found her. And I'm not sad enough about it. Because it's not love. What else is there to say?' The lack of apology rankled a little – 'Manners, as Ma would say, though I don't suppose I'd feel much better if he said, "I'm sorry for having sex with Lavender in our bed." '

The mechanics of the separation were resolved with very little effort on Linda's part and with a speed and ease that I privately found shocking. How terrifyingly little time it took to dismantle a marriage! Jassy, packing and removing for the plaintiff, and Lavender, lugging and ferrying for the defence, did their work in a matter of hours. Lavender had been red-faced and embarrassed and the fact that Jassy had insisted on addressing her as 'Comrade' throughout wouldn't have helped. By the time Linda returned to Dalston two days later, there was not a scrap of evidence of Christian's ever having lived there, apart from the emptiness of Jassy's old bedroom, which had been the setting for the unlamented salon. Christian's quasi-sociopathic lack of sentimentality coupled with his absence of interest in physical things meant there were no photographs, no pictures, no objects, no knick-knacks or keepsakes that could accidentally have been left lying around. His utilitarian wardrobe was modest and, Jassy said, fitted easily into the medium-sized wheelie suitcase that Lavender had trundled into a taxi; his collection of workmen's boots filled another. His books, files, papers and notes were already mostly at the Hampstead flat that doubled as the *Notus* offices, and what remained in the Dalston house – a tin of rolling tobacco, some hair pomade, a toothbrush and an old iPad with a smashed screen – took moments to scoop up. Christian had moved back into the Hampstead flat by the end of the day, as though he'd never left it, and that was the end of Linda and Christian's marriage.

25

'I think Lavender thought she'd be moving in with him,' Jassy said. She was making supper for us all a couple of weeks later at the Dalston house, the kitchen blissfully free, for the first time in years, of Christian's gannet-like acolytes. Upstairs, Jassy had delved into the Halloween decorations box – Moira loved Halloween in London and always came to her mother's for it – and zigzagged the door to the ex-salon with black and yellow barricade tape that read CRIME SCENE, DO NOT CROSS, which made Linda laugh every time she passed it.

'Oh dear, poor her,' said Linda, not sounding especially sincere. 'But maybe that sort of love is enough for her. I suppose it must be, for some people. You know, being OK with the feeling that you're so incredibly useful to someone that that's why they love you.'

'You were OK with it,' Jassy said. 'Weren't you? At the start.'

'Well, everyone likes to feel needed,' Linda said, biting enthusiastically into a cheese gougère. 'And he did teach me important things about myself. But I don't find it's enough in the longer term. These are delicious, Jassy, are there any more?'

'In the oven,' said Jassy. 'There's a whole other tray. But save space for your actual dinner.'

'It's so nice to be cooked for. I love a gougère,' said Linda. 'I love to know there are more of them coming.'

'I'm finding this a bit weird,' I said. 'Lin, do you really not mind even a little bit about Christian? You seem so serene about it.'

'Sanguine,' corrected Jassy. 'She's sanguine. And pragmatic.'

'Yes, sanguine is better,' Linda agreed. 'I'm sad it ended the way it did, but I don't think weeping and wailing would be a good use of my time, and anyway, as I've already explained, Fran, he sort of did me a favour.'

'Funny sort of favour,' I said. 'Your marriage is over.'

Linda rolled her eyes. 'I do know, Franny. My second marriage, to be exact, and me only a slip of a woman. It's not ideal, but there's no need to be so dramatic.'

'The scales fell from her eyes,' said Jassy, uncorking a bottle. 'At long bloody last.'

'Exactly,' said Linda. 'So although I can object to the manner of the scales' removal, I can't object to their actual loss, because who wants scales all over their eyes, in life? Though to be honest they were sort of dangling off anyway. Like that poor goldfish I had when I was little who bashed into his plastic castle, do you remember?'

She got the distracted, faraway look that always accompanied an animal reminiscence, so I rapped the table and said, 'Concentrate, Lino, come on.'

'Yes, sorry,' Linda said. 'It's just I loved that fish. Troy. He was incredibly clever.'

'That wasn't Troy,' said Jassy. 'The intelligent fish was Colin.'

'Don't be stupid,' said Linda. 'Colin is obviously a caterpillar's name. Colin was my caterpillar who pupated into an elephant hawkmoth.'

'Oh yes,' said Jassy. 'He was pink.'

'And gold,' said Linda. 'Divine colourway.'

The Radletts' ability to insert animals into random conversations sometimes drove me nuts. I knew that we'd be in for an exhaustive traipse around caterpillars of yore unless I intervened.

'Where were we?' I asked.

'What? Oh, we were on scales falling,' said Linda.

'The thing is, not every marriage is supposed to last,' said Jassy. 'As Auntie Bolts is so fond of saying.'

'I am well aware of that,' I said. God knows I'd heard my mother say it enough times. 'But shouldn't people at least try, just a bit? People who aren't, you know, actual Auntie Bolts?'

'What for?' said Linda. 'If neither of them wants to stay in it, then what's the point?'

'Spoken like the Bolter herself,' laughed Jassy as she poured the wine.

'Don't, Jassy,' said Linda, glaring at her sister, all good humour gone. Mention of the Bolter never went down well. 'Don't ever compare me with her, even for a joke.'

26

As it happened, Aunt Sadie and Uncle Matthew were not able to train their beams fully on to the demise of Linda's marriage, because shortly after her return from staying with me in Oxford we found out that Louisa was taking part in a reality show. True to her much-derided teenage ambition, Louisa had indeed become an influencer, and an enduring one at that, who now had half a million followers on Instagram. She had cycled patiently through various specialisms and personas over the years, starting off with cosmetics (via a blog optimistically called Get My Look!) and progressing through fashion, accessories, styling advice, books, travel, gardening, ceramics and interiors, before alighting on an Instagram-friendly mix of all of these, adding country pursuits and apparently artless – though in fact forensically conceived – glimpses into her enviable lifestyle. You could tap on her clothes, her cushions, her sofas, her kitchen gadgetry, the wine she was drinking, the veg box she was cooking from, and buy them there and then.

Louisa had been living happily in Scotland for years, ever since marrying Jonty Fort William, the laird of her dreams, and they occupied a remote, formerly crumbling castle with very narrow windows and no natural light to speak of on the east coast. This was now being renovated thanks to the impressive income generated by Louisa's influencing and brand ambassadorships. The persona she had settled on was pretty much her own – a well-to-do thirty-something lady of the manor, wife and mother of four, small-c conservative, cheerful, just the right side of tweedy, devoted to making life agreeable for her beloved, her children and her dogs. Louisa talked like the Queen in the 1960s, said 'air' for 'oh', and had wholeheartedly adopted her husband's vocabulary. Jonty Fort William was extraordinarily, hilariously posh, to the point where it was sometimes hard to understand what he was saying. 'Poor you, it's like a really niche speech impediment,' Linda had once said to him sympathetically, at which Jonty had guffawed heartily and with a slight look of puzzlement. Uncle Matthew said, to his face, that he didn't understand why Fort William seemed so much older than him despite being half his age; he had been saying the same thing ever since Fort William had first come to stay at Alconleigh. Jassy made the same joke – 'Knobless oblige' – every time she clapped eyes on him. Regardless, Jonty was the most amiable man imaginable. He and Louisa found each other enchanting and were happy among their mounted stag heads, hundreds of acres of gorse and enormous paintings of brown horses.

Every large family has one changeling child who seems to have inherited different genes from anybody else, and Louisa was that child. She was the sort of person who, on a rare trip to London, would look at an only mildly brightly coloured cushion in a shop and murmur, 'Yah, so fun,' who called ordinary tea bags 'builder's tea' without embarrassment, who always talked very slightly too loudly, thus making it impossible for anyone to have dinner with her in a public place (there were other issues, such as her enthusiastic deployment of the words 'yummy', 'yummers' and 'yummeroo'), and who hunted, shot and fished in a variety of flattering outfits, all of them clickable. Her cleverness lay in making her deeply traditional and oddly antiquated lifestyle seem modern and aspirational. In the summer she posted pictures of her children wearing Victorian-looking white dresses or sailor suits running through wild-flower meadows; in the autumn she made jam in her huge kitchen, a battery of vintage copper pans dangling from a beam in the ceiling; in the winter she showed her followers how she was styling her twenty-foot Christmas tree this year and told them what she was planning to make with the estate venison. Jassy said that you had to admire her for monetizing her incredible squareness rather than any connection to her dad, and for spearheading a Sloane Ranger revival almost single-handedly.

'Sloanes are always with us,' said Aunt Sadie. 'They just lie low.'

'They're all in bands nowadays,' said Uncle Matthew gloomily.

'Jonty wouldn't be in a band,' pointed out Linda. Everyone stopped talking to briefly howl with laughter.

'Yes, but I mean that people used to be embarrassed about being Sloanes,' said Jassy. 'They didn't go, "Yah, hi, I play the banjo, actually." Anyway, the music Sloanes are a whole other thing, and they do still mostly keep quiet about it. Louisa is like some sort of full-on 80s throwback.'

'Sometimes she looks like Princess Anne,' Uncle Matthew observed, frowning. 'She never used to. I can't understand it.'

'It is odd, isn't it?' mused Aunt Sadie. 'She is so very correct, like someone of a whole other generation. A whole other century, even. I suppose it's her way of rebelling.'

Having never engaged with social media in any shape or form – he barely knew his way around a website and took every misclick deeply personally – Uncle Matthew had signed up to Instagram, initially to monitor Louisa's output, which he did eagerly and with a sort of appalled, if fond, fascination. He used, for reasons no one ever quite got to the bottom of, the pseudonym Hubert Peruke and an old sketch of an extravagantly bewigged seventeenth-century gentleman as an avatar. Inserting the picture into the avatar space had taken him the best part of an afternoon, during which Aunt Sadie heard him bellowing such terrible obscenities from his study that she eventually felt compelled to go along and offer help, which was furiously rejected ('MONKEYS can use the internet, Sadie, it's not going to defeat me,' he'd roared). In the manner of these things, Uncle Matthew soon became fascinated – and quickly obsessed – with many of the strangers' accounts he came across and eagerly followed. His morning routine now consisted of walking the dogs, having a hearty breakfast, pretending to do the crossword and retiring to his study to scroll through Instagram for an hour. He commented under dozens of strangers' posts a week, and didn't mind at all when they blocked him, since the app's algorithm provided him with a bottomless supply of replacement accounts. Aunt Sadie, amused by this improbable new hobby, jotted down some of Hubert Peruke's comments at the back of the kitchen diary. When she first saw this list, Jassy recited the comments in the form of a rap, stabbing her finger at us and beatboxing badly in between.

Load of old arse
I dont believe you
CLOSE YOUR MOUTH WHEN YOU SMILE
You think it looks nice but it looks horrible
Nobody wants to look at your bare chest fella
NO
you think its sexy but its not sexy
Stop pretending
SHOW OFF 👎
I showed this pic to my dogs and we love it your dog is a
    GOOD BOY ♥♥♥
I love your dog
Twat
Wouldnt eat that if you paid me
Its not interesting
Lovely (under every post from a fan account called
    _streetcatbob)

Davey quickly got wind of Uncle Matthew's new hobby. He already had an Instagram account under his own name, commenting 'Divine!', 'You *are* clever' or 'I couldn't love it more' under every post made by his hundreds of friends and acquaintances. Now he created a second account, using the name Petronius and explaining to Uncle Matthew – he always prefaced his explanations with 'As you know, Matty' – that Tacitus had called the Roman courtier Petronius the *arbiter elegantiarum*, the arbiter of taste, and that Davey would henceforth 'have a little fun' adjudicating on matters pertaining to gracious living. Uncle Matthew bellowed his approval and invited Davey to join him in his study after their respective breakfasts for a little of 'the Instagram', which, he declared, really set you up for the day. Davey eagerly accepted and absolute gales of laughter now emanated from the study every morning between eight thirty and half past nine ('We have to ration it, otherwise it stops being a treat,' Davey explained, 'like me with cheese'). Whereas Davey in real life was charm personified, Petronius-Davey was waspier and took intense, giggly delight in writing things like 'reliably naff' or 'the proportions are all out, darling' or 'ghastly colour' under the accounts of several well-known interior designers and/or the people who'd hired them. The grander and more pretentious the house, the meaner he was. Either because the designers in question didn't read their comments or because Davey's suggestions – 'Needs another table lamp', 'Try a rose pink', 'I'd raise the skirting' – were perhaps occasionally useful, hardly anyone blocked Petronius, and many people started following him. Hubert Peruke, by contrast, had two followers, these being Louisa and Davey.

Aunt Sadie and Uncle Matthew had been bemused but accepting of their eldest daughter's online fame but were horrified when it was announced that Lady Fort William, née Louisa Radlett, influencer extraordinaire and daughter of retired rock god Matt Radlett, would be appearing on the third series of *The Conch*, a reality show whose strapline was 'Don't Be Piggy' and which was set on a small Hebridean island. The show promised to test participants in camping skills, self-sufficiency, team-building and leadership. While privately admitting that Louisa might be quite good surviving in the wild, since she was remarkably thick-skinned, used to the cold and could sail, swim, ride, hunt, fish and skin a rabbit in her sleep, Aunt Sadie nevertheless objected to her participation, and she and Uncle Matthew immediately set off to stay with her in Scotland for a week, with the express purpose of dissuading her from taking part.

This coincided with Linda deciding to go on holiday to Paris, a city she'd always liked but did not know well. 'Paris is really good for the soul, Fran. It's like medicine.' She booked herself a trip on the Eurostar, timed to fit in with the fortnight-long closure of the Sausage for its annual sprucing up before the summer season. She left on a Friday and was due back a few days later to supervise the work.

Things went wrong almost immediately, she later recounted. The carriage was not full, and Linda left her seat three times to go wandering off in search of a loo, and then coffee, and then an Emmental baguette. It was only when she disembarked at the Gare du Nord and had gone through customs that she realized that both her phone and her wallet were missing. She could picture her handbag sprawled appetizingly open on the table and was cross at herself for being so idiotically trusting and careless, but it took a few seconds for her to fully appreciate the scale of the problem. She was stuck. Her hotel booking was on her phone, as were her only methods of paying for anything. 'This must happen to people all the time,' she thought, as she wheeled her suitcase through the station and on to the pavement outside. It was a glorious day, late morning, the sky a perfect blue. People were bustling about purposefully in the sunshine and her spirits rose despite her quandary. 'There will be an obvious solution. I just need to think of it.'

But no obvious solution immediately presented itself, so she wheeled her case a little further, away from the taxi ranks and hawkers, and sat down on it. A passing man squatted next to her and offered her a cigarette, which she declined; he shrugged and walked away, followed by another man, who was more aggressive and got shorter shrift ten minutes later. 'This is ridiculous,' Linda said aloud, riffling uselessly through her bag again. Neither the phone nor the wallet had rematerialized. She couldn't even get back on the train and return to London if she wanted to, because her Eurostar ticket was on her phone too. What did people do in these situations? Would the hotel help? She couldn't entirely remember its name – something long to do with chestnuts, or was that the one that had been fully booked? All she could remember was that it was in the 6th arrondissement and that she had ticked the option to 'pay at hotel' on the booking website. No lovely prepaid room was waiting for her. How far was the 6th arrondissement on foot? She could see from the street sign that the Gare du Nord was in the 10th, which didn't sound nearby. Or perhaps she should walk to the British embassy. The thief hadn't pilfered her passport, after all. She could produce it, explain what had happened and throw herself on their mercy. But throwing yourself on diplomats' mercies seemed overly dramatic, and anyway where *was* the British embassy? She should go back to the station and try to find someone who could help her. There would surely be someone there who would know what to do. Find a passenger list with her name on it, perhaps.

But she didn't move. She had started to feel a gnawing sort of panic. She kept returning to the idea that this sort of thing must happen all the time, and was getting more and more annoyed with herself for not coming up with the solution – the solution that, she felt, ought to be glaringly obvious, *would* be glaringly obvious to anyone else. The sun was so hot, and now she was thirsty. The pavement outside the Gare du Nord was dirty and littered. She would find a phone box – did such things still exist? – and reverse the charges to Aunt Sadie. A pathetic, childish move – she could almost hear Christian's voice telling her so – but Aunt Sadie would know what to do, and if she didn't, then Davey definitely would. Davey would probably know someone charming who would come and rescue her. Linda cheered up, before remembering that Aunt Sadie was in Scotland and that she didn't know Louisa's phone number by heart – or Aunt Emily and Davey's, or even mine, come to that. Or anyone's. The gnawing panic grew and began to bite her. 'This is how someone ends up begging, or sleeping on the street,' she thought. 'Or becomes prey for bad people.' She looked up and around her: there didn't seem to be any especially bad people ogling her, but the problem was that bad people sometimes looked quite nice.

Suddenly Linda felt very sorry for herself. What was she doing in Paris on her own anyway? She'd mislaid two husbands and a child, and the people she loved were happily living their busy lives without her. What had she done, scooting off to Paris on a whim? She should be here with Tony – well, no, not actual Tony as such – or with Christian, though not really Christian either, but anyway, with someone, someone who would have ordered an Uber, one of the nice luxey ones, as the train pulled into the station and would right now be whisking her off for an aperitif at the lovely hotel they'd thoughtfully booked with love in their heart. Instead, she'd opened booking.com by herself late at night, ticked the only neighbourhood she was familiar with and booked the first – or was it the second? – nice-looking hotel that had a garden. She couldn't even be sure of its name. She felt like crying.

A gendarme! Of course. She should find a gendarme. The French police wouldn't shrug and leave tourists stranded, forced to spend their days begging outside train stations or being bundled into vans by pimps. Would they? She sniffed and opened her handbag again to look for a tissue. There was no tissue. Why was she so stupid, so unprepared, so idiotically bad at life? The absence of anything to blow her nose on tipped her over the edge and she began to cry.

'Ça va?' said a voice. Another sleaze with another cigarette, Linda thought. She didn't even bother looking up.

'Obviously fucking not,' she said. 'Since I am crying. Go away. Allez-vous-en.'

'OK,' said the voice, sounding amused rather than concerned. This made Linda furious, so she looked up.

'Je ne veux pas être prostituée,' she said. 'Or in fact traffiquée either. So go away, please.'

'I understand. But you do seem to be in some sort of difficulty,' the man said, 'and perhaps I can help. Here. So you can blow your nose, at least.' He handed her an immaculate, ironed handkerchief and, seeing her hesitation, laughed. 'It's OK. There's no chloroform on it. I don't want to traffic you. It's just a mouchoir. Pour se moucher. Which you need to do because the tip of your nose is dripping.'

Linda snatched the handkerchief and blew her nose.

'Wow,' said the man. 'So inelegant.'

'I know,' Linda said, 'but my mother always says there is absolutely no point in blowing one's nose daintily. You know, um, avec finesse. You just end up having to do it more than once, which is hopeless. You might as well really go for it.'

'You have certainly done that,' said the man. 'May one sit next to you, or would you prefer to stand up?'

Linda considered this and held out her hand. 'Up. Pull me up, please. I'm so tired and hot and it's not nice to be at pigeon level for this long, looking at their poor horrible feet. Your English is very good.'

'Thank you,' said the man. She could see him better now the sun was no longer in her eyes and they were both upright. He was tall, green-eyed, brown-skinned, black-haired, about her age, wearing a blue tailored jacket, jeans and a pale pink open-necked shirt.

'I am at your service for about fifteen minutes,' he said. 'After that I am catching the train to Brussels.'

'Oh,' said Linda. 'Is that where you live?'

'No,' said the man.

'Good,' said Linda. 'I mean . . .'

The man was laughing again. 'We need to speed this up,' he said. 'I really can't miss my train. What is the problem here?'

'I am English,' said Linda.

'I had deduced,' said the man.

'Oh,' Linda said, annoyed at the idea of being so identifiably a French person's idea of a British one, like some sort of wandering rosbif. 'Actually I am very European in my general outlook, and I would have thought in my appearance.'

'You are an English bobo,' said the man. 'It's short for bourgeois-bohemian. You bear all the external signs.'

'Do I?' asked Linda, further put out. 'I mean, I suppose it's not the most inaccurate description in the world, technically, but I can't say I like it. The main thing is, I am completely respectable. Completely. And honest. My phone and wallet got stolen on the train from London, you see – I left my bag on the table, so stupid – and now I don't have any money, or any means of getting money, or getting anywhere, and I can't even remember the name of my hotel and I don't know where the British embassy is. It is an absolutely ridiculous situation to be in, but I am in it and I don't know what to do.'

'I see,' said the man.

'On top of that I'm becoming aware that I sound like a scammer. Do you have them here? You know, a person who says the sort of thing I'm saying right now and then runs off with your money – people who knock on your door and say they've been mugged and can you lend them twenty quid so they can get home, and you always *do* lend them the twenty quid because if it was true even just once . . .' She trailed off. She was rambling. Was she even making sense? Desperation seized her, and she said the thing she made a point of never saying. 'But I am not someone like that. I am . . . I suppose I might as well tell you. Je suis la fille d'un rock star anglais. Très fameux.'

'I see,' said the man again. He still sounded amused. He looked Linda up and down and seemed to make up his mind about something. 'Come with me,' he said, grabbing the handle of Linda's suitcase. 'We have about eight minutes. On dit plutôt célèbre, by the way. Ou très connu.'

'Aren't you going to ask me *which* rock star anglais?' Linda said as they half-walked, half-jogged past the cab rank. 'And isn't connu some sort of swear word?' They were heading for another line of cars beyond the taxis, towards a row of people carriers with smartly dressed drivers.

The man didn't answer but was talking to the driver of one of the cars in rapid French. The driver took Linda's suitcase, smiled at her and put it in the boot.

'I mean, you seem nice, but this scenario is very like the bit in a film where the woman heads off to her new life as an au pair only to find herself in a sordid basement,' Linda said.

'Yes, I admit it is exactly like that. Here are some euros,' said the man, handing her a slim fold of notes. 'The driver will take you to a hotel that I sense you will like. It is not very far away. I will meet you there for dinner this evening at eight.'

'What, just like that? What if I don't want to have dinner with you?'

'Then you don't have to, of course. I will have dinner somewhere else. But do you want to have dinner with me?'

Linda thought. 'Yes,' she said.

'Donc,' said the man, as though everything were self-evident. 'I'm going now. À ce soir.' She watched him run back to the station as her taxi pulled out. She didn't even know his name. She realized she could hardly breathe.

27

Linda maintained meerkat-like vigilance during the journey to the hotel, in case the car suddenly veered off the leafy boulevards and headed for a dank, abandoned storage facility somewhere in the outskirts. Despite feeling exceptionally thirsty, she did not help herself to the bottled water that was within reach. She was acutely aware of the oddness and potential danger of her situation, and of the fact that she would normally never in a million years let a strange man put her into a strange car and send her to a destination of his choosing, like a parcel. But there were no alarming detours, just Paris going about its daily life outside her window, and within ten minutes or so the taxi had pulled up outside a smart cream-coloured town house at, as far as she could make out from street signs and their angle, the foot of Montmartre. The facade was plain, like a private house's, with nothing to indicate a hotel. There were two red glass lanterns flanking the front door. The driver said, 'Voilà, madame, on y est,' parked the car and went to open her door. Linda stood on the pavement and peered at the street. She could see the Moulin Rouge, and nearly laughed aloud at the Paris-ness of it all. Then she remembered that the Moulin Rouge was in a famously seedy area. 'Where are we?' she asked the driver. 'Comment s'appelle cette area?' She gestured around her and then remembered the word. 'Ce quartier,' she clarified.

'Soapy,' said the driver.

'Soapy?' said Linda.

'Oui, madame.'

'Are you sure?' asked Linda.

'Oui, madame.'

'OK,' Linda said dubiously. 'How strange.' She reached in her bag for the euros the man had given her, but the driver waved her cash away, informing her that the fare had already been taken care of. 'Right,' said Linda. 'Well, then. Thank you. And you're quite sure that this is the place – this is the hotel?'

'Mais oui, madame,' the driver said, more emphatically now.

'I suppose I'd better go in, then,' Linda said doubtfully. The driver shrugged and said, 'Et bien oui, quand même,' before smiling at her encouragingly, as one might smile at a child, and driving away.

Behind its sober facade, the interior of the hotel – it now became clear to Linda that this was indeed a hotel, though unlike any she'd stayed in before – was all dull golds, dark red velvets, foxed mirrors and dim lighting, the insistent, low-slung sexiness of the decor contrasting with the high, gilded ceilings and intricately enamelled wall panels, and with the grand proportions of the space. A number of small salons branched off the central foyer; Linda could glimpse squashy, voluptuous seating in inky-coloured spaces lit by muted light. There were candles burning everywhere, even in the early afternoon, and the air smelled delicious, of tobacco, flowers and something faintly leathery. The floor of the foyer was chocolate-brown marble and now she walked across it, feeling half anxious and half enchanted, to the reception desk. She was about to try and explain that she had been sent here by a man whose name she didn't know and that she had no booking or credit card to check in with – God, what if they had no rooms? What if they laughed at her and shooed her away? – when the concierge turned from the colleague he had been speaking with, beaming at her as he said, 'Ah, madame, here you are. Welcome. We have been expecting you.'

'Have you?' said Linda.

'Of course,' said the concierge. 'My name is Hervé and I am at your disposal throughout your stay. Ah, here is Patrick. He will take your luggage to your room.' A fresh-faced young man appeared at her side and picked up her case. 'Would you like to go straight up, or perhaps rest your feet down here first, have some tea, some coffee, un petit snack?'

'I'd love a glass of water,' said Linda. 'What is this place, please?'

'This is the Maison Chéret,' said Hervé with a tiny inclination of his head. 'We are a small hotel of twenty rooms.'

'It's amazing,' said Linda. 'I've never seen anything like it. It's like a film set.'

'Thank you,' said Hervé, looking pleased. 'It is a very special place.'

'But don't you need me to check in? I don't have my cards with me, but I do have my passport. Right here.'

'We can do all this later,' said Hervé, waving the passport away. 'So, here are the numbers you need to call to report your stolen cards.' He pushed a vintage postcard of a recumbent woman at her, the numbers neatly handwritten on the back in ink. A waitress had appeared with a bottle of iced water on an antique, Moorish-looking golden tray, and now Hervé poured Linda a glass, which she gulped down in one. He poured her another.

'God, I was insanely thirsty,' Linda said. 'My mother says that sort of thirst is exactly how you get urinary tract infections.' Hérve looked blank, but an ancient childhood memory hurtled out of nowhere to the front of her brain. 'Les voies urinaires,' she said triumphantly.

'Ah oui,' said Hervé, suddenly grave. 'Là, il faut faire très attention.'

'They're a nightmare. Right, so – well, I suppose I'll go up to my room, then.' She laughed slightly wildly. 'Thank you for being so welcoming, Hervé, and for the phone numbers.'

'Of course. Would you like me to show you up, or just give you the key?'

'Just the key, please, if you don't mind. I always feel embarrassed standing about gormlessly oohing and aahing while people show me the curtains or the minibar, and it must be even worse for you,' said Linda.

Hervé laughed. 'First floor,' he said, handing her an enormous golden key on a dark green tassel. 'No room number. The stairs are behind that curtain, or there's a lift to your right. Dial zero if you need anything at all.'

Linda cancelled her credit cards, asked for new ones to be sent to her care of the hotel, put a block on her phone and then had a deep bath and a wonderful sleep. After that she spent a long time getting ready for dinner, telling herself that she was only taking such care because she had nothing better to do. She congratulated herself on having packed one glamorous dress, even if it was ancient. It was one of Merlin's, a high-necked, form-fitting, ankle-skimming number, the colour of blackberries. She wondered whether Merlin knew this hotel from his time in Paris, because he would love it. She was ready at seven p.m. but spent another ten minutes putting her hair up, then down again, then up again, then removing her lipstick so that it looked more like a stain than an effort. It was nice to get dressed up, she thought. She hadn't really dressed up in years. She waited until exactly four minutes past eight before leaving the room and heading downstairs.

'Ah,' said the man, rising from the table to greet her. 'Hello again.'

'Hello,' said Linda.

'Fabrice El Hassane,' he said, holding out his hand.

'Linda Radlett,' she said, shaking it and sitting down. 'This is . . . this is absolutely amazing. All of it. You should see my room – it's insane. It's the whole first floor and I've never been anywhere so luxurious in my life. It's so opulent. But cosy, you know? Sort of cocooning. There are loads of places to lie down and nap, and I really love naps. It's the sort of place that makes you want to recline because it's so incredibly comfortable.'

'Good,' said Fabrice. 'I'm glad.'

'I'm trying to avoid saying sexy because my first husband, Tony, used to call inanimate things sexy all the time and it made me feel physically ill, but it really is. So sexy. I mean, it drips sex, it's borderline indecent. And the colours! My room – well, it's really more my giant apartment – is this divine shade of green and then the bedroom has this extraordinary golden wallpaper that shimmers.'

'I am delighted you like it,' said Fabrice. 'I thought you might.'

'And *this* room!' said Linda, looking around her in wonderment. The domed ceiling had been painted the darkest navy blue and gilded to look like the night sky. 'Whoever designed this place is a genius. Because it's sexy and louche but also just so quilty.'

'What is quilty?'

'Cosy, you know, like quilts. Comme un gilet? Padded. Soft.' She stroked the arm of her velvet chair as though it were a pet. 'I'm as snug as a bug in a rug. I can't thank you enough for rescuing me and bringing me here. Thank you so much.'

'You are more than capable of rescuing yourself, I think,' he said with a broad smile. 'But I'm delighted I could be of use.'

'I really was stuck, though,' said Linda. 'I was starting to freak out. I'd have thought of something eventually. But not,' she gestured at the room, 'of anything like this.'

'This building used to be a maison close,' said Fabrice. 'In the early 1900s. The interior designer paid tribute, if that's the right word, to its origins. The red lanterns outside, for example. The whole Belle Epoque thing.'

'What's a maison close?' asked Linda.

'A high-end bordello,' said Fabrice. 'For socialites and aristocrats. Employing courtesans rather than prostitutes, if you want to make that kind of distinction, which I'm not sure one should, poor women. I don't know if you've looked out of the window, but the Moulin Rouge is just over there.' He gestured. 'Which may have had something to do with it. Entertainment after the show, you know.'

'Well, that makes perfect sense,' exclaimed Linda, 'now you say it, because that's exactly what it feels like in here – a mixture of an Edwardian gentlemen's club and, as you say, a brothel, but really friendly. Goodness me.'

'Will you have a drink?' asked Fabrice. 'Champagne?'

'Yes please,' said Linda. 'How lovely.'

Fabrice raised one finger and was immediately attended by a waitress, who called him Monsieur El Hassane.

'Merci, Élise,' he said after a brief discussion about vintages that Linda couldn't quite follow.

'What is your relationship to this place?' said Linda. 'If you don't mind me asking. Are you a regular?'

'No, I own it,' said Fabrice. 'What are we eating? I can recommend the bream, but perhaps you are vegetarian? In which case, the miso aubergine is very good.'

'It's your hotel?' said Linda. 'This whole place? How absolutely extraordinary.'

'Not really,' said Fabrice with a shrug. 'I could see the potential in the area before other people, that's all. It used to be squalid. Parts of it still are, as you may have noticed. Even now, I wouldn't go for a walk at two in the morning.'

'What is the area called?' Linda asked. 'Are we in Montmartre?'

'Not quite. We're near the beginning of Montmartre,' said Fabrice. 'The main part of it is up the hill. This is called SoPi. It's an abbreviation of South Pigalle.'

'Oh! So Soapy was right.' Linda chewed thoughtfully on some bread for a while and then said, 'I mean, it's funny, isn't it – at least, I hope it's funny and that there isn't going to be some really hideous punchline trundling along later – but actually you really did pick me up from a station and send me to a house of ill repute, in a way,' Linda said.

'I can assure you that this is simply a hotel,' smiled Fabrice. 'I have two others, rather more sober, on the Left Bank, but I thought you'd like this one the most.'

'I do,' said Linda. 'I love it.'

'I'm glad. Oh – I bought you something. Here. I guessed that you had an iPhone?'

'Yes,' said Linda.

'So here is another one. Once you've set it up it should download all your content, including your banking app and so on. So you will be unstuck.'

'This is all unbelievably nice of you,' said Linda, even as it occurred to her that she was no longer in any particular hurry to be unstuck. 'Above and beyond, as my mother would say. Thank you so much. And, well, I don't know how to say this delicately but I am not, um . . . without means . . .'

Fabrice raised both eyebrows at her and smiled.

'. . . and so I will obviously refund you for everything, the taxi and the lavish suite and the dinner and the phone. Give me your details and I can do it later tonight. Or now, even?'

'It's not urgent,' Fabrice said. 'Or even necessary,' which made Linda blush, because she liked the way he said it even though she did not like the idea of being paid for, finding it indistinguishable from that of being bought.

'My God, this food,' she said. 'It's so good. I wouldn't have thought of turning butternut into beignets. I cook myself, you see. I have a cafe. In my house. Called the Sausage. Mind you, I cook there less than I used to. I have a little team now.'

'How charming,' said Fabrice. 'Though I would not obviously have placed you cooking in a cafe called the Sausage.'

'Well, I've done other stuff too,' said Linda.

'Racontez,' said Fabrice. 'Tell me everything.'

'You first. For example, where is El Hassane from? Are you Algerian?'

'Moroccan,' said Fabrice. 'On my mother's side. My father was French. He was called Sauveterre, but I use my mother's surname.'

'How nice,' said Linda. She thought that Fabrice's mother must be very beautiful.

'And do you have brothers and sisters?'

'I am an only child,' said Fabrice.

'Oh, poor you,' cried Linda. 'That's so sad.'

Fabrice looked nonplussed. 'It is not so sad,' he said.

'It is, to me,' explained Linda. 'But I'm glad not to you. I'm glad you're not unbelievably lonely, I would be. How come you speak such good English?'

'This is a very English question,' laughed Fabrice. 'Most of the world speaks English, and usually another language too, as well as their own. It's just the British who don't speak anything else, as if it was beneath them.'

'Oh dear,' said Linda. 'I'm afraid you're right. We find the idea of people speaking other languages slightly show-offish and funny, I think. Do you speak Arabic?'

'Passably. Your French shows promise, by the way, the accent is not disastrous. But also I lived in London when I was at the London School of Economics, many years ago. And a lot of my business is conducted in English, so . . .'

'But you don't have an American accent,' said Linda approvingly. 'People usually do, with business English.'

Fabrice shrugged.

'And are you married? I've been married twice.'

'Not at the moment,' he said. 'For me, with love affairs, it generally lasts five years.'

'That seems about right,' said Linda. 'Five years is quite a long time. I've never managed it. Do you start petering out slightly halfway through year four?'

'Not always,' said Fabrice, slurping an oyster. 'But please go on. Tell me more things.'

'I have a daughter. Called Momo. Well, Moira. She lives with her father and his wife, Pixie. They're moving to New York soon.'

'Oh, I'm sorry.'

'It's fine. It's only for a year.'

'OK. The father is the sexy Tony?' Fabrice asked.

'Ha ha, yes, exactly.' She leaned forward conspiratorially. 'Sometimes he said "woof",' she added.

'Woof? Comme ouaf ouaf?'

'Yes.'

'To express approbation?'

'Yes,' hooted Linda. 'Can you imagine the awfulness?'

'A little,' said Fabrice. 'I sometimes observed it when I was in London. Was he rich, this Tony?'

'Yes, very,' said Linda. 'Indiscriminately rich, if you see what I mean?'

'I do, yes.'

'But my second husband was more or less a communist. Posh, though.'

'They play at being poor, this genre of people,' remarked Fabrice. 'It gives them real pleasure.'

'Yes. Were you poor, before you owned hotels?'

'You are very direct,' Fabrice observed. He didn't appear to be displeased by the thought. 'But no. We were normal, ordinary, both my parents worked. The British like to see everything through class terms, it's like an incurable malady that is completely perplexing to the rest of the world, so I will say upper working class, if that helps you situate things.'

'And you grew up in Paris?'

'Yes, in an area called the Goutte d'Or, in the 18th, not far from where we met. It was very North African in those days. Now it's much more mixed.'

'What a British politician would call "vibrant",' Linda said.

'Yes, exactly,' Fabrice laughed. 'I think you also say "communities". But the whole neighbourhood is becoming quite hip, in the manner of these things.'

'And are your ma and pa still there?'

'My father died five years ago. My mother lives in Brussels now, near her many sisters. I was on my way to see her, earlier, with the train. It's her birthday. You would like her, I think, and she you.'

Linda felt disproportionately pleased by this.

'If we were speaking in French, would you say "vous" to me?' Linda asked later, over coffee.

'Of course,' said Fabrice. ' "Tu" implies a certain amount of intimacy, and we have after all only just met.'

28

'Allo, good morning. You were awake, I hope?'

'Wide awake. I'm in bed with my sublime breakfast. Congratulations on your mattresses, by the way, this one is like puffs of cloud. We had awful mattresses at home, so saggy and soft, so I always particularly appreciate a good mattress.'

'I'm glad it meets with your approval. A British make, in fact. And so, apart from enjoying the mattress, do you have plans for the day?'

'Well,' she said, putting her pain aux raisins down and sitting more upright, 'I suppose at some point I'd better go and check into my real hotel. Now that I am unstuck.'

'I see,' Fabrice said.

'Yes,' said Linda. 'So.' There was a tiny pause. 'Goodbye, mattress of dreams,' she added to fill it, with a little laugh that sounded less carefree than she intended.

'But do you want to check out?'

Linda thought. He had, after all, complimented her on her directness last night.

'No,' she said. 'I love it here.'

'So, then. Stay there. Hervé can call the other place up and cancel it for you. Have you remembered the name yet?'

'Yes, it was on my phone.'

'So there is no problem.'

'Well,' said Linda, great happiness rising in her like a tide, 'I suppose not.'

'The room is yours for as long as you want it,' said Fabrice. 'Though eventually you might consider a proper apartment.'

'What?' laughed Linda. 'How long do you think I'm planning to stay for?'

'I suggest five years,' said Fabrice. 'Or thereabouts. Now, will you meet me for lunch?'

They talked and talked. She didn't remember ever talking so much to one person in all her life. Fabrice seemed to find no detail of her past too trivial or dull. He wanted to know about everything and everybody – Aunt Sadie and Uncle Matthew, Alconleigh, the dogs, the hens, the donkeys, Jassy, Louisa, Robin, me, Aunt Emily and Davey ('Ah oui, Davey Warbeck,' he'd murmured in passing), the Bolter, Mr and Mrs Hopkirk, Creepy Jared, Merlin, Tony, Pooper Carmody, Pixie, Moira, Christian, Lavender, Morag, modelling, the cafe, the novels, the poetry, the politics – the lot. 'Aren't you bored yet?' she would ask, and he would reply, 'Not even a fraction.'

'So you were saying your father hunted you when you were little?'

'Yes, for a treat, with really sweet dogs.'

'Weren't you frightened?'

'Oh yes, always. Terrified, to the point of wanting to pee. We screamed with fear. It was wonderful.'

'Tell me some more things that Pa detests.'

'Any euphemism for death, especially "passed". Any euphemism for the toilet except the lav or the loo. If you wanted to make him ill with rage, you'd say, "I'm afraid he passed in the little boys' room." Men who wear pyjamas. The nicer the pyjamas, the greater the hate.'

'But it's OK for women?'

'Yes. Moustaches. Those very geometric thin beards. Soap that doesn't come in a bar, and also the word "pump". Craft beer in wacky tins, do you have those here? Women who read the weather on regional TV stations wearing tight, sexy party dresses. Those very white LED light bulbs, he has to leave the room. Adults who wear T-shirts with catchphrases from TV shows on them. Older men who have haircuts that suddenly make them look like lesbians. Emus and ostriches.'

'They are too big?'

'He hates their legs. Oh, raisins. He doesn't really eat puddings but if he does and there's an accidental raisin, he loses it completely. Vests. Limoncello. Cutlery with square edges to the handles, as opposed to curved – won't eat with them, he claims they hurt his palms. Have I said hats?'

'All hats?'

'Yes.'

'Tell me more things.'

'I liked modelling for Merlin – I liked the catwalk, it was fun for a bit. But I didn't really enjoy modelling for anyone else.'

'It seems a limited use of your considerable talents.'

'I hate not talking, and obviously when you're modelling you're paid to not speak. Actually, what I hate most is talking and talking and not feeling heard.'

'I understand,' said Fabrice. 'When someone close to you says, Oh, you are like this, and you don't recognize yourself from the description.'

'Yes!' said Linda. 'And sometimes you accidentally become the person that is being described, which is not at all the person you are. That's even worse. It takes years to unravel. I've done a lot of that. The whole period when I was modelling and partying too much because I wanted to show people that I was fun, but also when I was married to Christian. I really tried my hardest to become this whole other person, because he kept telling me that the person I was was awful. I mean, why fall in love with me, if I so needed changing?'

'It should not be a requirement in a relationship,' said Fabrice.

'Never,' said Linda with feeling.

'I mean, take Jassy,' Linda said a little later, returning to her theme. 'People always comment on how funny she is. And she is funny, sardonic, you know, very quick. But she's about ninety-five other things too. Or Pa, for goodness' sake. He is mostly known – well, apart from the music – for being this roaring, intransigent person. But no one is born roaring, are they? He didn't have a very nice childhood, so a lot of the roaring is about that, and I don't think he enjoyed the druggy, groupies-y bit of being famous – I mean, he loved it at the beginning, obviously, who wouldn't, I'd have gone absolutely apeshit, but you don't want to be stuck in that scene for ever, half out of it in quite a squalid, pee-stains sort of way. Luckily he met Ma. She completely has the measure of him. She sees that he is vulnerable. Roaring people often are, aren't they?'

'I hope I will one day meet Ma and Pa,' said Fabrice.

This made Linda very pleased.

'Isn't it funny to think that no one knows you exist?' said Linda. 'I mean, here we are, naked on a bed, and everyone thinks I'm in Paris dutifully trotting round the Musée d'Orsay. Or Versailles.'

'You should see Versailles, though,' said Fabrice. 'Let's go tomorrow.'

'Is today Wednesday? I'm supposed to go back to London tomorrow.'

'Today is Thursday.'

'Ah, well,' said Linda.

Versailles enchanted Linda, who told Fabrice everything she knew about Marie Antoinette – quite a lot, thanks to Aunt

Sadie's vivid history lessons – and cried twice at her own narrative. Fabrice said to remind him never to take her to the Picpus cemetery.

'Now I have to know why,' she said.

'It's where the people who were guillotined during the Terror were dumped, in pits,' said Fabrice. 'Minus their heads. The guillotine was in what is now the Place de la Nation, five minutes away.'

'I wish you hadn't told me.'

'Their descendants are the only people allowed to be buried there.'

'Well, that's something at least, for the poor beheaded to be with their families at last.'

'The last use of the guillotine in France was in 1975,' said Fabrice.

'Please kiss me,' said Linda, 'before I cry again.'

'Fabrice, don't you have things to do? Business meetings and things? Friends to see?'

'Yes,' said Fabrice. 'But I have cancelled them.'

'I don't want to be in the way.'

'You aren't.'

'Who are your friends, actually? What sort of people?'

'A lot of them are people I went to school with. Then there's another tranche, which is cool people.'

Linda burst out laughing. 'Cool people?'

'Yes. People who are cool. Fashionable. Out a lot.'

'You can't say your friends are cool people, it sounds ridiculous,' said Linda, snorting with laughter. 'And massively uncool. French people shouldn't say cool at all.'

Fabrice laughed too. 'I don't know how else to say it,' he said. 'I suppose I mean interesting people who are part of particular cultural scenes – designers, architects, artists, that sort of thing. And then more social people, journalists, politicians. And a lot of food people.'

'You're like Davey,' said Linda. 'I bet you know everyone.'

'Not everyone, but a lot of people,' said Fabrice matter-of-factly. 'Who I have no interest at all in seeing at this time.'

They were squashed up side by side in Chez Georges, on the rue du Mail, which Fabrice said was full of tourists but authentic, and which Linda would enjoy for its old-fashioned charm.

'Tony had a friend called the Yak. I can't remember why he was called the Yak, but he had been called it since they were about fifteen. That was just his name, the Yak.'

'But in conversation, did Tony say, "The Yak, would you like a drink?"'

'No, he'd say, "Yak, G&T?"'

Wild laughter from Fabrice.

'And then what?'

'Wouldn't you like me to be quiet? I feel like Scheherazade, though now I can't remember how the story ends. Or starts. Can you?'

'Yes.'

'How clever of you.'

'The king was married, but his wife was unfaithful.'

'It happens, I'm afraid.'

'Yes. But he did not like it. So he resolved to marry a virgin every day and have her beheaded the following morning, before she too could be unfaithful to him.'

'Men are so ridiculous. Look at Henry VIII, same sort of choppy-offy principle.'

'But eventually the kingdom ran out of aristocratic virgins. Or perhaps they hid. Either way, there weren't any. So the vizier offered up his own daughter.'

'Ugh,' said Linda.

'Who was Scheherazade. And who, that night, told the king a story that he liked very much. But she stopped at dawn, before arriving at the end. He spared her for another day, so he could find out what happened. Etc., for a thousand nights.'

'Poor Scheherazade, not much of a reward for her inventiveness,' said Linda. 'Being allowed to keep her head on.'

'On the thousand and first night, Scheherazade said she had run out of stories. But by then the king had fallen in love with her, so he married her and made her his queen.'

'Phew,' said Linda. 'I couldn't remember, and fairy tales often have such dreadful endings.'

'There have been several operas written about it, but I find them rather too Orientalist,' said Fabrice. 'Do you like the opera?'

'I'm not sure.'

'I will take you, so you can decide.'

They went to the opera. A striking, soignée blonde woman was staring at Fabrice from one of the boxes.

'Why is that woman staring like that?'

'Because we were engaged until I broke it off.'

'Poor her, she can't forget you, I don't blame her. When was it?'

'Five or six months ago.'

'Oh.'

'Fabrice?'

'Yes, Linda.'

'The woman at the opera. Am I prettier than her?'

'Dramatically so. But less chic.'

'Because more bobo.'

'Yes.'

'That's fine. Though I do need to buy some clothes at some point, I only brought enough for three days.'

'I wouldn't change a thing.'

'Alors, raconte.'

'So you know how bored we were, me and Fran, when we were teenagers?'

'Yes,' he said happily. 'I have never heard of such boredom. It is almost unimaginable.'

'We were once so bored that we spent a whole week discussing our favourite letters. Alphabet letters, I mean.'

'And what was the result?'

'It varied from day to day, but generally we felt that you wanted something solid, with a bit of a tummy, for friendliness, a D or a B. But not a complete fatso like an O. O says, "I'm a fun guy."'

'O is too much,' agreed Fabrice. 'I like E, with his arms held out.'

'Ah yes, E is endearing. But we felt too plaintive.'

~

'As you know, I've had a lot of sex,' said Linda. 'With quite a lot of people. But never like this.'

~

'I actually had no idea it could be like this.'

~

'I mean.'

29

No one had heard from Linda. We knew she was safe and well, because she'd left voicemails for Jassy and me telling us so, but there had been no further communications. She'd explained that she'd lost her old handset, but calls to the new number that had stored itself on our phones went unanswered.

'Don't you think it's at all odd that both of our voicemails arrived at a time when she knew we'd almost certainly be busy?' Jassy asked. 'And also, I mean, voicemail! She's not Ma. Send a text! No, she's up to something.'

'But what could she possibly be up to?' I replied. 'I think she's just hanging out and enjoying wandering around Paris. She's regrouping. It's completely normal.'

'Regrouping for two weeks?' said Jassy. 'Closer to three actually. Nobody goes to Paris for a mini-break and ends up still there nearly a month later. The hotel would need the room back, aside from anything else.'

'It is quite a long time,' I said. 'I don't think I've ever not spoken to her for more than a few days. It feels strange.'

'Me neither,' said Jassy. 'Which is proof. And what's with the new phone number? Something's happened. I'm not saying it's anything bad – but something's happened.'

'She probably borrowed a phone from the hotel for five minutes. You're reading too much into it. Her marriage has just ended, Jassy. I don't think anything's happened, as such. I think she probably just wants to be somewhere else, breathing new air and clearing her head. Have Aunt Sadie and Uncle Matthew heard from her?'

'A postcard,' said Jassy. 'Who still sends postcards?'

'Well, people with lost phones might. What did it say?'

'Something inane like "Here I am in Paris having a wonderful time, vive la France,"' said Jassy. 'Nothing useful. No clues. No address, obviously. But at least the postcard makes a certain kind of sense, because she still hasn't talked to Ma and Pa about how it ended with Christian, and she probably doesn't want to have that conversation right now if she's having a nice time in Paris. So I get that.'

'Yes, me too.'

'I did get one email from her, about a week after she left, but it was weirdly technical, all about the Sausage and not at all about what she was actually doing with her time, even though she must know that I am dying to know, bursting, practically. I emailed back but she didn't reply. She is definitely up to something. Ma would be all over it if she weren't so obsessed with the Louisa situation.'

Louisa was one of only six remaining contestants on *The Conch*, and the bookies' favourite to win the show outright. Aunt Sadie and Uncle Matthew had gone from utmost horror to rapturous pride and spent their entire time watching the live feed on a new sixty-five-inch television that they had bought for the purpose. 'They live on the sofa, basically. They're glued to it. They barely sleep. Ma says she's sure Linda's fine and that she'll pop up when she pops up.'

'It is slightly odd to leave you with the Sausage without asking first,' I said.

'That's not the odd bit – it pretty much runs itself, these days,' said Jassy. 'And anyway it's been closed for redecoration – I've just been going in a couple of times a week to keep an eye on things. She knows I can do it with my eyes shut when it reopens. The odd bit is the silence. But

232

she's going to have to come back at some point and explain herself to us.'

Linda finally checked out of the Maison Chéret a month after checking in. She had found a sparsely furnished flat on the Left Bank, on the rue Monsieur, and snapped it up on a six-month lease, her heart pounding. Six months! What was she doing, renting flats in Paris for six months on the basis of a new love affair? But she knew, with implacable certainty, that this was the love affair of her life, the defining event of her whole existence, the greatest happiness that she would ever know, and that, whatever happened in the future, she was doing exactly the right thing.

She didn't want to live with Fabrice. She didn't want to fast-forward to the part where they were settled and companionable, two comfy peas in their familiar pod – perhaps one day, but not yet, not when every moment spent with him still made her feel like a bell that had just been hit by a gigantic clanger, happiness reverberating so loudly that it thrummed through every part of her like a sound. She stayed over at his flat in an old hôtel particulier in the Marais all the time, but always left at some point in the morning, unwilling to rob herself of the agonizing pleasure of a few hours' break before she saw him again.

When Linda suggested she look for a flat in Saint-Germain-des-Prés, Fabrice said that it was fun to visit but too full of the too-rich denizens of the haute bourgeoisie, and that you could walk for kilometres and only come across well-heeled tourists and exorbitant antiques shops. 'The philosophers went a long time ago,' he said. He suggested that Linda look at places like Belleville, in the 20th arrondissement, or around the Canal Saint-Martin, 'your spiritual home, I think'. But Linda pointed out that she *was* a well-heeled tourist, and that although she loved both Belleville and the Canal Saint-Martin, both of which Fabrice had shown her during one of their many expeditions around the city, they felt to a greater or lesser extent like Paris's equivalent of east London, and therefore too familiar. In her mind's eye she'd also pictured herself in a bohemian garret somewhere vine-covered high up in Montmartre. After his remark about philosophers, she was too embarrassed to admit to Fabrice that her fantasy included Toulouse-Lautrec giggling over absinthe in the bar downstairs, and Linda greeting gold-hearted, maternal streetwalkers called things like La Grosse Berthe by name. But walking about the Left Bank one afternoon on her way to the Grande Épicerie to buy McVitie's chocolate digestives, she stopped by a A LOUER sign taped to the imposing grey doors of one of the grand houses on the rue Monsieur.

She pushed at the doors tentatively, not expecting them to open, and found herself standing in a big, cobbled internal courtyard, filled with pots of flowers, giving the formal space an almost rural feel. On the far side of the courtyard stood the building itself. It was white with green shutters. Linda texted Fabrice: 'Rue Monsieur? Do you know it?' His reply said: 'Your near neighbour would be the prime minister. Very safe.'

The combination of the shutters and the address itself – Linda had, as a child, developed a brief obsession with Monsieur, the high-heeled, libertine brother of the Sun King, naming her favourite mouse after him – meant she knew in her bones that she was in the right place. Her ardour was not dampened when the estate agent later explained that the street was named after a later Monsieur, the brother of poor Louis XVI, but Linda said that the Monsieur-ness mattered more than the genealogical specifics – it was a sign, pure and simple – and that she couldn't quite remember but didn't this later Monsieur anyway survive the revolution and indeed become king much later, after Waterloo? The estate agent stared at her and said, 'Ça, j'aurais pas prévu.' Linda explained that she knew literally no other history to speak of, but that her mother was pretty hot on pre- and post-revolutionary France and that her father couldn't watch *Les Misérables* without weeping all down his cheeks. In that case, the estate agent said, Linda might like to know that the duc de Saint-Simon lived in what was now the discreet Hôtel Saint-Simon, two doors down. 'Ma will die,' said Linda. 'Like living next door to Pepys! Can I move in tomorrow?'

The flat, which Fabrice had to admit was charming, if minuscule and in a ridiculously buttoned-up area, was on the ground floor. It was south-facing, sunny, with high corniced ceilings and mellow old parquet flooring that gleamed from a century's worth of floor wax. 'A lot of these apartments have ultra-modern interiors,' the estate agent had said. 'Everything opened up and denuded. But I think you perhaps prefer this older style? So, you are lucky.' The sitting room was painted a warm yellow, with a fireplace flanked by two bergère sofas upholstered in linen. The kitchen was just about big enough to eat in. The bedroom had old-fashioned flower-sprigged wallpaper, an armoire, a sink and an antique brass bed frame. This now contained one of Maison's Chéret's sublime mattresses, which Fabrice had had delivered on the day she moved in, along with armfuls of garden roses, some bedlinen, a full set of copper pans and a note saying they would go shopping at Merci or Ailleurs for everything else.

Best of all, the bedroom, like the sitting room, backed on to a walled garden – the whole street had served as royal stables in the eighteenth century, Fabrice said, which explained all the courtyards. This was la cerise sur le gâteau, because Linda now had a dog, a scruffy mongrel puppy called Claude who never left her side. One morning, Fabrice had informed her that they were off to the outskirts of Paris to collect a surprise. Linda had an inkling that the surprise might be a dog, and blurted out that although she was exceptionally grateful and pleased by the thoughtfulness of this idea, it was imperative that the dog should be a rescue dog. 'I couldn't bear it otherwise,' she said. 'I would love any dog passionately, obviously, but I would love a dog who had been unhappy or lonely or both even more. Especially if he was ginger. I really do love ginger animals the best.'

'I am sorry because I should have thought of this,' said Fabrice. 'But I am not sure we will find such a dog today. Especially if he must be orange. You do not see many orange dogs in Paris.'

'Perhaps they all get abandoned and end up in rescue. I'll get on the phone,' said Linda gaily. 'Leave it with me. When we meet tonight I expect I will have someone very special to introduce you to.' Enter Claude, who was tufty, chipper, very ginger indeed and who had exceptionally endearing round button eyes. He was probably largely terrier, Linda said, and maybe he had a bit of poodle in him too, which would explain his exceptional intelligence (it took Claude mere days to learn his theme tune, in this instance the first four bars of 'Non, je ne regrette rien' – 'Cheesy but apt,' said Linda). She asked Fabrice to speak to Claude only in French, to encourage full bilingualism.

The weeks went by, the summer ended and a routine of sorts established itself. Fabrice and Linda saw each other for dinner every night unless Fabrice was away on a business trip; if time allowed, they sometimes had a quick lunch together too. They spent weekends in either his flat or hers, getting up for excursions to neighbourhoods, small museums, notable churches, out-of-the-way shops, flea markets, street markets, parks and squares, and always with pit stops in cafes, bars, restaurants.

They did a lot of walking – no one in Paris drove unless they absolutely had to, Fabrice said, and she could see why – and Claude went everywhere with them. Fabrice said that there were thousands of different Parises, and no such thing as a definitive version of the city, but that he wanted to show her his, which encompassed everything from the Chapelle de Notre-Dame de la Médaille Miraculeuse in the rue du Bac to a tatty van in Ménilmontant dispensing ambrosial merguez sausages in pillowy flatbreads. They strolled the Coulée Verte, the inspiration for New York's Highline, and swam in a pool that floated on the Seine. Fabrice showed her a street in the 13th that looked almost English, in the Cité Florale, where the cobbled, garden-like streets were named after flowers and the brightly coloured houses were covered in wisteria and clematis. And all the time, they talked.

'Normally the conversation runs out,' Fabrice said. 'Especially when you spend this much time together. But not with you. It's bizarre. Great, but bizarre.'

Linda was so happy that sometimes she laughed while they were having sex, which Fabrice said was disconcerting but ultimately tolerable.

30

Linda knew that she should contact her family, whom she missed talking to terribly, but she didn't know where to start. The bald facts – that she had met a man and was living in Paris because of him – were so unequal to the vastness of her feelings and the heights of her happiness that she became discouraged every time she tried out the conversation in her head. Aunt Sadie and Uncle Matthew were especially difficult because, as Jassy had pointed out, they hadn't yet properly discussed the demise of Linda's marriage to Christian with her, and now there was already Fabrice. She should at least find out if Christian had started divorce proceedings, though she doubted it; if she knew him at all, the memory of her would have evaporated like summer rain from a hot pavement, just as hers had of him. Christian, who had been the centre of her world, now didn't enter her mind from one month to the next.

Linda, uniquely in my experience – the phrase was more usually a platitude or an aspiration – really did live entirely in the moment and had little or no interest in the past or the future. She minded about what she was having for lunch, and about where she would walk Claude that afternoon. She minded about seeing Fabrice for dinner. Beyond that, who knew? When a problem presented itself, she would try her best to solve it, but why worry about problems before they materialized, why invent hypothetical disasters to agonize over, as so many people seemed to? The idea had always seemed unreasonable to her, being both a poor use of time and a waste of her emotional bandwidth. Nevertheless, she felt uneasy about her vanishing act, and knew she would have to explain it sooner rather than later. (Moira, spending the summer with the Kroesigs at their villa in Sandbanks, near Bournemouth, was having a lovely time and was only dimly aware of her mother's new situation. Linda FaceTimed her three times a week. If Moira noticed from the background that her mother was clearly not in London or Norfolk, she never mentioned it, too busy excitedly listing her daily adventures and the ice-cream flavours she had been sampling.)

'They are broad-minded people, Ma and Pa,' Fabrice pointed out when Linda told him about her qualms.

'Yes, very, but even they might think this was all happening a bit fast,' said Linda. 'I don't want them to think it's, I don't know, indecent,' she explained. 'I don't think they would think that at all, but they might think that this is a mistake that I am making because I am on the rebound and therefore not really myself. Do you know rebound?'

'Like rebondir?' asked Fabrice. 'Bouncing?'

'Yes, exactly, how clever you are, Fabrice. Bouncing like a flea from the marital mattress straight to another one. The thing is, I *am* myself. I have never been more myself in my life. I am essence of myself, like a stock cube or the reduction for a béarnaise.'

'Maybe you should invite them?' said Fabrice. 'It might be easiest. They can stay in your suite at Maison Chéret. It's actually my suite, so it's always free.'

'You never said! Did you keep it for assignations?'

'Usually for my family and friends,' said Fabrice. 'Or to put up colleagues from abroad.'

'I note the "usually",' said Linda.

'The point is,' said Fabrice, 'it's there if your parents want it.'

'Maybe,' said Linda doubtfully. 'But not quite yet. I'll call them next week.'

*

It was obvious to Linda that Fabrice's love life before meeting her had been rich and varied. Yet it never occurred to her to enquire about the details, the whos and the wheres and the for-how-longs. He was clearly a person who liked having sex with people and so, clearly, was she – so was everyone. What else was there to say? You would have to be someone differently made from Linda to give passing thought to his, or her own, list of former conquests, let alone to strap on a head torch and mount archaeological excavations of the rubble of past love affairs. Her relationship with Fabrice was something out on its own, a shining brave new world, and the idea of constantly craning her neck to see what the people in the old world looked like, or what they were doing or wearing or saying, did not interest her in the least. She loved Fabrice, simply and wholly, and in loving him now understood that she had never truly loved before.

31

In the end, it was Merlin who found her. Linda had once idly wondered whether he knew the Maison Chéret, and it now turned out that he not only knew it but loved it as much as she did, and used it as his base when he was in Paris for Fashion Week. Making small talk with Hervé one evening while waiting for an Uber to take him to dinner at Caviar Kaspia, the concierge mentioned that an Englishwoman of great beauty and charm had stayed at the hotel for a whole month earlier in the year and still dropped in to say hello, that he adored her and that perhaps Merlin knew her.

'Don't be ridiculous, Hervé, of course not. I don't know every English person that passes through Paris! That's like someone in Armpit, Alabama, asking you if you know their Auntie Tammy-Jo because she also lives in France.'

'Yes, and I understand this pejorative comparison, of course,' said Hervé patiently. 'But I might know their Auntie Tammy-Jo if she lived in Paris and frequented this area and bought her bread at Mamiche, like me. It's possible.'

'Hardly,' said Merlin, rolling his eyes.

'I would remember her Alabama accent, for example.'

'Did the Englishwoman have a strange accent?'

'No.'

'Well, then.'

'OK,' shrugged Hervé. 'It was just an idea.'

'Oh, for God's sake, Hervé, don't look so dejected. Tell me the name if you really want to. I won't know her, I guarantee.' He glanced down at his phone. 'Ah – here comes my car.'

'Mademoiselle Radlett,' said Hervé. 'Linda.'

It later turned out that it was Davey, rather than Aunt Sadie or Uncle Matthew, whom Merlin called the following morning.

'Dear Merl, how jolly to hear from you. You find me feasting upon my morning millet. Heaven for the microbiome. All well at Merlinford?'

'I'm in Paris,' said Merlin. 'And you're putting me off my croissant. Is Emily in the room?'

'No, she's outside deadheading the dahlias. Why do you ask?'

'Because I don't want you to start shouting about it yet. Davey, I've found Linda!'

'Good God,' said Davey, putting down his spoon. 'What marvellous news. And she's quite well? In the pink?'

'I haven't seen her yet, but pinkissima, from what I hear,' said Merlin. 'I thought you might want to come and see her with me. I was going to call Alconleigh but then I thought that she might not want the entire Radlett clan racing for the Euro-star and descending on her with six million questions. Or at least, not yet. But could you? Race for the Eurostar?'

'Well, not race, it's so bad for one's joints,' said Davey. 'Bru-talizes the poor cartilage, and the absolute tragedy is that cartilage can't heal itself. But I'm on my way.'

'How on earth did you find me?' asked Linda. There had been a brisk rat-a-tat at her window and there, incredibly, were Davey and Merlin, large as life, standing in the courtyard in the afternoon light and peering in at her. She was so delighted to see them, she later told me, that she nearly cried. 'I was going to let everyone know where I was, I really was,' she said once they were inside and she had kissed them both. 'I just kept chickening out. Oh, it's so incredibly lovely to see you. I like your tricorn hat, Merlin, gorgeous braiding.'

'First things first,' said Davey. 'I found a vegan patisserie on the rue Voltaire.' He waved a paper carrier bag. 'I've got miniature mango tarte tatins and lemon tartlets and a kind of sumptuous éclair called a Trianon, and I can eat them all because they won't bloat me. I'm madly excited – and to see you too, darling Linda, of course, and looking so exceptionally well. But let me just organize the cakes and put the kettle on and then we can chat for hours.'

'It was Hervé at the Chéret,' said Merlin when the tea was ready. 'Who mentioned you. Insisted on mentioning you, in fact.'

'Ha,' said Linda. 'I knew you'd know the Chéret. It's so much your sort of place.'

'I've known Hervé for literally years,' said Merlin. 'He used to be at the Hôtel Costes and when he told me he was leaving there to work at Chéret, I knew it would be beyond fabulous. Anyway, we were chatting last night while I was waiting for my car and your name came up.'

'The world is tiny,' said Davey happily. 'I'm not a bit surprised. The mango on these is sort of candied, you must have one before I eat them all. I hope you're not cross with Hervé for telling us how to find you, Linda? We did have to plead a bit, but I said we were related and apparently you'd told him all about my fragile inner apparatus, so then he could place me, and of course he knew Merl of old, so it was fine. And he didn't tell us anything else about your circumstances (whatever they may be, one has one's theories). He was very discreet.'

'He knew you lived on the rue Monsieur,' said Merlin, 'and that it was on the ground floor, but he didn't know the number.

He remembered you mentioning the green shutters, though, so Davey and I have been wandering about opening courtyard doors and looking inside, like burglars.'

'You look more like a pirate today, Merly, I adore your get-up. We've only been nosing about for ten minutes,' said Davey. 'I might nose more later, I do love a good nose at the French in their sparse houses, so madly chic, such an unparalleled understanding of negative space. I must say, Linda, I wouldn't necessarily have pictured you in the 7th. But you look very at home.'

'I am,' said Linda. 'I am extraordinarily happy.'

'And this is all charming,' said Davey, waving an arm at the room, 'in its sweet little way. The former flat of the concierge, I think? Are we to assume from this young fellow . . .'

'Oh, sorry, this is Claude,' said Linda. Claude let out two joyful yips, as though to say, 'Yes, that is I.'

'. . . that you are well and truly ensconced? I must say, that's a terribly sweet dog – no, not too close, Claude darling, mes allergies. Does he speak English, Linda?'

'Yes,' said Linda. 'You can call him Claud, if you like.'

'What a good boy,' said Davey.

'And yes, I am truly ensconced.'

Merlin was looking at her with a smile on his lips, his cup of tea balanced on his satin-clad knee.

'What's his name?' he asked. 'Not the dog.'

'Fabrice El Hassane,' said Linda. It gave her pleasure just to say the words.

'Nice one,' said Merlin, at exactly the same time as Davey gasped an amazed 'No!'

'What?' said Linda. 'Oh, come on, this is too much. Don't tell me you know him too?'

'Of course I know him!' said Merlin. 'For a start, you couldn't miss a person who looks like that, especially when they're wandering around your hotel. Or rather their hotel. But I also know him from parties. We were always bumping into each other when I lived in Paris. Well, well.'

'I know him too,' said Davey. 'Linda, you sly fox.'

'You know everyone,' said Linda. 'So I don't even know why I'm surprised.'

'I don't know him *very* well,' Davey elaborated. 'I'm old friends with his decorator, you know, who does up his hotels, so we've had lunch a couple of times. I'm rather an admirer of Fabrice El Hassane. And of course – well, his looks, so distracting even for the red-blooded heterosexual male.'

'Dear Davey,' said Linda. 'How I've missed you.'

'Fabrice is very hot,' said Merlin.

'I know,' said Linda happily. 'He's boiling. He's wonderful.'

'So what's the deal?' said Merlin. 'Last time I looked, he was running around with, what's her name? That singer.'

'I don't know,' said Linda truthfully.

'Oh wait, that's not right – no, last time I looked, which must have been last Fashion Week, everyone was talking about how he'd got engaged to – tsk, I can't remember her name either. Jacqueline de something. Society beauty, bit chilly. Used to buy from me when I worked here. It'll come back to me.'

'How did you meet?' asked Davey, so Linda recounted the stolen phone, the suitcase and the Gare du Nord.

'Sweet,' said Merlin. 'Romantic. But he's quite . . . he runs about, you know, Lin. Bit of a shagger. You do know, don't you?'

'He is notorious. His reputation precedes him,' agreed Davey. 'Ha, what a hilarious thing for me to say, like someone in a Georgette Heyer novel, I do make myself laugh sometimes.' He chuckled appreciatively to himself. 'But it's that neck of the woods, darling. He is a rake.'

'Oh, I know all of that,' said Linda breezily, even though she didn't, quite. 'The thing is, dear Merlin and dear Davey, that I love him with all my heart, that I feel so completely alive that it's almost obscene, and that nothing else matters to me. Now, tell me everything that's been going on while I've been away. Start at the beginning please. I need all the details. And then stay for supper, won't you. Fabrice is coming at about eight and he'd love to see you.'

32

'YOU'RE ON SPEAKER,' said Uncle Matthew.

'Well?' said Aunt Sadie. '*Well?* What did you think? And we want to know what you thought too, Merlin. Try not to talk over each other.'

'DAVEY? MERLIN?' said Uncle Matthew.

'Yes, hello,' said Davey.

'Hi,' said Merlin.

'GOOD TO HEAR FROM YOU, MERLIN,' said Uncle Matthew.

'Eh?' said Jassy. 'Since when?' She'd FaceTimed me to join the landline conversation and her disembodied face was peering up from the kitchen table, where I'd laid my phone. No one answered her question.

'I think that she's euphorically happy and a damned good cook,' said Davey. 'Though the gastrointestinal tract, so wretchedly farouche, did pay for it later.'

'NOT NOW, DAVEY, WITH THE TUMMY THINGS,' said Uncle Matthew.

'Davey, darling, perhaps the gastric detail can wait,' said Aunt Emily.

Merlin laughed. 'Davey did shots last night,' he said.

'Not *shots*, Merly. Medicinal sips to aid digestion of the richer proteins. Vieille Prune, Matthew, eau de vie, you know, so delicious.'

'FOR GOD'S SAKE, DAVEY,' said Uncle Matthew. 'STAY ON TRACK. WHAT WAS LINDA LIKE? WHAT WAS *HE* LIKE?'

'We can hear you,' said Merlin. 'No need to shout.'

'EVERY NEED,' said Uncle Matthew.

'Linda . . .' said Davey. All of us leaned forwards to hear him better. 'Linda was like the happiest person in the world.'

'Radiant,' said Merlin. 'She looks wonderful. She's incredibly happy.'

Aunt Sadie exhaled.

'Merly, don't you think Linda's started looking slightly French? It's funny how that happens, with full immersion,' said Davey.

'Davey, you and Merlin are in the same room,' said Aunt Sadie. 'You can chat to each other any time, can't you? Like after this call, when you've filled us all in?'

The sound of Jassy laughing came from my upturned phone. Her picture had frozen.

'I have a friend, Billa Toft-Monks, you might know her, whose son was a robust pinkish English boy who read Chinese at university,' said Davey, wholly unperturbed. 'And then he went to study there for a few more years. Now he's back and still robustly pink but somehow much more Chinese than English.'

Uncle Matthew actually punched the worktop.

'NOW I'VE HURT MY HAND.'

'Davey?' said Aunt Emily. 'Do you think you could fast-forw –'

'Same thing with Linda,' Davey continued inexorably. 'She has absorbed some of whatever it is that makes Frenchwomen look French. I can never exactly put my finger on it.'

'Oh, I can,' said Merlin. 'It's because . . .'

'YOU'RE FADING OUT, MERLIN,' said Uncle Matthew.

'Oh, sorry, I'm in the minibar, getting us cocktails,' said Merlin. 'Hang on a sec. There, is that better?'

'We were on Linda looking wonderful,' said Aunt Sadie.

'Yes. It's because of better hair – all the millions of women

248

who buy those books about looking French just need to go to Paris for haircuts,' said Merlin. 'And then it's just much better skincare, less make-up, higher necklines, flatter shoes, minimal jewellery, a good handbag, an oversized blazer, flattering jeans and the total absence of any item that a woman in the UK would buy because it was "fun" or "cheery".'

'Aren't you clever,' said Davey.

'It's my job, Davey,' said Merlin.

'IF YOU DON'T STOP GOING ON ABOUT HAND-BAGS I'M GOING TO GO AND SET FIRE TO MERLINFORD,' said Uncle Matthew. 'JUST SO WE'RE CLEAR.'

'He actually would, Merlin,' said Jassy.

'Keep your hair on,' said Merlin. 'Was that Jassy? Hi, Jassy. So anyway, yes – Linda. Linda is basically in seventh heaven, and so is Fabrice. Turns out we both know him. It was quite strange to see him in such a domestic setting. I've only ever seen him socially in bars or clubs, or at rooftop parties.'

'YES, BUT WHAT IS HE LIKE?' asked Uncle Matthew.

'Also wonderful,' said Merlin. 'Really.'

'He was at supper,' said Davey. 'Rather like going into a room and finding a lion sitting on the sofa with his paws nicely brushed, nibbling an olive. He also looked very happy,' said Davey. 'He adores her, I think.'

'Yes, I do too,' said Merlin.

'THANK GOD,' said Uncle Matthew. 'I TRUST YOU BOTH TO BE ABLE TO TELL.'

'I could cry with relief,' said Aunt Sadie. 'In fact, I'm going to.'

'I'm still not that into the set-up,' said Uncle Matthew. 'But we'll see.'

'Get a drink, everyone,' Davey said later, when all the questions had been answered. 'Me and Merl have got Negronis.'

The conversation paused while Uncle Matthew went in search of a bottle of wine and Aunt Sadie found clean glasses.

'READY,' said Uncle Matthew. 'IT'S NOT CHAMPAGNE BECAUSE I'M STILL NOT SURE.'

'We're raising our glasses. To Linda and Fabrice. Of whom we entirely approve,' said Davey.

'Linda and Fabrice,' said Merlin. We heard their glasses clinking in Paris, and clinked ours in Norfolk. 'Yes, I do too. Long may it last.'

33

After that, of course, we all raced to Paris. Aunt Sadie and Uncle Matthew went first. The phone call had brought relief, but they still had questions and were eager to assure themselves that Linda hadn't been installed in a French flat 'like a bloody tart' and at the 'beck and call', Uncle Matthew had said, 'of some bloody Pierre or, or, or Jean-Luc in a bloody beret. Because that's plain wrong, is what it is.' Aunt Sadie had had to shush him quite sharply when he started making hee-hon hee-hon noises and weighing his own imaginary breasts with his hands, and reminded him that there *was* no Pierre or Jean-Luc, but rather a Fabrice who'd already met with family approval.

They left trepidatious and, in Uncle Matthew's case, if not quite up to the boil, then certainly simmering, and came back two days later enchanted. They were utterly persuaded of Linda's happiness, and utterly charmed by the Paris she'd shown them. Fabrice had been away on a business trip, but this hadn't seemed to matter: Uncle Matthew declared on his return that Fabrice was a prince and that he now looked upon him like a son.

'But you never even met him!' said Jassy. 'Pa, have you gone mad?'

'Didn't need to meet him,' said Uncle Matthew triumphantly. 'Got the measure of him from Linda. What a guy, Jass. What a guy. Talk about knowing how to live. That's Fabrice all over.'

'I can't tell you how wonderful she looks and how really happy she is,' said Aunt Sadie. 'It's quite something. She's radiant.'

'Oh my God,' said Jassy. 'Is that your way of saying she's pregnant?'

'Of course not, darling. It's my way of saying she's glowing with love and contentment. Mind you, she will need to do something with herself, eventually,' said Aunt Sadie. 'She can't just spend the whole day walking about looking at paintings and sitting in cafes and the whole night having very good sex.'

'Well, I don't see why not,' said Uncle Matthew. 'She's allowed a break after slogging at the Sausage for so long, and there are worse ways of passing the time. Eh, Sadie?'

'I suppose that's true,' said Aunt Sadie.

'I wish you two had even the tiniest concept of boundaries,' said Jassy. 'Imagine what it's going to be like when you're properly old and become increasingly disinhibited.'

'Naturism, I should think,' said Aunt Sadie. 'So make the most of us now, darling.'

'And anyway, she's educating herself with all that trotting around looking at stuff,' continued Uncle Matthew, ignoring both of them. 'And she suddenly seems to be able to speak fluent French.' He said this with wonderment. His own idea of speaking French was speaking louder English and feeling annoyed when his fluency was not remarked upon.

'Yes, that's true, though I did teach them all quite a bit of French; she had the foundations. I suppose in a way it's a bit like she's gone on a language course at an especially nice university,' said Aunt Sadie. 'Like the Sorbonne.'

'That's right,' said Jassy. 'She is a very mature student, with very mature and horizontal tastes. I wish you'd met him, Ma, so you could report back.'

'And a university history course too,' mused Uncle Matthew. 'She knows a ton of interesting stuff, all the dates, everything. I must say, Paris is an amazing city, everyone leaves you alone and you can take dogs into restaurants. The waiters kept bringing

Claude treats. Claude is one of us, Jassy. And he's bilingual. Bloody clever. Shall we buy a flat in Paris, Sades?'

'Don't be silly,' said Aunt Sadie, but her eyes lit up.

'Lino said there was a huge dog cemetery on the outskirts,' said Uncle Matthew. 'Really civilized, the French, I've always said so.'

'Maybe Linda could become a tour guide,' said Jassy. 'She could shack up with an Italian next, or someone Spanish, and then she'd be all set. Or a German.'

'Don't you be silly either,' said Aunt Sadie. 'And anyway, she's not shacked up, she's in her own flat.'

'I liked staying in that brothel,' said Uncle Matthew. 'I liked the vibe.'

'It's not a brothel any more, Matt,' said Aunt Sadie.

'Could have fooled me,' said Uncle Matthew, winking at her.

'Yeah, OK,' Jassy said on her return from a week-long stay with Linda. 'I take it all back. I completely get it. They're made for each other.'

The endless demands of family life meant that I could only get away for a weekend. I stayed at Linda's flat, the two of us hunkered in her unusually comfortable bed while it rained outside, chatting for hours on end, croque monsieurs and glasses of wine to hand.

'What do you do when Fabrice isn't around?' I asked. 'Don't you get lonely?'

'No,' said Linda. 'Isn't it funny? You'd think I would – I'd think I would. But I never do, or at least not so far. Paris is just so interesting. You keep stumbling across amazing things by accident, like a whole, perfect medieval cloister near Fabrice's flat. The other week I followed a tourist sign to the oldest house in Paris and discovered it had belonged to Nicolas Flamel, who

I'd always thought was a fictitious alchemist from *Harry Potter*, hadn't you? I must tell Robin, he'd die. And there's a secret speakeasy behind a launderette, and a ruined Roman amphitheatre hidden in the rue Monge – oh and not far from here there is an incredible Art Nouveau building and the entrance is the shape of an upside-down cock.'

'I can't picture that at all,' I said. 'What, feet up?'

'No, silly, not a cockerel, a penis. And such good churches everywhere, quite often with relics, I do love a relic. I mean, London is hugely interesting too, obviously, but you stop paying attention when you've lived somewhere a long time, don't you? Whereas here everything is a new treat. And French history is so much juicier and feels so much closer for some reason, like it's only barely out of reach. I could walk about all day and never get bored.'

'Jassy was right, you know. You could actually be a tour guide, a quite specialized and boutiquey one.'

'It's not the worst idea anyone's ever had,' Linda conceded. 'Hervé could recommend me to people. And I could do foody ones too, off the beaten track, places with no tourists.'

'I want to know more about your life. What about seeing actual people who aren't Fabrice? Do you do any of that?'

'Yes, Franny, of course, what a question. I have two girlfriends now, Héloïse and Olympe. Hëloise is gay and Olympe is married to a man called Eudes. Isn't that the most hilarious name?'

'How do you spell it?'

'E U D E S and you pronounce it uuughd, obviously, as I just have been. The S is just sitting there silently for extra pompousness, it's a French thing, as though one George or Eude was not enough and they had an invisible twin.'

We laughed at poor Eudes.

'Don't worry about my social life, Franny, it's pretty active.

Fabrice is like Davey, he knows everybody, and we go out and see people, for drinks and suppers and things. I get the feeling they think I might be temporary, but that they'd be sorry about it if I was. They're very nice. And then Merlin hooked me up with a couple of his friends too. So I have people to go to lunch with if I want, or to an exhibition, or to ask where to get my hair cut and so on.'

'That's a very good haircut, I must say.'

'Thanks. It's quite a bit shorter. I can see if they can fit you in tomorrow, if you like?'

'Could you?' I had been acutely aware of my great dowdiness ever since I'd arrived. 'Davey said you'd started looking French, and it's true. Well, part-French.'

'I now use very expensive face cream religiously, including on my neck,' Linda laughed. 'Which is quite French of me. Do you know, they even have special cream for the snowy orbs. Oh, what a shame it is that you won't meet Fabrice. He knows every last thing about you and is dying to finally meet you, but this hotel he's opening in Auckland is taking up all his time.'

'As in New Zealand?'

'Yes. He has his hotels but then he and his friend Jacques, who does the interiors, also have a company that does consultancy work. They're also consulting for a hotel in Byron Bay, in Australia, either before or after Auckland, I can't remember. That one's a sort of hippy-luxe affair, on the beach. The other one's more towny and glam. He has so much work on, it's nuts. He's not there now, he's in Milan looking at furniture, but he has a great big trip to Australia and New Zealand coming up in December. He's going to be gone for ages – weeks, in fact.'

'Oh. What will you do?'

'Well, the lease on here comes up at about the same time. I need to decide whether I'm going to stay in this flat, in which case there's no issue, or whether I'm going to move somewhere else, which I quite feel like doing now I know Paris a little bit better. There are such divine tucked-away little neighbourhoods, almost like villages, really green and bosky and I could keep hens. I'll show you tomorrow, if you like.'

'Yes please, I'd love that.'

'And then if I do move, I might wait for Fabrice to help me when he's back, rather than do it on my own. So when he goes on his trip, I thought I might come back to London for a bit and get to Alconleigh in good time for Christmas.'

'Oh do, that's a brilliant idea. We'll all be there too. It would be so nice, and we can help Aunt Sadie get things ready.'

'It's a plan. Now, shall we get up and make our way to Les Halles? I booked at La Poule au Pot, which you will love more than life, it's proper French classics but done in a modern way.'

'You're so at home here, aren't you?' I said. 'You know where to go and what to eat and how to get there, and how to speak and what to wear, and I feel slightly jealous.'

This was true. I was struck, quite forcibly, by how far removed Linda's life now was from mine: we were the same age, but we might as well have belonged to different species. I was contented, I loved my husband and two children dearly, I liked my job and earned enough money, and my life with Alfie was comfortable and harmonious. We were as happily married as married people can be: well suited, compatible, cheerful together. And yet when I thought about my daily life, with its endless pinpricks of irritation – trying to shoehorn work in between cooking, tidying, finding the swimming or gym or ballet kit, driving to a play date, driving back from a play date, constantly bending down to pick things up and put them on the stairs, knowing that I was the only person who would ever take them upstairs and put them away, wrestling the children away from their electronics, trying all the time to invent games and pastimes and hobbies for them, feigning interest when they said boring things at epic length, looking after them when they spiked a sudden fever or had a tummy bug; the way Alfie left his worn, curled-up socks on the floor, like the ghosts of feet, or his underpants, like the ghosts of bottoms; his occasional moodiness and preoccupations with work, the dullish drinks with dullish neighbours, the Sunday drives to country pubs or National Trust houses, the whole quotidian drag of it . . . Of course, what I describe is the grit of marriage, the grain in the wholesome wholemeal bread that nourishes and sustains. But Linda's bread was the bread of paradise, and that is an incomparable diet.

'I'm very lucky,' she now said. 'And I don't have to sleep with Englishmen who are useless at sex any more, so there's that too.'

'That's not at all fair,' I cried. 'Alfie is perfectly good at sex.'

'Perfectly good is what you say when you're Ma and the milk is out of date and still drinkable,' said Linda. 'Not in a carnal context.'

'Yes, well.' But I thought she was wrong. Perfectly good worked for me. It comforted and reassured me. I thought of good, kind, stolid Alfie in Oxford right now, wrangling the damp, squealing children into their pyjamas after their bath – he never dried them thoroughly enough – and tucking them up to read them a story in which he'd do all the voices, his loving patience never wavering. I smiled to myself as Linda and I headed out into the Paris night, and sighed a little too.

34

Fabrice left for New Zealand in mid-December. He would be gone for six weeks and fly back to Paris for the end of January. 'It's a disgustingly long time,' said Linda dejectedly. 'I don't know what I'm going to do with myself. Maybe Zoom you naked a lot.'

'I would like that very much, though it might be difficult given the time zone situation.'

Linda frowned. 'Well, there's always the phone. And sexting. And just think –' here she brightened considerably – 'how absolutely wonderful it will be to see each other again afterwards, reunited after nine million years.'

'You will have a nice time at Alconleigh,' said Fabrice. 'It will pass quickly.'

'Yes. It'll be really, really Christmassy,' said Linda, who loved Christmas passionately at the best of times and knew that she would love this Christmas best of all. 'I wish you could be there. Ma really goes all out with the decorating and the cooking, even someone who really hated Christmas couldn't help getting into it if they came to Alconleigh. I bet she gives you a stocking, I'll save it for you. Oh – but what will your mother do? Do you usually spend it with her?' Linda had not yet met Mme El Hassane, who despite what Fabrice had told her had been fond of his fiancée and did not seem to be champing at the bit to be introduced to Linda.

'She'll be at my aunt Faiza's,' said Fabrice. 'They don't really celebrate Christmas, but she'll have a nice time. Will Ma really give me a stocking? I am an adult man.'

'The age is not relevant,' said Linda. 'She always gives us stockings and she wouldn't dream of leaving you out. She'll make Claude one too.'

'This is what I love about Ma,' Fabrice said.

Linda left Paris a week before Fabrice's departure because Tony, Pixie and Moira were finally moving to New York, and she needed to say goodbye to Moira.

'See you in six weeks, my dearest dearest darling,' Linda said to Fabrice as the Eurostar pulled into the platform and her eyes filled with tears. 'This is quite romantic, isn't it, you waving me off for weeks, as though I were a soldier going to war. And almost as sad.' She did not say that the circularity of the thing bothered her: they had met at the Gare du Nord and here they were, saying goodbye in it.

Fabrice, who had paid for an extra ticket so he could see her off, carried Linda's suitcase into the carriage, put it on the rack, kissed her with some force and said, 'Goodbye, Linda. It will pass very quickly, you'll see. I will think of you every single day until we meet again.'

'I love you, Fabrice. You are everything to me. You are the whole world,' she suddenly said, holding his coat lapels and looking up at his face. 'Oh, I do wish the words weren't so naff.' She laughed, but her voice quavered. Fabrice had never told her he loved her, not in those three words, and she had been shy of saying it before now, even though she so often looked at him and thought 'I love you, I love you, I love you' so loudly in her head that she'd feel stupefied. But she had not said it out loud, until now, because she didn't want Fabrice to think she was clingy or in need of banal reassurances, and because saying 'I love you' when you mean it for the first time in your life is really a question, a frightening one to which there is only one possible answer.

The doors were closing now, with a soft little pffft, and

suddenly Fabrice was back on the platform, waving at her until she could no longer see him. If he had said it back, then she hadn't heard. She watched Paris recede, and wondered, later, as the train entered the tunnel, whether the whole thing had been a dream.

35

Moira arrived at Alconleigh in a chauffeur-driven car. 'Thank you, Adams,' she said politely as he saw her to the door.

'I like that dog,' she said, once she had kissed Linda.

'His name is Claude,' Linda said, kneeling down to unbutton Moira's coat and unbundle her from her various layers. 'I've been living in Paris, remember? In France. Although I'm back now, for a bit. But when you come and stay with me in the school holidays, you'll be coming to Paris. Won't that be exciting?'

'Yes, it will. So is Claude a French dog?' asked Moira. 'I didn't realize it. Will he understand what I am saying to him?'

'He's bilingual,' said Linda. 'That means he speaks two languages.'

'He is a very clever boy, isn't he?' said Moira, kneeling down to scratch Claude's neck with great enthusiasm. 'Do you know, Daddy doesn't like France. He says it's full of French people and that we're well out of it.'

'Daddy is a bit silly sometimes,' said Linda, 'but never mind. Now, come and say hello. Everyone's excited to see you.'

'OK. Is Uncle Robin here?' Uncle Robin was Moira's most looked-up-to person in the world, so infinitely cool that she was sometimes incapable of speech in his presence.

'Of course,' said Linda. 'He's looking forward to seeing you. He has blue hair at the moment, can you imagine? Rather suits him, actually.'

Moira gasped as she digested this. 'Is Monaco in France?' she asked as Linda hung up her coat, scarf and mittens in the boot room, where, she now noticed, a new child-height coat rack had recently been affixed to the wall. 'Papa Leicester goes to Monaco sometimes.'

'No,' said Linda. 'Very much not. France is wonderful, the most wonderful country in the world, as you will see. You'll love it. We could go to Disneyland Paris! Would you like that?'

'The main Disneyland is in America,' said Moira. 'The best one. Daddy and Pixie are taking me. But I would like to see the French one too,' she added kindly, taking Linda's hand. 'Can we go and see Uncle Robin's hair?'

Aunt Sadie had strung Stars and Stripes bunting across the beams of the kitchen and made a particularly extravagant and US-themed tea for Moira, who now stood at the threshold, delighted and suddenly shy.

'Moira!' cried Aunt Sadie. 'My darling girl! Don't you look lovely! Come and give me an enormous hug.'

'Ah, Moira,' said Uncle Matthew, ruffling her hair as she clambered on to Aunt Sadie's lap. 'There you are. I've bought you a harmonica, and if you're very good I might teach you to play it this weekend. You'll have to practise outside.'

'It's really a present for Daddy and Pixie,' said Jassy. 'Hello, Momo, you little sausage.'

'Yo, Momo,' said Robin.

'Yo, Uncle Robin,' said Moira, blushing pink. 'Yes please, Grandpa, I would like to learn the harmonica. Hello, Aunt Jassy, you *big* sausage.' She giggled as Jassy feigned outrage. 'Hello, Auntie Franny!'

'Moira, darling,' said the Bolter, who was just back from a ride and wearing eye-wateringly tight cream jodhpurs and dark red lipstick. 'Are you excited to be moving to New York? I lived in New York for a couple of years, you know. Do you remember, Frances? I think you came out, didn't you? Once or twice?'

'Yes,' I said. 'Someone the Third, wasn't it?'

'Second, I think. Or was that the father? Can't remember. Wonderful thighs. The son, I mean. He had that pretty cottage in the Hamptons.'

'Anyway,' said Linda, shooting my mother a look. 'Isn't this lovely, Momo?'

'Yes,' said Moira. 'Who is that man?'

'What man, darling?' said Aunt Sadie. Moira pointed at the hulking figure who'd just appeared at the kitchen door.

'Oh, that's Hoooan,' said Uncle Matthew with no great enthusiasm. 'Hoooan, this is Moira.'

'Yeah, it's me, Juan,' said Juan. He was an impressively built man and he furrowed his brow when he spoke, taking an inordinate amount of time to answer even the most banal questions. Juan hadn't smiled since arriving two days previously. 'Done your coat rack for you earlier, Sadie,' he now said. 'All right, Moira? Nice to meet you. I'm not very good with kids.'

'Juan is Auntie Bolter's young friend,' said Aunt Sadie. 'Thank you, Juan, for the coat rack.'

'He's a cage fighter,' said Jassy. 'Do you know what that is, Momo?'

'I don't know,' said Moira.

'No, I didn't either,' said Aunt Sadie. 'Have a doughnut, Moira, darling, I made them myself. Those ones are apple and cinnamon and those ones with icing are raspberry jam.'

'It means he's very good at fighting,' said Jassy. 'He fights for money.'

'In a cage,' said Linda.

'Mixed martial arts, Moira,' said Juan. 'Bit of boxing, bit of judo, ju-jitsu, karate, Muay Thai, that sort of thing. Yeah?'

'It's actually highly skilled,' said the Bolter. 'Have a doughnut, Juan.'

'Can't, babe, it's a protein week,' said Juan, patting his rock-hard stomach.

'But is fighting *good*?' asked Moira, confused.

'Depends,' said Uncle Matthew.

'You need someone taken out, say the word. I'm your man,' said Juan to Moira.

'I didn't know fighting was a job,' said Moira.

'No, well,' said Linda.

'I wouldn't hurt them if they were a kid,' Juan said. 'I'd just be *assertive*.'

'Good to know,' said Jassy. 'Reassuring.'

'I don't know what assertive means,' said Moira.

'Hop down off your chair for a sec,' said Juan. 'I'll show you.'

'Do I have to?' said Moira.

'Yeah,' said Juan, at the same time as Linda said, 'No.'

'Right,' Juan said to Moira. She barely reached his waist. 'Say you were a kid who stole my sandwich, yeah? At school. Cos you'd forgotten your lunch.'

'I don't have packed lunch,' said Moira.

'Yeah, but say.'

'OK,' said Moira.

'And you wouldn't give the sandwich back. You just sat there eating it. Chewing it. Looking at me. And it was doing my head in. Really winding me up. Because my mum made me that sandwich and it was my favourite. Nutella. Yeah?'

'Yeah,' said Moira, who loved Nutella.

'Right. So what I'd do is, I'd come up to you, like this –' here Juan, who was six foot four and who seemed to have expanded dramatically widthways in the past five seconds, loomed gigantically over Moira – 'and I'd look at you like *this*.' His eyes, which were ordinarily perfectly normal and a perky blue, suddenly looked completely dead and empty.

'Whoa,' said Jassy.

'I don't like it,' said Moira.

'That *is* actually quite intimidating,' said Linda. 'You look like a complete psycho, Juan.'

'Isn't it good? I make him do it all the time,' said the Bolter.

'In what possible context, I wonder?' said Jassy.

'Ha ha,' laughed the Bolter delightedly. 'Bingo, darling. Ding-a-ling.'

'Can you undo your eyes now?' asked Moira.

'Nah, mate,' said Juan, sucking his teeth and slowly rolling his shoulders back, first one, then the other, so that they actually rippled beneath his T-shirt. 'Cos YOU took my Nutella sandwich and YOU need to give it back.'

'I didn't, though,' said Moira anxiously.

'She doesn't even have packed lunches,' said Robin.

Moira looked at him gratefully.

'So then,' continued Juan, 'if you still weren't listening, I might come closer. I might say, OI, and give you a little tap.'

'That's quite enough of that,' said Aunt Sadie briskly. 'Who's for milkshakes?'

'In a bit,' said the Bolter. 'I just quickly need to show Juan something in my room.'

'Here, Momo, this is for you. A present. Look, there's a gold teddy on it with little blue eyes. It was a wedding present, from when Daddy and I got married, so it's nice for you to have it. I had it resized.' Linda didn't add that the charm bracelet, a gift from Blanche, had never been worn.

'Thank you, Mummy, I love it,' squealed Moira. She held out her wrist. 'Can I wear it right now? Will you put it on me?'

'Of course, darling,' said Linda. 'Now, Momo, I want to tell you something, which is that Daddy and I loved each other very much, when we got married, just as Daddy loves Pixie very much now. It's important for you to know that, because sometimes when children get older they wonder if their mummies and daddies ever liked each other, and it makes them feel sad. Will you always remember?'

'OK,' said Moira. 'Are the teddy eyes real jewels?'

'Yes, they're sapphires. There. It looks lovely on you. Now, Adams will be back to collect you in about five minutes – we've said goodbye and see you soon to everyone, and here's your suitcase, but have you got all your extra things?'

'Yes, and here's my car picnic that Grandma Sadie made, and my harmonica is in my pocket, and the money from Auntie Bolter, and the fake tattoo from Uncle Robin. I just need to kiss Claude, can you pass him? Also, Mummy?'

'Yes, Momo?'

'Can I show you something really cool?'

'Yes please.'

'OK. Pick me up, please. Look *right* at me.'

'Oh my God, Momo, that's horrendous. How are you doing that?'

'I asked Uncle Juan to teach me dead eyes. The first time he said no because he was having an afternoon nap with Auntie Bolter, but the second time he said yes.'

'Gosh. You can stop now, Momo, it's so unsettling.'

'YOU took my Nutella sandwich,' said Moira. 'And YOU need to give it back.'

'Well, I don't anticipate any trouble at your new school,' said Linda, 'so at least there's that. Goodbye, darling.' She hugged Moira tightly and put her back down. 'See you very soon.'

'Goodbye, Mummy.'

'Are you all right, Linda?'

'More or less,' Linda said, wiping her cheeks. 'She'll be OK, won't she, Franny?'

'I really think she will be, yes.'

'I tried, you know, when she was little. Littler. I tried and tried to connect. I had good intentions. It just didn't seem to happen.'

'But it has now.'

'Oh yes, it has now. Better late than never, I suppose.'

'Juan,' said Aunt Sadie the following day, 'I've only just been in the boot room – you made a whole *new* coat rack!'

'Found some bits in the barn,' Juan said, shrugging. 'The one you gave me was pony, so I knocked up another one. I used the same coat hooks and rawl plugs. It's just better wood.'

'Juan is incredibly good with his hands,' said the Bolter.

'It's a work of art!' cried Aunt Sadie. 'That's proper craftsmanship, Juan.'

Juan considered this at some length. 'Not really,' he said. 'My dad – now *he's* a craftsman. I just picked up a few basics from him.'

'Nothing basic about *you*, Juanito,' said the Bolter.

'You actually are eating him with your eyes,' said Jassy. 'I thought it was just an expression.'

'She's got a good appetite on her,' Juan said matter-of-factly. 'Haven't you, Georgie?'

'Chomp!' said the Bolter gaily.

'Hang on, who's Georgie?' said Jassy.

'Auntie Bolts,' said Linda.

'Me. I'm actually called Georgina,' explained the Bolter. 'Remember?'

'Are you? I swear I've never heard you called that in my entire life,' said Jassy, amazed.

'Bolter is Bolter,' said Uncle Matthew.

'Yeah, I prefer Georgie,' said Juan. 'Bolter is bolts, isn't it? Makes her sound like a toolbox.'

'It's from bolting, darling,' said the Bolter. 'You know, like a horse?'

'Don't know any horses,' said Juan. 'Don't want to either. Don't trust them. Their ears are too small.'

'How come you're called Juan, Juan?' asked Linda. 'Is somebody Spanish?'

'Hoooan,' said Uncle Matthew. 'Hoooan.'

'Nah,' said Juan. 'My real name is John, but I go by Juan.'

'Hoooan,' said Uncle Matthew. 'Am I saying it right?'

'Pretty much,' said Juan.

'I don't suppose, Juan,' said Aunt Sadie, 'that after your triumph with the coat rack I could ask you to move a couple of pictures round for me? I always make such a mess of the walls, you see, and I'm too embarrassed to get someone in especially.'

'Happy to,' said Juan. 'Any little jobs like that, just ask. I can do basic electrics, as well.'

'Oh my God,' said Linda. 'You are about to become Ma's favourite person in the universe, Juan. You have no idea.'

'When you say basic electrics,' said Uncle Matthew, 'would that include telephone things? Like modems and routers?'

'You're in luck, mate,' said Juan. 'Used to work for BT before I went pro. Broadband engineer, wasn't I?'

'HOOOAN!' shouted Uncle Matthew. 'Do you think you could make the broadband in this bloody house work properly? Sometimes me and Davey can't get on Instagram.'

'Maybe,' said Juan. 'I can give it a shot.'

'It's very hit and miss,' explained Aunt Sadie, 'depending on the room, even though we have those discs everywhere. No one can seem to get to the bottom of it.'

'Wi-Fi extenders,' said Juan, and nodded. 'Leave it with me.'

'Hoooan,' Uncle Matthew said, coming very close and looking into Juan's eyes with terrifying intensity. 'Hoooan. If you can make the broadband work in every room of this house, I will marry you.'

'Yeah, steady on, mate,' said Juan.

36

Fabrice's mother slipped off a chair while changing a light bulb and landed badly. She lived on her own and couldn't move to call anyone for help for two hours. Out of the blue, Linda got a message from Fabrice saying that he'd just come from the hospital in Brussels, having flown in overnight. Mme El Hassane was now conscious and the scans and X-rays had revealed nothing more catastrophic than a broken ankle and badly bruised shoulder – 'The head is good, thank God.' The doctors said that she was on the mend and would be discharged within a week into the care of her sisters, the youngest of whom had been a nurse. Now Fabrice was at Bruxelles Midi. The Eurostar to London left in forty minutes and he had a seat on it. Did she have plans for tonight, and if so might she cancel them? He would fly back to Hong Kong from Heathrow tomorrow.

Life, thought Linda, was sometimes sad and often dull. But there were raisins in the cake, and here was one of them.

'Bonsoir.'

'Fabrice!'

'How beautiful you are, Linda. Shall I come in?'

'What? Yes, yes, of course, sorry. I was just staring at you.'

She was watching him dress through half-closed eyes the following morning, as she had so many times before. Now Fabrice came to sit on her side of the bed.

'Coffee?' Linda asked, raising herself up on one elbow. 'Do you have time?'

'My car is on the way,' he said, 'and it's much too early for you to get up. Stay in bed.'

'I am very tired,' she smiled. 'In the nicest possible way. I don't suppose you want to quickly . . .'

'Linda,' said Fabrice, taking her hand, 'I came to see you, of course, but also to tell you something.'

'I don't like the sound of that one bit. It feels ominous.'

'I came to tell you that I love you.'

She felt light-headed; if she'd been standing, she'd have leaned against something.

'I was going to tell you, that day on the train, but the doors closed and then it was too late.'

'You never said it in Paris.'

'I have said it so many times before in my life, in so many romantic and not romantic situations, automatically, like a robot. When I knew that I loved you – which was very early, by the way – I couldn't bring myself to say those same old words to you. They were too small and stale. But I knew that this was real and that all the others were false. When I met you, it was like recognizing somebody. Do you understand?'

'Yes,' said Linda. 'It was the same for me.'

'When your train pulled away I felt desperately that I wanted to tell you. I thought about it all the time, in bed when I couldn't sleep, in the middle of meetings, first thing in the morning. It became a sort of obsession. But it is not something I wanted to say on the phone or in an email or a text. So here I am, telling you now.'

Linda leaned her head on his shoulder. They stayed like that for a long time.

'Fabrice, when you come back, when we're back in Paris – shall we live together?'

'Yes, my darling,' said Fabrice. 'We shall live together for years and years and years.'

'For more than five years,' Linda said.

'I love you ten times more than I've ever not-loved anyone else,' said Fabrice, 'so that's at least fifty years. And when I am ninety we can re-evaluate the situation. Now I am going or I will miss my plane.'

37

It was two days before Christmas and everyone who wasn't already there had started converging on Alconleigh. The weather was filthy, grey and slushy, not nearly cold enough for snow. The fires were all lit regardless, giving the whole house the feel of a gold-tinged, nostalgic illustration in an Edwardian picture book. In the sitting room, the tree was twelve feet high, every branch covered in lustrous baubles and dozens of ancient, wonky decorations made by the Radlett children during every stage of their childhood. Linda and I had spent much of the afternoon at the kitchen table, cutting and gluing extra paper garlands at Aunt Sadie's behest because she didn't feel that the hall looked festive enough to really make an impact, this despite the entire house being beautifully festooned with trails of ivy, holly, eucalyptus, old man's beard and every kind of berried branch known to man. Aunt Sadie started raiding the hedgerows in September like a soldier on a mission, wearing leather welder's gauntlets and wielding enormous shears, before storing her haul upside down in the barn to dry, and she netted the holly bushes as soon as their berries appeared, to stop them being pecked away by the birds. There were red pleated-paper Christmas trees hanging from the ceilings, glass baubles dangling from the chandeliers, huge vases of mossy, wintry branches everywhere, and pots of forced narcissi, whose scent mingled with that of the cheese stars that Aunt Sadie was currently very patiently showing my children how to make.

Louisa and Jonty were arriving from Scotland at the

weekend (Louisa, runner-up in *The Conch*, was now famous). My husband was due any moment, and next door Aunt Emily and Davey's cottage was, this year, sporting a modern Alpine chalet theme that Davey had been working on for weeks, based, he said, on the Chalet Zannier in Megève. 'Do you know it, darling? No? Never mind.'

Linda was five months pregnant. I'd found her throwing up in the children's bathroom, right at the top of the house. She said she'd been feeling nauseous a lot, but put it down to missing Fabrice.

'Linda, don't be ridiculous. Missing someone doesn't make you physically ill,' I said.

'That's where you're wrong, Fran. I do feel physically ill from not being with Fabrice. Sometimes I feel physically ill if he's away for two days, so imagine what it's like in this situation – weeks and weeks to go.'

'When did you last have a period?'

'I never really keep track,' said Linda. 'They're not regular. I see them when I see them, a bit like boring friends.'

'But you use contraception?'

'Oh yes,' said Linda. 'Well, usually.'

We got in the car and drove to Holt, where we purchased two pregnancy tests from the Boots on the High Street, to make sure. Both were positive. Linda was ecstatic, all the more so when I told her my news, which I'd kept a secret until then: I was three months pregnant myself.

Fabrice finally rang on the afternoon of Christmas Eve, and got Uncle Matthew.

'Ah, Fab, there you are, my boy. What? Yes, this is Matthew, but you can call me Pa.'

We all stared at each other in disbelief.

'You too, dear Fab, you too. Onchontay right back. Yes, at long last.'

'Pa, let me talk to him and stop calling him Fab,' Linda cried.

Uncle Matthew waved at her to be quiet. 'Linda sends her love,' he said. 'I'll put her on in a minute. What? No, you won't have been able to, the signal's shit, always much better to call the landline. Our broadband works brilliantly now, though. Juan fixed it. What? Spanish fella. Bolter brought him. Fabreece says he's tried you twice, Lin.'

'Only twice?' said Linda.

'Now, I've put together a lot of good stuff to show you, Fab,' Uncle Matthew continued relentlessly. 'In my study. For when we finally meet. Just things I'm into and that I know you'll be interested in too. Do you like cats, Fab? Ha! I knew it, me neither. But I'm going to show you a cat that you won't believe. A cat that is more like a man.'

'Pa, for heaven's sake, pass me the phone,' said Linda, somewhere between laughter and tears. 'Ma, make him stop.'

'Matt, let Linda talk to him,' said Aunt Sadie. 'And give him my best love.'

'I'm being yakked at by a load of women, Fab,' said Uncle Matthew. 'Can't hear myself think. Where are you, exactly? Sydney? Very nice.' He pointed at the handset for our benefit and did a thumbs up.

'Matt,' said Aunt Sadie, 'give Linda the phone.'

Uncle Matthew eventually peeled himself away, with great reluctance. Linda grabbed the handset and took it to the snug for privacy.

'Man speaks better English than I do!' Uncle Matthew exclaimed.

'I wish he could have joined us,' said Aunt Sadie. 'Such a shame for Linda.'

'For all of us,' said Uncle Matthew. 'This is Fabby we're talking about.'

Linda and I went to Da Sty, in part to get away from the Bolter and Juan. Earlier that afternoon, Louisa's six-year-old daughter, Sorcha, came down to the kitchen and informed her mother and Aunt Sadie that 'Juan and Auntie Bolts *live* together'.

'I don't think so, darling,' said Aunt Sadie. 'Do they? I'm not quite sure. Maybe some of the time.'

'They live together every afternoon,' Sorcha said. 'Before tea. I hear them.'

'Oh, I see,' said Aunt Sadie.

'You told him, right?'

'God, yes,' said Linda. 'I did consider waiting until I saw him again, but I couldn't help myself.'

'And was he thrilled?'

'*Thrilled*. At first he couldn't speak in English, just gasped and laughed and shouted in French, and then he said it was merveilleux and that he couldn't be happier. We talked for hours, his poor phone bill. I love his voice. Fran, do you think it's weird that he told Pa he'd only tried to phone twice?'

'Not really,' I said. 'In the circumstances. You text, right?'

'Oh yes,' said Linda. 'All the time, although we can't often have back and forth conversations because, aside from the time difference, he's always in meetings. We email too.'

'Well, then,' I said.

'Sometimes,' Linda said, 'I wonder if I've made him up. Do you know what I mean?'

'Not really, no.'

'The more time passes, the more my Paris life seems to recede. Like when they change the scenery at the theatre. One minute you're in a sitting room and the next you're in an orchard. You know?'

'It's only geography,' I said. 'Alconleigh is so incredibly familiar to you, to all of us, that when we're here it's almost impossible to imagine being anywhere else. I feel like that too, when I'm here. Like only this is real, and my Oxford life is some sort of blurry fabrication. It's normal to feel like that. And then when I'm at home, it's Alconleigh that becomes dreamlike.'

'I know,' said Linda. 'You're right, and that's exactly it. But every now and then this idea comes into my head, that maybe Paris and – and everything that happened in it – was a chimera. It wasn't, was it?'

'No,' I said. 'And it's ki-mera, not shi-mera. I think.'

Linda laughed. 'Here we still are, all these years later, with no idea of how to pronounce things.'

'Nadir,' I said.

'Auspices,' said Linda.

We drank our hot chocolate, like the children we no longer were.

'You know how you were with Moira?' I said. 'When she was born?'

'I've been thinking about that a lot,' Linda said. 'I really don't think it was post-natal depression – I know you do, Fran, but I absolutely don't. I just . . . I don't know. I wasn't very well. I felt outnumbered by the Kroesigs. They seemed so much more in control of my life than I was, and I hated them, by that point, and I felt angry and trapped until Tony went off with Pixie. It won't be the same with this baby. I feel like I've bonded with it already, and I never felt that with poor Momo until she was about three.'

38

Linda went into labour five weeks early. Fabrice, his phone turned off, was in a meeting with an architect on the outskirts of town. By the time he saw his missed calls and raced towards the Hôpital Franco-Britannique in the architect's borrowed car, Linda was dying from a post-partum haemorrhage. Fabrice, unaware, turned much too fast on to the rue de Villiers. He crashed into a plane tree and was killed instantly. His body was taken to the same hospital. The sun shone imperturbably on Paris. The Seine glittered in the pale April light. Their child, a strikingly beautiful little boy, was adopted by me. His name is Fabrice and I love him as much as, perhaps even more than, I do my own children.

At Linda's funeral, my mother, black-veiled and weeping, holding Claude in her arms, remarked that the occasion was sadder than she could bear, but that growing older only made life harder for women like Linda. 'She died at the age when you still think you'll live for ever,' she said, 'and that nothing will ever change. She was still so beautiful and happy.'

I shook my head. 'It wasn't like that. He was the great love of her life,' I said. 'And she of his, I think.'

'Oh, darling, one always thinks that,' said the Bolter sadly, taking my arm. 'Every, every time.'

Acknowledgements

Thank you to dear Juliet Annan, formerly of Fig Tree, for her faith and support over the past two decades. It's discombobulating when the only publisher you've ever had retires, so an especially enormous thank you to her successor, Helen Garnons-Williams, for being simply wonderful from our very first email exchange. Thanks, as ever, to Georgia Garrett, who is so much an old and beloved friend that I always slightly want to laugh and go 'Eh?' when she starts saying agenty things. Thank you to Lesley Levene for her impeccable copy-edit, and to everyone at Penguin Random House, especially to Ellie Smith, Olivia Mead, Ella Harold and Kyiah Ashton. Thank you to the ludicrously talented Holly Ovendon for making my favourite book jacket of all time. Thank you to Clara Strunck for doing such a good job of filleting *The Pursuit of Love* when I first embarked on this project seven and a half million years ago. Thank you to Eleanor Sykes for knowing about things like Twinkle 12s, and for being such a pal. And thank you most of all to Nancy Mitford's estate and trustees for giving me completely free rein to reinvent things in my own way, and for trusting me not to balls it up too badly.

Linda's cork-and-shell-covered kitchen cupboards are lifted from life and belong to stylist Maud Smith, whose lovely house was featured in the July 2020 issue of *House & Garden*. The ancient corgi who makes Uncle Matthew cry is real and lives (still, I hope, but let's not dwell on that) on the west coast of Ireland, so thank you to him too. I've also taken liberties with the geography of glorious north Norfolk.

India Knight
Suffolk, 2022